Burning Questions

a novel

The Volcano at St. Miguel
Book 3

Jeremy Harmer

WAYZGOOSE PRESS

Editor: Maggie Sokolik

Cover Design: Getcovers

Wayzgoose Press

Eugene, Oregon, USA

wayzgoosepress.com

Print ISBN: 978-1961953338

This is an original work of fiction, written without the use of AI. Any resemblance to real events or characters is purely coincidental.

V91325

Contents

Old Stories, New Beginnings

Anselmo

HE LOOKED at himself in the mirror, slicked back his hair, and wondered if he was presentable for what was to come. He couldn't do much about how age was creeping up on him, but given that, he thought, he didn't look too bad. Perhaps that was because life was pretty good. He didn't work much anymore. He was officially semi-retired. Instead of being out on the street or holed up in his office he now spent most of his time in the club he'd managed to be accepted in or, with his wife, going out to restaurants, attending the occasional concert or municipal event, and once a year, heading off for a foreign holiday or a cruise specially designed for people of their age. When asked how he was, he would reply, 'never better,' or 'I can't complain. Getting older isn't much fun, but the alternative is worse,' and people would pretend to laugh even though they had heard the witticism countless times before.

He had chosen an open-necked light blue shirt, typical of the region, with white trousers and the shiny brown shoes that he was particularly pleased with. He couldn't decide whether to wear glasses or not. Would they shine in the lights — would there be lights? — but if he didn't wear them, would his eyes look all small and 'piggy' as his grandson had called them once? This was an insult that should have perturbed him, but because it came from a favourite child, he couldn't be upset.

They had said they would be here at eleven o'clock, but in the end, they didn't arrive until about a quarter to twelve, not an unreasonable delay by local standards, but these were out-of-towners. He hadn't quite worked out exactly who they were, but he knew why they were coming, and he thought, *I have a good story to tell*. I just hope I don't forget names like I seem to do often these days.

His wife showed them into the sitting room. There were four of them. Three were carrying boxes of various kinds, but the fourth, who was obviously in charge, came up to him and, holding out her hand, said, "*Señor Gonzalez de Luna, es todo un honor.*"

He took the proffered hand. "Anselmo," he said. "You can call me Anselmo. It is an honour as well, madam. At your orders. You must tell me what you want."

After looking around the house, the visitors ultimately chose the sitting room. They set up two lights angled to shine onto two white parabolas — "reflectors," the director said — and two chairs. There were microphone booms and two cameras strategically placed to capture them both. He had a radio microphone attached to his blue shirt, the cable disappearing behind the collar and into the power pack in his left-hand trouser pocket.

"This seems an awful lot of trouble just for a quick conversation," Anselmo said.

"We want it to sound and look good," one of the cameramen replied.

The director was clearly agitated. She kept looking at her

2

watch and muttering. But the doorbell rang in the end, and the director went with Anselmo's wife to answer it. Anselmo heard a woman who wasn't his wife or the director saying hello, and a moment later, he was surprised and rather pleased to see the well-known Gaby Aguirre walk into the room. He had seen her on the screen for at least the last thirty years, and here she was in his sitting room. He'd tell them about that in the club.

He stood up as she came towards him. "Señor Gonzalez de Luna, may I call you Anselmo?"

"You may," he said, a ridiculous smile that he couldn't quite control suddenly appearing on his face. He caught his wife watching him, amused, and tried to control himself.

Gaby Aguirre did her professional best to put him at his ease. "Just act normally," she said, "don't worry about any of the other people here. Just talk to me. Concentrate on me. It'll be fine."

He suddenly felt nervous. People would watch this. What if he sounded stupid? His mouth was suddenly dry.

She seemed to sense this and called for one of the crew to bring him a glass of water, which he drank gratefully.

"Anselmo," she purred, "you know why we are here. We are making a documentary about the devastating earthquake and the volcano. Now, after all these months, we are hoping to piece together the story of what happened and how a volcano suddenly turned up just down the road. We are interviewing lots of people to talk about how it all affected them, and you are important, of course you are, because according to our research, not only were you here when the volcano erupted so dramatically — provoking that earthquake — but you were also there close by when the volcano suddenly appeared."

"Yes, yes, that's true. I was only a boy when the mountain — it wasn't a mountain yet, of course — suddenly blasted out of the ground on Don Artemio's land. That's why we called the volcano 'Artemio's Fire', you see, and then, you know, of course, it erupted like that, and there was an earthquake. It was dreadful, you see, those destroyed buildings, that boy in the street. That thing, Artemio's Fire, seems to have been a part of my life, and sometimes it feels as if—"

"Perfect, Anselmo, that's perfect," said the famous Gaby Aguirre, placing a reassuring hand, over familiarly, on his knee. "Let's save it all for the filming, shall we? Cristina, did we get any of that? Are we running?"

The cameramen and the soundman agreed, and someone produced a clapperboard to hold in front of one of the cameras. Cristina, the director, silently counted five seconds down with her fingers, and the interview began.

Federico

Sitting in his flat in the big city evening far away, a glass of beer next to his chair, smoke curling from the cigarette he held between his fingers, Federico tried to take stock of his life and the massive changes that had shaken his once settled world. His father, to name just one, had died, leaving his old and slightly quirky aunt and her mentally challenged daughter rattling around in the hacienda in San Miguel de Las Colinas, far to the north. That was a significant change. His daughter, his lovely daughter on whom he doted, had got married and moved out of his home, and he missed her like hell. That was a big change, too. And then, thanks to his father's passing, he had inherited a substantial amount of money and obtained a more spacious flat, which was nice, and yet another change, indeed a welcome one. He was determined not to let that change change him, though. He would continue to do his legal work, most frequently representing trade unions and advocating for workers' rights in an unequal world.

The huge thing, however, quite apart from everything else

that had happened, and something which had taken him completely by surprise, was that now, for the first time in years, he was yearning hopelessly for a woman who had already gone and whom he might never see again.

He shouldn't be smoking. It was stupid to threaten his health like that, as Angelita told him almost daily. At least she used to when she lived with him, but now she and Martin, the strange foreigner who was his new son-in-law, had a flat of their own, and that was right and proper. But the echoes of her absence seemed to haunt his new world. He took another drag on his cigarette. He would give up, he would. Not tonight, though. Not after the year he had been through.

He was still trying to adjust to being fatherless. Now that Don Esteban had gone, he missed the old *pendejo* in a way he would never have expected, given their stormy relationship, antagonistic on both sides. Of course, he had always admired him. It was obligatory after all. Many other people showed their fading respect for the old revolutionary as he ambled towards the grave in the hacienda outside San Miguel, rattling around with his disappointed sister and her damaged woman-child. But love? Even now, he didn't know if his father had ever truly felt that way about his son. True, the old man had loved Angelita — everyone did — but most grandfathers Federico had encountered felt a special affection for the children of their children, so he supposed that was not something enormously special. I, though, I was denied, he wailed to himself and then felt guilty for such self-absorbed absurdity.

Loving Angelita? That was a given for him, but it also seemed to be so easy for many of the men who circled around her. There was Martin, of course, and looking at the two of them, he was sure it was the real thing, at least for now. They had met on that bus journey to San Miguel de Las Colinas as they made their way to the Volcano festival to commemorate the fiftieth anniversary of the young mountain that had erupted near the town such a relatively short time before.

What a festival it had turned out, so shockingly, to be. The concert, the parade, the joy, the sudden agony, death everywhere, all just after he had made it to his own father's deathbed in time. By the time his father had wheezed out his last stuttering breath, however, it was almost a minor event in the cataclysm that had engulfed the town. It had started at that concert where Angelita played the violin truly like an angel, duetting with that beautiful young man, Julio. They looked more like a couple at that moment than his daughter and Martin, the foreigner who had been sitting next to him, his leg encased in plaster after the bus crash that had nearly killed him and Angelita as they made their way to San Miguel. Yes, Julio loved Angelita too. He understood, but they were good friends, not lovers — more like brother and sister.

Then there was the professor who was conducting, the old lech. Disgusting. He wanted to hate him. Professor Jacinto Perez, the world-famous violinist, Angelita's teacher, and — he could still hardly bear the thought of it — his daughter's seducer. What could she have been thinking? How on earth could Perez have sunk so low and abused his position in that way? It didn't bear thinking about. He wouldn't think about it. He couldn't stop thinking about it. But Perez had been punished for his sin, it seemed (if you believed in that kind of thing), damn near killed on the rim of the volcano as it blew its heart out the day after the concert. The maestro would never play again, that's for sure, and would be severely disfigured for the rest of his life. To cap it all, he had that trouble with his weird twin sons to deal with now, not something that a person so badly mauled should have to face.

Federico still didn't know why he had agreed to represent the maestro's sons. He was a lawyer who argued for the rights of workers. The professor's sons, on the other hand, were ex-members of an abusive religious sect whose purposeful act of propelling the monstrous leader of that cult into the Volcano's pulsating fire looked pretty much like murder, however extenuating the motivation for their act might seem. Not his kind of thing at all. But the professor had lost everything he told himself. Then again, so had so many townspeople and visitors, still mourning for the victims of the earthquake, which the volcano's eruption had been a precursor of. How does anyone face a thing like that? How does anyone come to terms with such an appalling catastrophe?

I suppose we just do, he told himself as he felt again that sudden, unfamiliar lurch of longing, a new sensation after years of not feeling anything at all. He had been hurt and devastated when Angelita's mother had walked out all that time ago and disappeared from their lives so many years before. He hadn't understood it at the time and still didn't, and supposed he never would. Back then, though, and quite apart from his sense of abandonment, he had worried about the effect that it would have on his daughter. But she had never talked about it. She had been very young, after all, and it seemed their lives together had quite enough love to go round for her to be much preoccupied. He'd stopped worrying about it years ago.

Then, he'd met Martin's sister, Victoria, and even though she was married — admittedly to a man who seemed to be, at the very least, having some kind of nervous breakdown — he had no real defence against the sudden tsunami of emotion he felt almost as soon as he met her. He was far too respectful to do or say anything about it, given the circumstances, but he knew that she knew, and what's more, he knew that at some level, she felt precisely the same as he did. That's why he had agreed to help her (another desperate case) get her vulcanologist husband out of that stinking jail and out of the country on account of his bizarre behaviour at the concert that night. He couldn't *not* help her even if he'd wanted to. She had disarmed him from the moment she had arrived at his father's hacienda and pleaded for help.

Now she had gone back to her country, taking her children and that man with her. Try as he might to stop himself, he just kept thinking about her, awash with the almost teenage yearning this provoked in him so that the case he was due to work on tomorrow in the courts — an unfair dismissal issue — was practically impossible to focus on. He closed his eyes and pictured, yet again, Victoria's hurt look as she had said goodbye to her brother Martin that day at the airport and had vanished into Departures with tears in her eyes and a lingering glance back at him.

"*Señor*, is there anything else you need? I'm going to bed now."

"No, thank you, Maria. I'll see you tomorrow."

He stubbed out his cigarette, pulled himself up from his chair, and made his way to the bathroom for a pee.

Maria

She was almost used to her new room and her new existence. It was so different from her previous life. Now she was a widow living in the flat of her male employer. Then, she had worked for a well-off woman and her family during the day. But, she had lived in the chaos of a cramped flat in a miserable part of the city with a husband who drove a battered old taxi, that is, when he wasn't drinking too much and beating the hell out of her because life in the city had turned out to be so much worse than the unrealistic dreams they had both allowed themselves to believe in.

Despite all that, she had been lucky, she supposed. She had had a good job with a good employer. Señora Bicky (she knew that Victoria was her real name) was a foreigner who worked on the radio and was married to a scientist who travelled extensively to study volcanoes. But the señora paid her well, and Daniel and

Sarah, Señora Bicky's son and daughter, were like the children she had never had. She missed them all the time now that they had gone.

What is going to happen to my life now? she wondered for the thousandth time. Before, even when the increasingly unhinged Juan was thumping the crap out of her, she at least knew where she was, a respectable married woman in an unhappy, terrible marriage, working for a good employer, painfully fulfilling a role that society had ordained for her. But then Victoria Kassoniliki had persuaded her to leave her abusive husband, incurring the wrath of their sanctimonious neighbour, Esmeralda. It must have been Esmeralda who told Juan that she was going to San Miguel with Bicky (because it seemed she was worried about her husband Alexei, who was behaving increasingly erratically, and she needed someone to look after the children).

It had taken them some time to work this out when they eventually discovered that Juan had been killed in an accident with a long-distance bus at Mil Curvas (a thousand curves), a stretch of the highway on the long journey north, the same accident that had involved Angelita (her new employer's daughter) and her husband Martin, señora Bicky's brother.

She had been shocked to learn about Juan's death, but try as she might, she did not feel sad about it. She felt regretful about the slow erosion of the dreams they had both cherished, which began when he persuaded her to leave their village and head for the big city. He had assured her that they could live a better life there than the one they had started with, scratching a living from the dusty earth.

She supposed he had been right to be adventurous in a way, but when it hadn't worked out as he had hoped, he acted as if it was a personal insult. He shouted out his misery, disappointed by their childlessness, disappointed by the squalor of the polluted congestion he drove around in, and disappointed by the tiny flat they lived in. The more disappointed he became, the more irritated he became. And the more irritated he became, the more he seemed to need to take it out on her. It had started with shouting and progressed to a light slap from time to time, gradually increasing until by the time she had left him, getting out of the car one day in a monstrous traffic jam on the ring road so that he could not follow her, he had started to strike her. She had to get out.

She imagined she would live a lonely life now. She was done with trying to be a good and pleasing partner. God knows she had done her best. Maybe men were all like that after a bit, though her señora's husband seemed all right, just a bit strange to her eyes and often absent. Just occasionally back then, though, she thought of a gardener who worked for a lady a few doors from Victoria. The lady was a bit of a nightmare, señora Bicky always said. She was friends with people in high places, none of them very agreeable. At least that was her opinion after going to a gathering there. Still, the gardener who worked for the lady-with-not-very-agreeable-friends had kind eyes. Maria remembered him and how he always greeted her in a very friendly fashion when she arrived and left Bicky's house. He seemed like the kind of man she might like.

She got into bed and told herself not to be silly. She'd never see him again, obviously, and her youthful looks had long ago evaporated, she thought, and anyway, just because someone seemed outwardly friendly, you couldn't tell if….

She gave up, closed her eyes, and was asleep in a heartbeat.

Silvestre

It wasn't possible, was it? To be *president*? Of the *whole country*? The entire enormous great big country? In his life, he'd travelled around the republic, of course, been to conferences, holidayed at beaches (when he was younger), visited the sights, and though there were still places, even states, he'd never been to, still he knew his way round the land that he was proud to be a member of. What he was contemplating now was altogether different, however, and he wasn't sure that he was up to it.

San Miguel de las Colinas, where he was the mayor, and its surroundings were their own little world, after all. Even in that little world, he had found it hard to govern, beholden, as he was, to the landowners from the valley and to businessmen who had helped to realise his mayoral ambitions. Once he had achieved such great heights, they had been quite sure that he owed them and, as a result, called in favours all the time. That old monster, Heredia, for example, who managed his large estate in the valley, was a typical and prominent case. Don Vicente, as everyone called him, had once been a person Silvestre admired, despite knowing that he and all the other landowners treated their workers in a nearly medieval manner. But you get used to things, and once you've been sucked into the web that money and power spin around you, you have to learn to live with yourself some-how, so he did, shutting down his normal scruples to make it possible.

It was not possible anymore. The earthquake had been trans-formative in all its awful majesty, not just for the town and its surroundings, but also for Silvestre. In the aftermath of such a traumatic event on such a vast scale, there was no one pulling his strings for once. As a result, his essential humanity had suddenly escaped from the compromises he had learnt to justify, burying his guilt in a whirl of mayoral action. But when, in an instinctive response to an extraordinary situation, he had started scrambling over the ruins of collapsed buildings, tearing at obscene piles of concrete with his bare hands to try and reach people buried in the wreckage his actions, so instantaneous and so unlike the typical behaviour of a politician that people had become used to, had roused the public imagination and lifted him from the rut he had been trapped in and had seemed destined to follow.

The effect of his actions on himself was even more extraordinary. It was as if he'd woken from a corrupt and troubled sleep, realising suddenly, and with absolute clarity, that he could be better than he had allowed himself to become. There was a reason to be better, not only for himself but also for the people all around him, whether they were the Migueleños he lived and worked among or, if it came to that, anyone in this beautiful country.

When people started whispering that he was the kind of man who should be their national president, he had thought they were joking, but he soon had to accept that more people saw him as a way of turning the page on the old systems of government. Aurora, his loyal PA, agreed enthusiastically with all of this, but that shouldn't mean too much, he thought. She was dogged in her support of him, no matter what he did or said.

He supposed she was in love with him, but she never showed it or made him feel pressured, and even if she had, there was nothing he could have done about it. She was just 'there', always dependable, and apparently unshockable, never complaining and only ever looking unhappy if he seemed to be getting the worst of some exchange. In such cases, she would do her best to step in and deflect the attention of his adversary, especially if it was someone like the chief of police in San Miguel, Rivendeira.

Silvestre knew the chief was corrupt, like many of his law enforcement colleagues. He suspected, too, that the policeman was somehow in league with the more extreme right-wing forces, who, for people like the landowners in the valley beyond, seemed to offer the possibility of a future in which they could go about their business without being bothered by petty rules or social interference. But whatever he was involved in, the problem, of course, was that, like many corrupt people, he seemed to be able to cover his tracks remarkably successfully. Silvestre would give anything to get rid of his compromised cop, but now it looked as if he would just have to wait his time and hope for the man to go too far, too overtly.

Hope! It was a new emotion for the mayor of San Miguel. But it felt good! Anytime it started to fade, as it sometimes did when he was tired or low, he only had to look at the young man at his side, Silverio, who had become such an essential part of his life and who felt almost like the son he had never had. However, that was overly sentimental, he told himself.

How strange life is! A few months ago, this new and passionate supporter had been a thorn in his side — he and the gang he associated with. The 'Ejercito de Arturo Sanchez' (The Arturo Sanchez army), they called themselves, with their demonstrations and political posturing. Their most successful stunt had been to interrupt the concert for the Volcano festival, which he had worked so hard to bring about. Right there in the theatre, in front of the state governor and his repulsively condescending wife, the EAS had humiliated him and upset those lovely young soloists, both San Miguel born, playing their violins so beautifully. One of them, the young man, had been a victim of the earthquake the next day, poor guy.

Yet, he knew even then, at some level, that what they were fighting for — fundamental rights for the workers on the estates and in the factories — was laudable and that if he could only have seen it back then, he had a lot more in common with them than he did with the people who saw him as 'their' man. Silverio had been their leader but had moved away from them to support Silvestre's new and growing campaign for the presidency. His girlfriend, the lovely young nurse Genoveva, was still, he knew, an active member of the EAS and had taken part in that demonstration in the theatre. Still, she was now dealing with her own sorrow, the death of her brother, the young violinist who had lost his life the next day in the earthquake.

He felt tears come to his eyes at the thought of her sadness and marvelled at the open purity of such an emotion. How miraculous to feel this way again. Now, and with everything that had happened, he felt as if he had washed a lot of the dirt away from his previously unsatisfactory life and had a new chance to make a difference. What a prospect. What possibility!

"Silverio," he said to the younger man at the next desk in his office ('most irregular' according to Aurora), "have you got a minute? Something I'd like to run by you."

Part One
Battle Lines

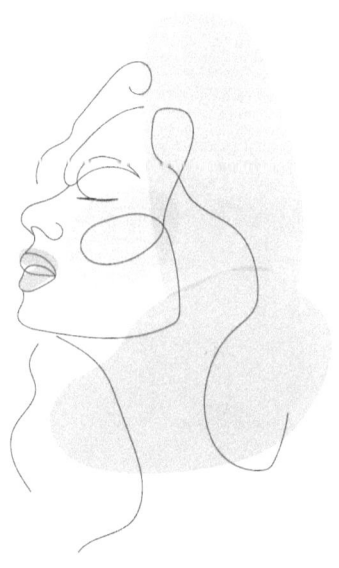

Chapter 1
Genoveva

THE FIRST TIME Genoveva and Silverio made love, she felt a contentment and joy unlike anything she had experienced before. It was so joyful that it was as if she could momentarily forget entirely about her brother, Julio, and though ever since his death he hovered around her like a spectre, his beautiful face with that little scar above his eye from a childhood accident. Still, she was able to almost ignore him in the ecstasy of her happiness.

At the hospital the next day, people would not stop asking her what had happened and why she was so different. But she didn't have any words to describe how she was feeling, so she just smiled enigmatically, without the almost hidden sadness that had masked her features since she had received the news about her brother's death back then, when it was too late to repair the damage to their relationship. To her friend Dolores, however, she said something of how she was feeling and why, and watched the look of amazed encouragement on the other nurse's face. Her friend looked slightly shocked by it all, or jealous. Or both.

Surprised by ecstasy as she was, the world seemed good to Genoveva for the first time in months. Colours were more vibrant, the air hummed with promise, and the sound of laughter all around her had a magical, sweet ring to it, as if the pain that had been visited upon San Miguel had been washed away by quicksilver streams and gorgeous music. She supposed that this was what real happiness felt like — a great joy that could accept and encompass not just the beauty but also the ugliness of life, neutralising it with its shafts of delicious sweetness.

She was still almost skipping as she went to the nurses' locker room and changed out of her uniform and into her regular clothes. She and Dolores left the hospital and made their way to the meeting place. Though everyone now knew about the EAS (the Ejercito de Arturo Sanchez), the movement founded to protest the medieval conditions under which some agricultural workers were forced to toil on the prominent haciendas down the valley. They still adhered to their secret knocks and codes upon arrival. They had had to change the location, of course, since they had discovered a spy, Dr Martinez, in their midst. Still, in general, they enjoyed a considerable amount of public sympathy, especially since the demonstrations and the resulting thuggery of the landowners' gangs at the volcano festival concert and the next day.

That threat had passed, or so they thought, when the thugs, overawed like everyone else by the cataclysmic earthquake, had left the town. When the old leader of the landowners, Don Venustiano, had sickened and then died, Silvestre Ocampo, the mayor, was significantly less hostile to them than before. Anyway, he appeared to be spending most of his time preparing for the presidential election in which he was planning to be a candidate. According to Silverio, it seemed as if he had a good chance of winning, too, though it was said the entrenched factions standing against him were gearing up to challenge him, and to do so with everything and anything they could find. Still, that's what you would expect, her boyfriend said, and we have to be ready for anything they might throw at us.

She and Dolores, who had joined the EAS because of her, took their seats. Most of the others were here today too, except for Silverio himself, who, now that he was helping Ocampo in his fledgling campaign, had stopped coming to the meetings. His place had been taken by number sixty-seven, Gerardo Villas, a young pharmacist who had joined the group just before the volcano festival and who had made himself incredibly useful immediately. For some reason, though, she didn't quite trust him. There was something too watchful and sinister about him, a quality a bit like the weasel Martinez. Perhaps, she told herself, it was simply that he wasn't Silverio. But she didn't think so. There was something suspiciously secretive about him, in her opinion, even though she didn't know anyone else in the group who shared her beliefs.

The meeting started. On today's agenda was their journey to Calixtlapan down the valley to demonstrate at a landowners' meeting, which was to be addressed by Don Venustiano's son, who had assumed a leadership role since the death of his cantankerous old father. The landowners were forming themselves into a powerful right-wing movement, allying themselves with some of the wealthy fossil fuel barons and evangelists who held significant influence over both local and national politics. As far as the EAS could see, these groupings aimed to chip away at all and any egalitarian laws that restricted them.

"What they want, what the rich always want," Silverio had said to her, "is to make more and more money and not have anyone or any regulations to get in their way." What they feared, above all else, was outside scrutiny of their behaviour, which might threaten the money they earned from their nefarious activities. It was an open secret that the growing drug trade was based in their haciendas and formed an increasing proportion of their crops. That meant, of course, illegality, and illegality breeds corruption, and that was precisely what the EAS was fighting against. They still cleaved to visions of justice and equality. However, Venustiano Heredia's son was gaining popularity in the region. He spoke the landowners' language, and by all accounts, he possessed a great deal of charisma and force.

The people round the table, and their followers, planned to go to this meeting and disrupt it, peacefully, of course, to make 'young' Venustiano look ridiculous and take the attention away from his growing stature.

By the time the meeting had broken up, they had made their plans. They would charter a bus and set off mid-morning, so they would be ready in the square at Calixtlapan when the meeting, rally, or whatever it was started. Secrecy about this was paramount. If people found out about their actions, they would likely do their best to thwart them. They knew they were running a considerable risk. They would not be popular when they arrived.

Chapter 2
Federico

AFTER HE ENDED his online video call and shut the lid of his laptop, the lawyer sat in his new office, in his new, bigger apartment, thinking. Anyone observing him would have found it challenging to determine whether he was sad, happy, reflective, or morose. It is doubtful that he would have been able to work it out either. He reached for another cigarette just as Maria knocked on the door and came into the room. He put the cigarette back in the carton and turned to face her.

"Hello Maria, what can I do for you?"

"I am sorry to interrupt you, señor Federico."

"You haven't interrupted me, Maria. I was just talking to Señora Vicky, but the call is finished now."

"How is she, señor?"

"She's well. The kids are well. They ask after you, you know."

"I miss them, señor."

"I know you do. But maybe you'll see them again sometime soon. Who knows."

"Señor?"

"And the best thing is you stopped me from having another

cigarette by coming in just now!" Angelita, when she came round, had started using underhanded tactics. 'If I have kids, *papi*, I'd like them to know their *abuelo!*'

That got his attention. "Are you pregnant?" he'd asked, surprised at the tiny flicker of joy that the idea sparked in him, but she assured him that no, not right now. Not after she'd got herself an agent and was beginning to be booked for small events, quite apart from the string quartet she had formed, which was starting to attract attention. But she had finally provoked him to do a bit of research. After some research, he'd come across advice about how to quit smoking, which suggested cutting out one more cigarette a day every fortnight. He was already down to six — with, he had to admit, occasional lapses — and though it was tough, still he longed to be able to look his beautiful violinist daughter in the eye and say he'd done it for her. And maybe for Vicky, too, though in what possible world she might be interested, he couldn't tell.

"Señor?"

He brought himself back to the present. Maria was still standing there.

"I'm sorry, Maria. I was thinking of something else. What was it you wanted?"

"Señor, about these classes you mentioned the ones about learning to read and write," (she blushed), "the first one is tomorrow. But señor I am not sure. I will never be able to read and write like you señor, like people do," (She had not got far in primary school), "and I don't want you to waste your money señor. So maybe I should not go?"

"Maria, I won't hear of it. I know you're nervous. I would be, too, in your situation. But this is important. It's the first step. Who knows where it might lead?"

She stood there uncertainly.

"You know what, Maria? What I would like most of all —

when you come back from that class — is for you to make those incredible stuffed peppers you do, and the rice and the spices and everything. I love the way you do it."

His phone rang. He apologised and answered it.

"Hija," he said in that loving tone he reserved for Angelita, "hold on a second..." He covered his phone's microphone, "You'll have a great time tomorrow, Maria," he said, holding the phone away. He put it back to his ear. "If you have a second sometime in the next thirty minutes or so, could you make me a coffee?"

She went out of the room.

"Papi, we haven't seen you since Sunday. Martin and I wonder if we could come over tomorrow for dinner."

"You have news?"

"No. Well, nothing important. But we'd like to see you anyway."

Again, he covered the microphone on his new phone.

"Maria," he called out into the corridor, "there'll be three for dinner tomorrow. Angelita and Martin are coming over."

Chapter 3
Jacinto

HE WAS GETTING STRONGER every day. His face was still criss-crossed with scars and burn marks, but that was something he'd just have to put up with, he supposed, and who knows, maybe it would look less awful in time, and then he'd be back — and watch out! He'd already spotted two beautiful young physios in the rehabilitation centre he'd been living in since he had been discharged from the hospital all those weeks ago. Stop it, he told himself, that's how you got into this mess, this disaster, in the first place. For a moment, a memory of Angelita's beautiful willing-ness flashed across the music professor's memory, but he swatted it away in frustration, guilt, and anger.

His hands were still a mess, but they had stopped hurting and had, to a large extent, healed despite the scars. And although he walked with a bit of a limp, he was going a little further all the time. Strangely, his almost insane journey to Artemio's Fire that night seemed, despite its tragic consequences (as evidenced in the injuries he had sustained at the crater), to have awakened in him the desire to wander. So, today he walked out of the centre and made his way towards the main square in the afternoon sun, life-affirming and warm upon the stretched parchment of his face.

A few people waved at him as he made his way. He had become something of a minor celebrity, though not like before, when he had been one of the world's most celebrated violinists on stages around the republic and the world. Now he was admired, and his fame as a virtuoso instrumentalist had been recast in the public's eyes as a brave survivor in his new role. There even seemed to be a hint of redemption in people's attitude to him since the story about his quest to save his twin sons from the clutches of that mad 'religious' sect had attracted sympathetic coverage from the media. It had dulled the rumours of his abusive behaviour towards his young students that had begun to surface just before the eruption. Now he was viewed with a mix of pity and admiration, neither of which he thought he deserved in the slightest. He knew, or thought he knew, that his devastating injury was some kind of punishment for his past indiscretions.

In the square, there was a seat he liked to sit on, just outside a café. He leant his stick against the bench and sat down, the wooden slats warm under his buttocks. Birds skittered through the colonnades to wheel in the square before heading off past the dome of the cathedral, still undergoing restoration work after the damage it had suffered all those months ago. He sank on the bench and closed his eyes, sensing, only a moment later, a shadow fall across him. He looked up.

"Hello, maestro!" Not many people called him that anymore.

"Marisol, how lovely to see you. Won't you sit down?"

"Only for a moment. I have a meeting with the mayor."

"He's still the mayor? Even though he's trying to get himself elected in the next presidential showdown?"

"Yes, I know. People are beginning to criticise him for that. But I wanted to know how you are?"

"I'm getting on, you know. I feel better. Really," he added, seeing her face.

"I'm glad to hear that. And what about the boys? Those poor boys?"

What indeed? They had their first appearance in front of a judge, scheduled for ten days later. He couldn't see how that would help, given that the twins were still hardly speaking, except to each other, though the psychiatrist had assured him that they were making good progress. But the fact is that they were facing the charge of murder. After all, they had pushed the leader of that terrible cult into the maw of the erupting volcano and watched with apparent disinterest as the man they called 'The Luminescence' evaporated in a bubbling hiss of flame and steam. There were witnesses, too, so there was no denying it.

"They seem to be improving, gradually. As far as I can tell, they are not overly displeased by my visits."

"I am so pleased to hear that." She looked at him with concern. "My poor, dear man, and it was all because of me you were here in the first place."

"Ah, yes, but…"

She was already getting up. "Let's talk properly later," she said, "you lovely man."

"Not so lovely now,"

"That depends on what's inside," she laughed and left, saying she didn't want to be late for her meeting.

He had no time to reply.

A waiter came out from the café behind him. He ordered a coffee and a small brandy.

Yes, the twins were making progress. He hadn't been lying. They no longer looked like blank stick figures. They wore regular clothes — jeans and T-shirts — and their once-hollow eyes had begun to register the world around them. They had hair on their unshaved arms. One of them had even smiled at him yesterday while the other looked on. They talked to each other, too, though he found it difficult to understand what they said. He desperately wanted to know how it had all happened, but as long as they wouldn't let him in, he remained in the dark. Still, if his recovery had taught him nothing else, it had made it abundantly clear that what was needed, above all, was patience.

Next week, for the hearing, Federico Hernandez, the lawyer father of his ex-student, was flying up to represent the boys at the hearing, and his daughter, the student he had seduced, the memory of whose naked beauty still haunted his dreams, would be giving evidence too. Perhaps even his estranged wife, Marisa, would be there as well, if she could manage to pull herself away from whatever commune or shamanistic gathering she was involved in, but he hoped she wouldn't show up. Her disdain was more than he wanted to put up with right now. What a disaster it all was.

He took a sip of coffee, dark, bitter, and seductive, and chased it down with a small amount of brandy, which warmed his throat as he swallowed. If he could only reach out to the damaged boys and prise them away from the madhouse, or worse still, the prison, then maybe he would be able to think about what to do with the rest of his own messed-up life.

Chapter 4
Vicky

AFTER THE CHILDREN had gone to bed, Vicky walked into the sitting room, far across the sea, where her husband Alex sat slumped in front of the television watching sport, which he didn't enjoy. But recently, sunk in the dark gloom of some kind of depression and unreachable as he had been ever since they had flown away from their old life — maybe ever since he had begun to lose his mind over there in San Miguel, even before he'd ended up in a prison cell — he had taken to staring at the screen for hours on end. She didn't understand it.

He had once seemed almost noble in her eyes, slightly strange to be sure, but she had always ascribed that to his ranging fascination with volcanoes and mountains and the earth's core, and she had loved him completely. She still did, she supposed, and the kids missed him, but he had been absent in more than just a geographical way ever since he'd got to San Miguel. She still hadn't got to the bottom of who he'd got involved with. There was a woman, she kind of knew, but it didn't seem to have been a typical affair, and then he'd ended up being part of that demonstration at the concert and been dragged off to a stinking prison where he'd been beaten up and seemed to have become seriously unhinged. Thanks to Federico (she smiled at the thought of him), they'd got out of the country before the police came for him again, and now here they were, far away, and she didn't know what to do.

She had tried to bring Alex out of his catatonic state. When she took Daniel and Sarah to school, she left him with instructions to do various tasks around the house until she returned. But he never did what she had asked, and after the first few times when she'd prompted him, unsuccessfully, to explain why not, she'd simply stopped and watched, wondering what on earth to do.

Vicky had found a part-time job at the local radio station, producing a couple of programmes. She did it remarkably well. They wanted her to start doing a daily show of her own, but she couldn't agree to that whilst Alex was in this state. It hurt to say no, but then everything hurt these days. The man she had relied on ever since they met, and who had fascinated her with his lean grace and air of mystery, had begun to get puffy and invisible. She tried to think of him as he used to be, striding up mountain scree, wildly excited by volcanic eruption, talking fumaroles and eruptions, magma and pyroclastic flow. He had always been an impossibly compelling maverick to her, and she wished for him to be that again. But that person had vanished before her eyes.

Thank God for Federico. Federico, who had persuaded her to get him out of the country, to stop him from spending years in courts and prisons. And even as this amazing man persuaded her, she could see the sadness in his eyes and feel a sharp stab of regret in her own heart. Now she was beginning to realise how much she needed the lawyer, whom she hardly knew in her present predicament. He had seemed the most sympathetic and reliable person she could rely on in the craziness of those last days.

Now, so far away, their frequent online conversations were her lifeline since Alex had drifted away to wherever he was. Federico seemed to understand her, and she found herself telling him everything that was going on in her life. He reciprocated with news about his own life, and, of course, about Angelita and Martin.

Martin! She missed him so much. She even missed his maudlin phone calls in the middle of the night, or whenever else he used to call her to bemoan his petrified life, as he saw it, and the guilt he carried about the death of his girlfriend back then, all of which led to his complete lack of self-worth. But that had changed since he'd met Angelita on that bus journey and they'd both nearly been killed. He had emerged from the wreckage of the bus with a badly broken leg and a wildly re-energised heart, and with a lovely young woman beside him.

She almost resented her new sister-in-law because now it was to her that her brother turned whenever he was troubled or in need of support, and his calls from across the ocean were increasingly few and far between. Nothing could break the bond between them, given their shared experiences, and she loved her brother, but she needed him, too. She knew she wanted to go and see him because, right now, given Angelita's burgeoning career, he was unlikely to travel this way. She still felt guilty that she had not been at their wedding, but given the circumstances, that had not been remotely possible. It was only right, therefore, that she should go now. Sometime soon, at least. And if she went to see him, she would also see his father-in-law. She smiled at the thought.

"I'm going to make us a bite to eat, Alex. What do you fancy?"

There was no answer.

"I'll rustle up some pasta and a nice salad. How does that sound?"

He might not be interested in supper, but she was. Lightly cooked pasta, a lovely salad with the new dressing she had come across, and some chilled white wine. She might even have a glass as she cooked.

She put a pan on the stove and prepared the pasta as she waited for the water to boil. Then she got a nice bottle of Macon Villages from the fridge and opened it. Pouring herself a glass, she took a delicious, cool sip, savouring the freshness in her mouth.

There was a massive crash from the sitting room and a groan — more like a shout, hardly human — and for a second, she stood rooted to the spot, unsure of what she had heard. Then she went into the room.

Alex was standing, half crouching, blood pouring from a deep, very deep, it seemed, gash in his arm. There was glass everywhere, and a cold draught had invaded the room. It came from what had only recently been the window but had now been reduced to a few shards of glass. She realised the television had gone and the coffee table was overturned.

"Alex, Alex, what the hell? Alex, are you all right? What the hell happened here? Let me look." She pulled his arm towards her, and the sleeve of her shirt turned red almost at once. The blood was virtually spurting out of his arm.

"Mum? Dad? *¿Qué está pasando?* What's happening?"

Daniel stood in the doorway, and on his face was a look of shock. From the corner of her eye, she could see the smashed television on the lawn in the light that spilt out from the sitting room. She didn't know where to look, what to do, or where to go.

"Mum? Mum?"

She snapped out of it then. "Daniel, lovely, don't worry. But quickly, run to the kitchen and get me two tea towels, the biggest you can find." As he ran off, she turned her attention back to her husband. "Alex, Alex, talk to me. What happened? What have

31

you done? What on earth's going on? Alex?" She forced him to look at her, tilting his head with her free hand. But the eyes that looked back at her were completely blank.

Now she was terrified. Daniel came back with tea towels. He stood there watching in fear and confusion, and she tried to create a tourniquet around his arm above the wound that, unless she did something about it quickly, would pump out blood until there was no more left to pump. She tied a second towel around his arm, and the blood flow slowed a bit, but she became conscious of just how much he had lost already. He looked pale and — she didn't mean to think this — quite mad. She sat him back down on the seat — they could clean the blood later — and ran back into the kitchen, Daniel following her. Oblivious of her soaking shirt sleeve, she washed her hands, dried them quickly on her jeans, and reached for her phone.

"Which service? Ambulance, please. Yes, he's breathing, but he's cut himself very badly. He's lost a great deal of blood. Fifteen minutes? Yes, we'll wait."

She hugged Daniel to her. She'd go back into the sitting room in just a second. She had to. But she just needed a moment. She started to cry.

Chapter 5
Silvestre

His office seemed to be full of people rushing in and out, paper flying in all directions. They were young, they were old, they were anywhere in between. Stacked in a corner were placards adorned with his face, others showing him scrabbling away at fallen masonry with his bare hands on that terrible day when the earthquake struck. The walls were hung with banners which said 'From the troubled past to a better future', the slogan they had chosen.

Aurora made her way through the melee in his inner office. "Señor Alcalde, Señor Alcalde."

"Yes, what is it, Aurora?"

"The representatives from the communidad del Arroyo Blanco have been waiting for twenty minutes, and it's only ten minutes before you are due to talk to the leaders of the *Syndicato de trabajadores de transportacion* (the transport workers union). Sir, you know I am the biggest supporter of your campaign, but something must be done. It can't go on like this." She had found a new sense of purpose and authority since the volcano had done its business.

"Okay, Aurora, I'm coming. Silverio, thank God," he called in relief as he saw the younger man make his way through the crowd of volunteers, "can you get some order into this rabble? I have to go and remember to be the mayor!"

"Yes, Sr Alcalde — Silvestre," he still seemed uncomfortable using the mayor's first name despite multiple invitations to do so. "Leave it to me."

Police Chief Rivendeira accosted the mayor in the corridor. "Señor Alcalde!" He was one of the people who had most decidedly not succumbed to the newfound gentleness of his nominal boss.

"What is it?"

"Them again, Sr Alcalde. We may have a problem."

"Them?"

"The woolly-hatted crazies."

Ah, Silverio's gang and that lovely girl of his. He'd steered clear of them and their activities, only saying what was politically appropriate or necessary. After all, they hadn't pulled any crazy stunts since the fracas at the concert that day. Just the occasional demonstration and some leaflets, that kind of thing, and what was wrong with that? But now Rivendeira was telling him something about a plan to go and demonstrate in Calixtlapan, and that would be like walking into the middle of a fire. Who knows what might happen.

"How do you know about this? Anyway, Calaxtlapan is some way away, so why do we need to bother?"

He saw the look that passed over Rivendeira's face and tried to ignore the contempt he saw there.

"I make it my business to know these things," said the police chief acidly, "and Sr Alcalde, you will not want trouble. Young Heredia, Don Venustiano's son, is getting stronger every day."

"Listen, Comandante, I know it could get a bit confrontational, but the day we stop people expressing their democratic rights is not a day I wish to see while I occupy this office."

"Well, as to that…," the policeman started, but the men were interrupted by Aurora clutching a folder full of documents. "Sr Alcalde, you are running very much behind schedule. We must get to the meeting."

"Okay, Aurora. Listen, Rivendeira, I've heard what you've had to say, and I will think about it. I'll let you know my position as soon as I can."

"Señor," said the disgruntled policeman, his indignation reflecting off the gold braid around his sleeves and the medal ribbons on his jacket.

Meetings, meetings. He got through both of them, unsure if people were aware of how little he was listening. However, the meetings continued, as meetings often do, and it seemed that an agreement had been reached. He was worried the bus drivers would go on strike. He would see if he could get someone on the city council to negotiate that away. He asked Aurora to make a note about it.

Back in the chaos of his office, he received a call from his wife, who wanted to know if he'd be coming home for dinner so she could instruct the maids. When he said he hoped so but could not be sure, she bore his reply with considerably more grace than she used to do. She had warmed to her new-seeming husband and, she was honest enough to tell him, was quite excited by the possibility of being a president's wife, a 'first lady' as she would be known if he did manage to succeed in the campaign that he worried was Quixotic but which seemed to be gathering momentum.

Silverio approached him to discuss plans, and they talked about the stages of the campaign, fundraising activities, and the numerous requests for him to make visits and appearances. "But

Se- Silvestre, I am worried that being mayor and at the same time fronting the campaign are just a bit too much for you."

"Because?"

"Well, it would be superhuman to be able to devote yourself equally to both things, and though you could do just about anything – "he was mocking the mayor affectionately — "still you are not yet, as far as I know, superhuman!"

"You think I should resign? Leave the mayor's office?"

"I think you should consider it. Then you could devote yourself one hundred per cent to the task of getting elected and along the way avoid," he paused," avoid any slip-ups as mayor which an over-extended schedule might make more likely."

One of the things he liked about the young man was his directness. He was always respectful, indeed, more than that, he was committed to the campaign they had started after the earthquake. Silvestre had come to rely on him more and more, and if — just imagine it — if he pulled this off, he would want Silverio at his side. So he didn't dismiss his suggestion lightly. In his heart of hearts, he knew he, like Aurora, was probably right.

"I'll think about it. Can we discuss it further over the weekend when you and your lovely girlfriend come over?" He had developed a fondness for the nurse, admiring her passionate convictions and easy nature, quite apart from the fact that she was stunning and cheerful. He found it impossible to be cynical about the state of politics in the country or the unpleasant compromises that anyone who practised its dark arts was forced to make when faced with the life-affirming affection that flowed between Genoveva and Silverio. It made him feel young and optimistic, and he looked forward to seeing them together again. But first, he needed to raise a complex subject.

Indicating that they should go into the small sitting room adjacent to the office, he pointed to a seat opposite the sofa, where he usually sat.

"Look, Silverio," he started after resting his head on his inter-locking hands. He looked down, trying to think of what to say and how to say it. "I had Rivendeira harassing me earlier on about your friends and their plans."

"Ah." Almost a sigh. This conversation had been a long time coming.

"You know I have kept away from this. I have not asked you or Genoveva about your activities. You well know that I am not unsympathetic with your aims and ideas – "*¡Dios mio!* Why was he sounding so pompous? "I mean, I like your crowd, if I'm honest, but keep that under your hat. However, I have my future to consider!"

They both laughed at that. Silverio was watching him intently.

"But I don't need what they, what you do to interfere in the campaign. I mean, I hope you understand that. Because I would hate for you to be compromised in any way."

Silverio understood. He pointed out that he had moved away from day-to-day involvement with the EAS precisely because of his participation in the campaign, something that Silvestre Ocampo had suspected, but was pleased to hear confirmed.

"And your girlfriend?"

"Well, as to Genoveva, she does what she wishes to do, and I will not stop that because I do not have the right. But she knows the score. I mean about her and the movement and about me and my closeness to your campaign, which she supports whole-heartedly, as you know."

"Yes, but still. "Look," he went on after a reflective moment, while the younger man sat and waited, "I know they are planning to go to Calixtlapan, don't ask me how, and I'm sure you will not be with them."

Silverio didn't reply, so he went on.

"But I'm worried. Heredia's son appears to have been

creating some kind of militia — I mean, his men are armed just like his father's thugs used to be. They're probably the same ugly bastards as they were then," (using bad words was not a habit), "and now that they seem to be getting more heavily into the drug trade, that's a real danger. I mean, look at the gangs in the far north and the south of the country, and the terrible things they are doing to each other. One of our main tasks will be to find some way out of that awful situation. Otherwise, God knows where this beautiful country is headed."

Silverio did not reply.

"But if our campaign means anything, it means to find our way out of this nightmare. It means finding a way to put kindness, humanity, equality, and basic justice at the heart of the way our country is governed."

"I know, Silvestre, and you know that is why I have joined you, because I, too, share this vision."

"So this is the thing. I worry about what will happen in Clalixtlapan. I worry for all those well-meaning young people — not all young," he added, seeing Silverio's raised eyebrow, "and what Heredia might do."

"Thank you. I mean it. Thank you. However, they are aware of what they are doing and the risks they are taking. We faced old Heredia's thugs that night at the theatre. If it hadn't been for the eruption, God knows what might have happened the next day." He remembered how he and Genevova had only escaped a severe beating, or worse, when the ground had started rumbling back then. "They have taken precautions. I am sure they have."

"Pleased to hear that. I can't help being worried, though. But if – "he held up his hand to stop Silverio talking — "if you can get them a message, just say from me that they should be careful, really careful. But of course, you can't say it came from me. We don't want that to get out."

"No, of course."

"Now we'd better get back to the madhouse next door!"

Chapter 6
Martin

HE WAS ALWAYS pleased to see his father-in-law. The two got on very well, like good friends, despite the age difference, and he loved witnessing Federico's devotion to his daughter, since it mirrored his absolute love for Angelita.

Martin had never been happier, and he was finding it difficult to adjust. He kept waiting for his tired miserableness to reassert itself, but it seemed to be staying away. He had lived with it so long that sometimes he felt a little bit lost. But then Angelita looked at him, or he watched her while she was practising, and he was grounded again.

He had gone back to writing. Not the self-indulgent, hardly disguised fiction he had been writing, which he now viewed with what one writer he had seen being interviewed called 'tender contempt.' Yes, he had written those things. They were part of him, but he was now able to read them objectively — something he had not been able to do before — and he knew how awful they were.

Additionally, a publisher of educational books had asked him if he could contribute material to help students learn English, and to his surprise, he found it quite enjoyable.

He missed Vicky and the children, of course, but less than he would have done if Angelita didn't occupy the centre of his life. For the first time in years, ever since their parents had killed each other in a morbid version of love and devotion without a thought for their children, he did not have to rely on his sister for his emotional equilibrium. As a result, he did not talk to her as much as, perhaps, he ought to. He knew she was going through a difficult time over there herself, but it had never been his role to comfort her because it had always been the other way round. He had not worked out how to change that, if, indeed, it needed to be changed.

But tonight, the fingers of his left hand interlaced in Angelita's right, his other hand clutching a bottle of imported wine — a brand he knew Federico was partial to — he waited for Angelita's father to open the door. It was Maria, however, who let them in. She told them that Señor Federico was talking to 'your hermana, señor' but we'll serve dinner as soon as he has finished.

Angelita looked at him, smiling. They both knew of the bond that had sprung up between her father and his sister, bitter-sweet because it seemed nothing would come of it. But it seemed somehow symmetrical given their situation.

They walked in. Martin gave the bottle to the maid, and Angelita went with her to the kitchen. He followed. They could hear Federico's voice coming from the room he used as his office. When Angelita asked Maria how she was Maria instantly started telling her about a class she had been to that day 'because señor Federico told me I should señora' and how it was the first classroom she had been to since she was a girl and how it was scary but how it was exciting too and she had liked it, if she was honest and what if–

"Martin," Federico "called from his office. "Martin, come

here. Your sister wants to talk to you. I think your sister needs to talk to you."

He found himself standing behind the older man. His sister was on the screen. She looked, frankly, a bit of a mess, Martin thought, which was unusual for her. When she saw him, she called out his name. "Martin, brother, Martin, I need you. We need you." And she started to cry.

"What? Vicky? Vicky?"

"I think I'll leave you to it," Federico said as he left the room. "Be gentle with her hijo, she's been through a lot." He had called him son!

He sat down in the seat that Federico had vacated.

"Vicky, Vicky, what on earth? What's the matter? What's happened?"

"It's Alexei," she said, wiping her eyes with the heels of her hands.

"Alexei? He's not—"

He was going to say *dead*.

"No. Yes. Worse. No, not worse, I don't know. Martin, I need you. *Martin*."

"Vicky, for God's sake, tell me what's happened. I don't understand. What's happened to Alexei?" He could hear Angelita talking to her father, asking questions, expressing surprise, or was it shock?

"He's been sectioned."

"Sectioned? What, like locked up or something? Like someone mad."

"Yes, exactly like that. Locked up. In a mental facility."

"Oh my God. Vicky. But how? Why?"

He was unprepared for what she had to say. She told him how difficult it had been since they left, something she had hinted at before, but she explained it properly: how Alexei had seemed to have lost his way, how his spirit had somehow been crushed.

42

How his eyes, once focused on distant landscapes and the wonder of the mountains and seas, now seemed to be looking at nothing as if he were somewhere else in his mind. Her voice trembled. She described how the ease they had together, the physical closeness and joy they felt (Martin wasn't hugely comfortable with that), had vanished in the mist — or in that stinking jail or whatever else, whoever else it was that had confused him in San Miguel.

Martin was in shock. Victoria Kassoliniki, his sister, was stronger, far stronger than he was. She had never talked to him like this before, laying her soul bare, it seemed, and he did not know how to react. He just sat there reeling, open-mouthed, hardly breathing.

"Martin?"

"Vicky. My God, Vicky. I'm having trouble taking this all in. I mean, honestly, I—"

"I don't blame you. But imagine, just imagine, you can't, of course you can't, just imagine what it's been like here. And Martin, I'm sorry to burden you like this," she had started crying again, "but I don't have anyone else to talk to you, anyone who knows."

He reassured her, almost in tears himself now, and told her to stop being silly and just tell him, please, please, what had happened that had got Alex — he stumbled over the word — sectioned.

So she talked about last night, about the crash from the sitting room and the blood and the television, "they're still trying to work out what happened and how, exactly, he cut his arm so badly, but he's not talking at all," and about how they took him away in the ambulance. She couldn't go because of the kids, and by the time she got to the hospital (a new friend of hers had come to babysit, but she hadn't left before she had lulled her troubled children back to sleep), the curtains were round Alex's bed. His arm had been bound up (the ambulance got there just in time, she was told, and he had lost a lot of blood. We've had to do a transfusion, the doctors said, and because of the overcrowding, we couldn't get a theatre, so we've done the repairs right here in cubicles. Not ideal, but we believe we've resolved the issue.

What they couldn't repair there and then, they told her, was his deteriorating mental condition. Throughout the whole ordeal, he had remained unfocused, almost comatose except for a brief outburst when he'd started shouting about the end of everything and the destruction of the universe. They'd had to restrain him without damaging the wound on his arm. When they'd done that, they'd sedated him, and then, before she got there, the psych team had come, and they had said no doubt about it, he's in some kind of psychotic crisis, and the best thing is to take him to a mental ward.

"When I got there, Martin," he heard her say, "they were waiting for transport to get him there, and then it seemed no time at all before he was being wheeled away. Martin was gone, and I'm left trying to explain to the kids what on earth has happened. I can't do it because (she was crying again) I don't know what's happened, and I don't understand anything.

As if on cue, he saw Daniel and his sister run into the room, and when they saw him on the screen, they cried out in excitement, 'Uncle Martin, Tio Martin'. For once, Vicky didn't even tell them off or quieten them down. And so, while he tried to live up to his billing as the beloved uncle, Vicky managed to put herself back together, and it looked to him as though it was possible that, in their excitement, the children might not have realised just how upset their mother was.

When Martin arrived in the dining room, the other two had already started eating. Maria had put his serving in the oven, so he went to get it and insisted on taking it to the table himself despite her protestations. Then they talked about what he had heard and what, if anything, he could do about it. The conversation ultimately proved fruitless because they didn't know how they could help. They ran out of things to say and ended up sitting in silence until Federico finally turned to Angelita and asked what news she had to share with him.

"Sorry, Papa, you are not going to be a grandfather yet!" Martin blushed, Federico play-acted, looking shocked, and said, "It's nothing."

"Well, it must be something."

"Well, no. Yes. Just that I've agreed to a concert invitation from home."

"You're doing a concerto or something?"

"No. We're taking the quartet," it was called the Delgadillo Quartet in honour of her departed friend and colleague Julio, "we're doing a concert to raise money for the San Miguel Foundation."

"That's good. Well done, *hija mia*. They need all the help they can get for the *fundación*. There's a lot of work to be done, even after these months, to repair the damage that the earthquake caused."

"The thing is — this is what I wanted to tell you - it's on the same day... the evening, as the deposition, the thing with the judge." She was talking about her and Martin going to court as witnesses to the events on top of the volcano that day when the leader of the weird cult had been killed.

"Ah." He was not looking forward to cross-examining his daughter and son-in-law, a possibility that had arisen since he had submitted the written evidence, making it perhaps unnecessary. But he was representing Jacinto's sons, so it would be his job, if called upon, to question his daughter and son-in-law.

"I don't want to speak in court, Papi, and with you there too. And you'll be asking me difficult questions. And Martin, too. Do we have to?"

"I hope it won't come to that, *hija*. You have sworn your statement, and we are not saying those boys did not do it, so I don't know why they would need to hear from you."

"But they could ask us to talk about it?"

"Yes, amor, I'm afraid you could. You were there."

"I know, and we were nearly killed. My hair," she said distractedly.

"Look, if it comes to it, I will ask you questions, and so will the prosecution guy — or woman, I don't know who it will be yet. But the only thing you need to remember, both of you, is to say exactly what you saw. You didn't do anything wrong. You just happened to be there."

The earth began to roar and smoke, as strange men appeared naked, marking the beginning of the pyroclastic fume, and terror ensued. She had relived the awfulness many times in lurid dreams that Martin had sometimes been forced to gently shake her out of.

Martin was trying to focus on this part of the conversation, but his mind was still preoccupied with what his sister had told him and its potential meaning. He shook himself away from that both for his own sake and for hers.

"Federico," he said, "do you think your aunt will mind us staying at the hacienda?"

"She'd better not! After all, it is our house, too. Anyway, I feel I ought to check up on her and see just how crazy she has become."

Angelita looked at him. They laughed.

Chapter 7
Rosario

She applied her lipstick as carefully as she could, given her increasingly shaky hands. It was bright red. She appreciated the way it offset the lined pale skin of her face. *Quite dramatic*, she thought, looking at her old features in the mirror. If she could only do something about the skin that fell from her jawline in a great fold. Maybe I should have that plastic surgery, she thought for the thousandth time. I can afford it now.

It was true. Her brother, Don Estaban, had left her a substantial amount of money, more than she had expected, even after the sum he had set aside for Marcela. He'd left the bulk of his estate to Federico and her niece, of course. Still, the house was hers for as long as she lived, after which it would belong to Federico, with the legal requirement that Marcela be allowed to live in it for her lifetime as well.

She took up a tissue and used it to remove flashes of red where her hand had been unsteady. Looking this way and that, she tried to make sure she hadn't missed any rogue blotches. Satisfied, she crumpled up the tissue and placed it on the surface of her new dressing table, a luxury she had awarded herself and about which she still felt guilty. She had spent so long being resentful of the way her life had turned out, and then feeling guilty about feeling resentful, that guilt had become a constant refrain in her life, even where it was not merited.

She removed the piece of muslin that she always put around her shoulders to ensure no makeup ever escaped onto her clothes. She hung it on the hook to her left. She stood up, somewhat unsteadily, and moved backwards to admire her handiwork. Not too bad, she thought. I may be a *viejita, una abuelita* — old granny, except I never will be! But, I look as good as I can at this vast age. A bit crumpled and stooped, but I'm not like those black-veiled old crones who hang around the cathedral all the time. At least I have a bit of class! Her brother's death seemed to have unleashed a newfound intolerance in her, and, guiltily of course, she was enjoying it. If she shocked some people, that was all to the good. It amused her. After all these years, she'd earned it.

Downstairs, in the newly refurbished rooms that had been set apart for her, her daughter Marcela was vocalising, apparently contentedly. It was difficult to tell if she was aware of the changes in her life: the death of the old man, her new room, and the girl who was with her so much now that her mother was spending increasing amounts of time outside the house. But Tia Rosario had managed to convince herself that Marcela was content and well cared for. After all, she didn't have much time left to enjoy herself, and she was determined to make the most of it. Later, her family wondered how early her mental decline first manifested itself. Still, for now, in Angelita's fond regard, she was just becoming a bit more eccentric, and that was rather wonderful.

She heard the bell ring at the main entrance, and her maid answered the door. A man was there, apparently, saying that he was there to collect her. She brushed the side of her dress, shook the bracelets that adorned her wrist, enjoying the sound they made, and walked to the stairs from where she called out for Marcela's carer. By the time she had reached the bottom of the stairs, Tiacuri was standing outside the room where she had been feeding Marcela.

"I'm going out," Tia Rosario barked.

"Sí, señora," the girl replied without expression.

"Look after Marcela. She's well and happy?"

"Sí, señora."

"I don't know when I'll be back. Please call me if you need to, but only if necessary. Do you understand?"

"Sí, señora."

Tia Rosario walked through the door and took her seat in the expensive-looking car that was waiting for her. Expressionless, Tiacuri watched as she was whisked away.

She was greeted warmly when she arrived at the club. Situated on the north fringe of San Miguel, it had escaped damage when the earthquake had ripped up the centre. It was a typical dining and social club for the well-heeled (and usually older) Migueleños. Before Don Esteban's death, Tia Rosario had never been here. Still, she had found herself invited, and as the weeks turned into months, she began to enjoy the rarified atmosphere in the lounges and dining room. No campesinos here, only people of refinement and tradition, she told herself. It reminded her of something, but she couldn't quite recall what it was. She was sure it would come to her later. She enjoyed the attention too and the slightly heightened sensation of risk, as if life was inviting her for the first time. Ridiculous at her age. *But was it?*

"Doña Rosario, hola, bienvenidos, ¿Cómo está Usted?"

"Don't be silly, Arnulfo. You don't have to be so formal. Call me '*tu*' like I do you."

"Really? A señora of your standing? Such a beautiful lady?"

49

He was flirting. It was rather lovely. She laughed modestly, unconscious of her coy suggestiveness.

"Come, Señora, come and join our little group. They are all dying to meet you." He took her hand and placed it on his arm as he led her to a circle of deep armchairs, occupied by a mixed group of men and women, some easily identifiable as wealthy ranchers, others more comfortably and obviously town dwellers. They were not young, but with one exception — an old gentleman with slicked-back white hair and a rather fine jewel-studded waistcoat under his smart formal jacket — they were all somewhat less advanced in age than she was.

She looked at the chairs and thought that if she managed to sit down in one of them, she might never get up. She was finding that kind of thing quite difficult and preferred it if no one was around to watch her exertions. At home, she kept a stick by her side, just in case, and she could always call the maid. But she didn't use the stick in public. It made her look ancient, she thought.

Reading her thoughts, Arnulfo indicated an empty chair and helped her into it. "I won't leave you there," he said quietly, so that the others could not hear, and she squeezed his hand gratefully.

Arnulfo, a prominent local businessman in earlier times with a lifestyle to match his extravagant success, introduced her to all the people in the circle. A club servant was called, and drinks were ordered. She had developed a taste for champagne, something she had hardly ever touched before, except for the occasional wedding she had attended over the years. She had mostly been abstemious except for the occasional Blanquita on special days, but in his will, her brother had told her to enjoy herself for once, and now she was determined to do just that.

"Everyone," Arnulfo announced while they waited for their drinks, "I would like you all to welcome the estimable Doña

Rosario. We all remember her dear departed brother, Don Este-ban. For those who have not had the pleasure of meeting Doña Rosario, I commend her kindness, her intelligence, her views, and, of course, her beauty."

There were noises of approbation. If anyone was embar-rassed by the man's oleaginous flattery, they did not show it. She smiled at them all. Furthest away from her was a woman she didn't recognise. She must have been in her late fifties or early sixties, she thought, though she found that age difficult to judge these days. The woman was handsome with blond hair (dyed obviously, she thought cattily, ignoring the black colouring that masked her white mane). She wore a sharp blue suit, a simple necklace over an expensive white shirt, and rather fabulous earrings, probably from a local silversmith. If she was wearing any makeup at all, it was very skillfully applied. All this, Tia Rosario noticed in an instant before finding the woman's gaze directed at her, a smile hovering on her lips.

Arnulfo was speaking again. She didn't follow everything, but it seemed that they were all bound by their worry about the campaign being run in favour of the mayor of San Miguel, who was running for president of the country.

"He's not even very good at being a mayor."

"He's a friend of those left-wingers — the crazies."

"He tried to stop old Don Venustiano from doing what was right with those idiots. They would have beaten the crap out of them — begging your pardon, Doña Rosario — if the bloody eruption hadn't happened, and that would have been less than they deserved."

"Mi amigo Rivendeira, the police chief" — they all nodded — "he says they're off to cause trouble at that gathering in Calixtlapan. Heredia's son is due to speak. He's going to try and build a movement, you know."

"Maybe he should run for president." Rosario saw the blond

woman smile knowingly. However, it seemed that no one else was paying any attention to her.

"No. He's too hot-headed and a bit thick, frankly. His heart's in the right place, though. We need someone cooler and better with the media — someone plausible. Someone the party will accept." The party was the national ruling party from whose ranks the last seven presidents had emerged.

"What do you think, Doña Rosario?" Arnulfo was asking her. She wondered what to say. Politics was a bit much for her, and she'd never been that interested. She left all that stuff to her brother. Heredia's son? He could have been her son, too, if it hadn't been for her brother standing in the way. Her eyes blazed with a sudden fury. It took her by surprise.

"What I think doesn't matter, does it? I'm just an old woman — 'they all cried out at this, saying 'not true' and 'you are anything but' — "maybe, but I tell you what,' she began to enjoy this, 'I think we need a bit of order around here.' We need someone strong. We've been through a lot, haven't we? We need someone to lead us out of it."

They murmured their agreement. Tia Rosario sat there in shock at having spoken so assertively. Not something she was known for. But this sensation of possibility, like a gathering wave, was warm and seductive. She felt slightly dizzy. She blinked a few times.

The drinks had come. It took a bit of time to sort them out, but finally, everyone had the proper glass in their hand.

"I propose a toast," Arnulfo cried, "to the future of our glorious republic built on law and order in the service of God."

"Law and order in the service of God," they cried before drinking thirstily.

"There's someone else here I'd like you to meet," Arnulfo interrupted them. "From the ruling party. Trying to decide whether to make a run for it" — he paused for effect — "not to escape, *haha*, but to lead, to be our man," he winked conspiratorially, "Isabela Gutierrez. Please give her a welcome and tell her she has to enter the race to put an end to the dreams of that weak liberal," they sneered, "Ocampo."

All eyes swivelled to the woman in the blue jacket. "Hello, everyone," she said, eyes icy blue, her blonde-dyed hair perfectly cut, "it is a privilege to be here. I don't know if I'm 'your man' or not," they laughed, "but someone has to bring this country to its senses and just because someone can crawl over rubble and take part in ordinary acts of humanity, it does not make him a good leader. It does not make him the man for the job. This country needs a very different kind of person. Not some kind of fake provincial." (Ah, yes, Tia Rosario thought, so typical of people from the capital, but still). "It needs someone who believes in business, in entrepreneurship, who will not allow unnecessary rules and regulations to stand in the way of our prosperity, our glorious future. We need someone who believes in God, in family, in people's freedom to write their destiny."

Arnulfo took over. "It needs you, Isabela Gutierrez, it needs you!" She smiled.

Later, as the car dropped her at the hacienda, Tia Rosario wondered at the world she had been invited into. It was so exciting. It refreshed her. *I am someone*, she told herself.

The maid opened the door for her. She saw Tiacuri standing just outside Marcela's 'suite', watching her as she arrived. What a sweet girl she is, she thought. "Hello Tiacuri, my dear," she said, "how are things today? Is Marcela all right?" She saw her daughter approaching, and she noticed her leaning her chin on the girl's shoulder. For a minute, she felt a bit jealous, but not for long. "She is so lucky to have you, and so am I." She smiled sweetly and made her way up the stairs. She needed a bit of a lie down, she thought — four whole glasses of champagne. Imagine!

Tiacuri watched her go, irritated again at her employer's wild mood swings. She thought she knew the reason for this and wondered how long she could stand it. But she had developed a fondness for Marcela, whose inchoate mumblings were now the music of her days.

Chapter 8
Angelita

SHE LAID her violin lovingly back into her case, the same violin that had been passed on to her by Perez, the professor who had seduced her. It had been an act, she admitted to herself, in which she had been complicit. Martin, though, wasn't having any of that. He was sure that Jacinto Perez was an abuser and should be made to pay for it, even if what more you could do to a man whose life had been laid waste by the injuries he had sustained at the volcano's rim, he could not articulate. His dislike of the man — and he wasn't alone in this — was softened by the pity he felt for him. He did at least acknowledge that his handing over of his precious violin to his wife, even if it was an expiation of his guilt, was nevertheless a beautiful thing. He loved how she made it sound.

There was a knock on the door.

"Come in!"

It was David, a promising young violinist, whom she was helping. He had needed guidance with some problems of technique. She loved working with him. He reminded her of how Julio used to be: eager, gifted, and gentle. How she missed Julio.

But at least she would see Genoveva when she went back to San Miguel.

They worked through some passages, and then he left, and she was free to pack up and start the journey back to the flat. On the metro, she sat clutching her precious instrument. It was a journey she took nearly every day. Occasionally, she remembered that Martin had seen her that day, the day that she couldn't stop thinking of as her disgrace, which Martin told her was ridiculous. But how strange that he should have noticed her then, of all days, and then they had met on that bus, and now she was going back to him.

She had returned to her studies immediately after the 'Volcano' concert with a zeal bordering on the manic. But she was in love, for one thing, and she was doing it not just for herself but for poor dead Julio as well. And suddenly the violin, the sleazy professor's old violin, overlaid with a patina of all the great players who had made it sing, started to sing for her, to sing with joy and passion. Every day, she knew it better, knew what it could be made to do, knew its quirks and oddities. She added it to the other meaningful relationships in her life. Her husband, her father, her increasingly eccentric aunt, her friends, especially Genoveva. This extraordinary instrument was now part of that family, close to her, a part of a sacred circle.

She had completed her studies in record time, and two things had happened: she had immediately been offered teaching work at the *conservatorio*, and after a concert she had played in, she had been approached by an agent. As a result, her career was taking off. She had already performed three different concertos in various parts of the republic and had achieved success as a recitalist, so far only in the capital. Additionally, the Delgadillo quartet, which she led, was carving out a name with its daring programming of contemporary compositions alongside some of the most famous and revered pieces in the repertoire. They were getting reviews. Critics were calling them 'the future'.

When she got back to the flat, she only had a couple of hours before she had to go out again. The quartet was going to perform a programme in one of the smaller halls of the arts complex, which housed the national auditorium. Federico was slumped on the sofa, a book he had been reading in his hand. He looked up when she walked in. She saw immediately the worry and perplexity on his face.

"Not teaching, *mi amor*?" she asked him.

"I called in sick. I know, I shouldn't have, but I just don't feel in the mood. I'm still trying to process what Vicky's going through. And the kids. And Alexei. What a mess."

"Come to the concert. It'll take your mind off things."

"I wish I could. But imagine if one of our students or teachers saw me."

"That's what happens when you tell *mentiritas*, those little lies!" she laughed. "I'm going to have a shower," she said, peeling off her top as she headed for the bathroom. It affected him — it always did. He followed her.

"Honestly, Martin!" she complained later, "now I'm running late." She was wearing her concert clothes. All black. A long skirt. Shoes with modest chunky heels.

"I love you!" He went up to her and took her in his arms.

"¡Por Dios!," she exclaimed, laughing. "Not again! Control yourself!"

He was about to reply, but a phone started ringing.

"That's yours."

"Yes, but where is it?"

She found it, eventually, and when she answered, she heard a familiar voice.

"Genny," she exclaimed, "we haven't spoken for too long. I'm so sorry. When are you coming to the big city?"

"Soon, I promise."

"Look, Genny, I have to rush. I have a concert. If I don't get a move on, I'll be late." Martin called a greeting. "But listen, I'm coming to San Miguel in a week or so for that court thing. Can we meet up? The quartet's doing a concert. You could come to it. If you'd like to, that is!"

"That sounds so good, Angelita. And I love that you called the quartet the Delgadillo quartet. But look—"

"You'll have to hurry."

"Thing is, I'm going to a demonstration that day. It's a big one. Don't tell anyone. But I should be back by the evening. And if not, we'll see you the day after? How is Martin?"

Angelita wanted to tell her how Martin was, and about Vicky and her dad and all the news. She wanted to share her stress about her appearance in front of the judge and ask her about Silverio's work with the alcalde. But all she said was," *Lo siento*, Genny, I'm sorry. I have to go. I'll call you, okay?"

She ran out of the house, blowing a kiss at her husband, who smiled back, satisfied.

Chapter 9
Federico

"Maestro Perez. Good day. I hope you are well. How is your recovery?"

"Good day, Licenciado. Forgive me if I don't shake your hand while I sort myself out." He was struggling with his walking stick while taking off his coat to hang it up. They were in the hotel room Federico had hired for their meetings, as he didn't intend to invite the man up to the hacienda, not while Angelita was there. Even now, he couldn't be sure how Martin might react to the man's presence in their San Miguel home.

Federico, like many others, but in his case with more piquancy, was conflicted in his view of the ex-violinist. Here, after all, was the man who had seduced his daughter, but maybe that wasn't the whole story, he thought. After all, at their first meeting in the business section of that plane, as he was dashing north to reach his father on his deathbed, and Perez had been on his way to the Volcano festival, Federico had seen something vulnerable and confused in the famous artist. Rationally, he was appalled by the man. Still, the wreckage he had become and his efforts to rebuild his shattered life had erased Federico's disgust, and if anything, excited his admiration.

When the professor asked him to help with the case of his sons, he said no, and he was sorry. Not his kind of thing at all. On the other hand, Angelita and Martin had told him something of what they saw, which was not much, and it had intrigued him. It sounded unusual. But he still didn't want to take the case on. The injured man, however, had protested, kept on at him, talked about cults and weirdness and loss. He seemed so desperate and needy that the lawyer had finally agreed to look into it. "I can't promise to help you, but I'll do a bit of burrowing around and see how I feel then. Will that satisfy you, Professor?" It would. The man's gratitude was almost embarrassing.

The first thing he did was to obtain a complete account from him. This wasn't easy. The professor's recollection was somewhat confused, and he was trying desperately to make the twins' action seem accidental, so that it took all of Federico's tact and experience to piece together his first clear picture (he hoped) of what might have happened.

A few members of the 'Sons of Perpetual Light' who had survived that eruption on the mountain were still being held by the local police, so he went to speak to them. They were confused young men. Two of them clung to the teaching of the 'Luminescence', the cult's leader, and spouted rubbish, as far as he could see, atheist as he was. They had no hesitation in venting their hatred of the twins and, in their opinion, their monstrous actions.

They were comforted, of course, by the knowledge that The Halo had achieved full luminescence and would soon wreak his celestial revenge, but that didn't stop them from hating his killers. On and on they went until Federico couldn't take it anymore. But there was another boy who began very hesitantly to talk about what went on at the Halo's command. He muttered about the shaving and the shriving, the whippings and the deprivations; the whole ghastly weirdness of it all, in the lawyer's eyes.

Then he went to see the twins in the secure unit where they were being held. But that was of little use, at least at first. They looked at him with a lack of interest, which was not exactly hostile, but they showed no warmth or welcome. He explained who he was and why he was there. It had no effect. After a bit, he left and went to talk to the psychiatrist in charge of their case. The man wasn't prepared to say much, of course, but he did say the boys were gradually emerging from their psychological 'hibernation'. The one notable thing, he said, was that the boys seemed to communicate with each other in a mixture of words, looks, and gestures. The moment they caught anyone watching them or trying to listen, they clammed up and reverted to their silent blankness.

Federico reported all this back to Jacinto Perez in calls and on his increasingly frequent visits to San Miguel. What he did not tell the former musician — because he did not think it would help — was that the psychiatrist had given him an idea. He had found a way of sitting close to one of the twins and, in his genuinely sympathetic voice, would ask him simple, gentle questions. They all followed the same format. "Were you happy?" he would say, and then, when, as expected, he got no reply, he would say, "Yes, that's difficult. Sorry. Maybe ask your brother if he was happy." Then some communication would take place between the two damaged boys.

At first, he could not make out much of what they were saying. But then came a day when someone started to open the door into the room where these sessions took place. Without thinking, Federico stood up and paced as the nurse came in. Asked how he was getting on, he noticed the boys observing him, and something told him to say that he wasn't having much luck. He couldn't get anything out of them.

He saw the twins register that, and it might have been his imagination, but he thought he glimpsed the shadow of a smile on both their faces. In the few visits since he had gradually begun to understand little bits and pieces of what might have gone on, and though it was still hazy and confused, if he added that to what the other boy had told him he felt he was beginning to understand something of the warping reality that the controlling leader and his lieutenants had imposed on the young men they had drawn into their twisted cult of fake religiosity and sado-masochism.

"My intention," he was telling Jacinto now, "is not to question the fact of what the boys did. You saw it. My daughter and her son-in-law saw it. Two of the cult members will testify to it."

"Then they are lost?"

"No, I don't think so, Professor. Not entirely. At least I hope not. I intend to build a case that your sons were damaged by a form of psychological bullying, coercive control, and cruelty of an extreme kind, which essentially altered their minds. As a result, they have diminished responsibility for what they did."

"It was not their fault?"

"It was most certainly their fault. But what I hope to be able to show is that because they were not thinking straight — they were, in effect, mentally ill at the time — they should not be punished too severely for what happened."

"Will it work?"

"We have to hope so. We have to hope so."

Chapter 10
Alexei

WHAT WAS HE DOING HERE, and where was *here*? What was going on? Where were the mountains? Everything was fuzzy in his mind. Every time he tried to remember how he had got to this place, he just couldn't.

He appeared to be injured. He had a bandage on his arm. He wondered why. He thought he might unwrap it to have a look. But every time he tried, he couldn't do it. He would start, and then he'd forget what he was going to do or why.

People visited him, but he did not know who they were. They seemed nice enough, but he couldn't understand what they said. They asked him how he was doing, and sometimes they would take him to another room and talk to him some more. They gave him food, drinks, and pills to swallow. They knew nothing about volcanoes. Now and then, he would ask them about fumaroles or different kinds of seismic events. They asked him why he was talking about those things. Since he didn't know, he didn't answer. They started talking again.

He wondered where Vicky was. Would she come and rescue him, like she did before when he was in that bad place? He couldn't recall why it was bad, but upon reflection, he remembered strange images and smells. This didn't make any sense, except that he did recall they were horrible. He started to cry. That was a problem because it meant that they'd come back and start talking to him again.

He had no idea how long he had been here. He slept. He was living in a strange cloud of shifting shapes and half-memories. He didn't know what to make of it. If Vicky came and got him, then he could go back out onto the mountain and feel the vibrations under his feet that rattled his chest and struck his stomach. The air, sometimes sulphurous, tickled the raised hair on his head. He was questing again — feeling the joy of searching. If only he could see something through the fog.

He couldn't feel anything.

Then one day, when another nice person gave him some pills and a glass of water, he realised he didn't want to have those people around anymore. Even in the murky world of half-light, he knew somehow that this was not what he wished for. As the days — he thought they were days — went by, and Vicky didn't come, one thing he started to obsess about amid his confusion was that he didn't want all the pills they were giving him. Increasingly, all his conscious thought now focused on how to stop taking their medication.

It was difficult. They stood and waited until he swallowed. *Very well*, he reasoned, he would try not to swallow. It wasn't easy. They watched him like hawks. He couldn't find a way to fool them. After each visit, the mist would ascend, and he would forget what he had wanted to do. Gradually, over the course of some hours, everything would become clearer. He would start to remember again.

He kept trying, until one day he managed to hide a pill against his lower teeth, or sometimes, his top teeth. He waited until the visitor had gone, then he would spit what was left of the pill into his hand. He stuffed it into his pyjama pocket. Later, he'd fish it out and drop it into the toilet.

If anyone had checked, they would have found a sticky, dry mess in his pockets. Luckily, they never did, so the evidence would disappear in the large washing machines that serviced the facility every day. Meanwhile, hiding the pills in this manner meant that some of the medicine seeped into his system, but much less of it did. As a result, his situation became clearer.

He had thought he was back in that former hellhole he'd been confined in, but this place did not seem the same. He had his own room, after all, and he had a bed to sleep on. But he could not leave, as he discovered after he walked to the main door one day. Before he reached it, he was stopped by one of the nice people and gently but forcibly escorted back to his room. That was that. But, as he had walked that corridor, he had seen a room to the right of the main door. It looked like a storeroom. It felt important to remember that.

He also noticed that the person who had restrained him wore a white coat. He also had a cluster of keys hanging from his belt. He started to wonder if these facts might be useful, but he lost that thread as he struggled to free himself from the suffocating fog.

As the days passed, however, his mind crystallised round two different, but overwhelming preoccupations. The first was, *When was Vicky coming to collect him?* When she failed to appear, this thought began to morph into anger over why she hadn't come. He began to resent her.

He could not know, of course, especially in the distorted reality of his confused state, that the medical staff had refused to let her visit. To bring about a cure and, hopefully, a return to some kind of normality, she had been told that she had to stay away. Any distractions or complications from his past would imperil his recovery.

"*Complications?*" she had protested, outraged. They had been unmoving, and as a result, she was excluded from whatever was happening to her husband and her children's father. She knew that something was wrong with him, as it had been ever since his time in San Miguel. She still thought that she should be the one to put things right. That's what she told Federico repeatedly in their long-distance conversations. The experts didn't agree, or they weren't listening.

The other obsession that had taken hold of Alexei was an absolute certainty that if he could get out of the building. The mountains were waiting for him — yearning to welcome him back. He looked out of the windows and thought he could see their corrugated sides, their peaks, the thousand eyes that beckoned him, and the bright mysterious light that emanated from them. He could hear the rumble of their subterranean eructations, which penetrated the safety glass of his room. He could sense the vibrations pulsating through the building.

He needed to get out there to find out how imminent the threats of more cataclysms were, like the one in San Migu—. His mind always skidded away from what had happened at that point, as if he were not strong enough to face it. Not yet.

He was sure that the nice people with their robotic gentleness would not let him outside, into the glory of his natural environment. He knew what he would have to do — and he was sure they would understand once they saw how important his work was. He had to get out of there without their help.

The medical staff noticed a change in their patient. He seemed more alive and less vacant. Not knowing that he was managing to take less of his medication, they assumed that the pills were working their magic. They looked forward to observing their continuing effects. Meanwhile, Alexei was busying his stuttering mind, planning and calculating his escape. After a few days — or was it weeks? — of thinking about this, turning it round and round in his brain in a maelstrom of plans and plots, he thought he might have worked out a solution.

He looked out the window at the city buildings, which looked like sharks' teeth of spikes and mountains that stretched as far as his eye could see.

Soon, if he was clever enough, he would be back out there.

Chapter 11
Genoveva

SHE LOOKED up at the clock on the wall of the operating theatre and saw that they had been here much longer than she had anticipated. It was all because of her. Well, and him.

She had managed to avoid Dr Martinez, a surgeon at the hospital, for weeks now. He was the spy who had infiltrated the meetings of the EAS and informed the authorities about their plans before their protest at the volcano concert. Like other members of the nursing staff, she was repulsed by his air of entitled brilliance. The knowledge of his duplicity had enhanced that repulsion. Now, though, because another surgeon had been obliged to pull out at the last moment, here he was operating in the theatre where she was working. She wanted to leave, but she knew they were short-staffed and so she could not, in all conscience, abandon the team. As a result, she had no option but to endure his lizard-like nastiness.

It was only her professional training that enabled her to continue with her customary efficiency. Luckily, perhaps, her mask mostly hid the disdain that was written all over her face. Or maybe the real thing that allowed her to disguise her revulsion was the excitement she felt about what was to come.

She should have been on her way already, but an unexpected bleed from the patient on the table in front of them had provoked an emergency, and it had taken some time to bring it under control and to ensure that they could go ahead. And now, as a direct result of her obstinate persistence, they were delayed again, and she was desperate to get going. But the trouble with being a good nurse — in the theatre or anywhere else — was that patient care placed obligations on you that were impossible to resist.

The atmosphere around the table was toxic. Dr Martinez's face was flushed with barely uncontrollable fury, which had silenced everyone else present so that the only sound was the tock tock of the monitors helping the anaesthetist to keep a track of the patient's unconscious state, increasingly important now that they were to be opened up again. Of all the people in the operating theatre, Genoveva should have been worried. If she had made a mistake, God only knew what would happen next. But it was something else that was preoccupying her most at this moment. Unless things came to an end quickly, she and Dolores would miss the bus that the EAS had hired to take them to Calixtlapan for the demonstration they were planning to mount to disrupt the landowners' meeting.

The press had been alerted, and as one of the 'brains' behind the whole thing, she needed to leave the hospital in time to be with her colleagues. They intended to make a statement that would be impossible to ignore. They would face the entrenched interests of the old families and other reactionary forces, on top of which the growing drug industry with its accompaniment of bestial violence posed a massive threat. The EAS, however, believed passionately that right would triumph, and if justice wasn't worth fighting for, what was the point in anything? She knew that Dolores was waiting for her outside so that they could go together.

"Nurse Delgadillo," the surgeon spat out, interrupting her thoughts, "once I have proved that you have made a mistake, that you have not only accused me of professional incompetence and wasted valuable time with your stupidity, quite apart from putting this patient through unnecessary suffering, your time at this hospital will be over and good riddance. You and your kind should never be tolerated. You contaminate everything you touch with your juvenile whining, and here, in the sacred surroundings of this operating theatre, you are no better. Scalpel!" he barked. She looked him full in the face as she passed the instrument over. She could swear he flinched. The others in the room were busy looking at dials, the patient, or the floor, desperate not to catch anyone else's eye.

Of course, she was full of dread, but she had been certain. When you counted the used instruments on the tray, including the gauze and any other items, and compared it with everything they had started with, it didn't add up. There weren't enough swabs. And if the missing one wasn't on the tray and it wasn't anywhere else in the theatre as far as anyone could see, then it must still be inside the patient. She couldn't understand how they might have missed it, except that Martinez had insisted.

He had been in a hurry himself, too, for whatever reason, and not inclined to listen to a nurse he hated after his unmasking and rough treatment by the EAS all those months ago. He had a critical engagement he needed to attend, and he wanted to get away as soon as possible. "Come on," he told them all, "it's time we finished up here. So, against Genoveva's protestations, he sewed the patient up. But she wouldn't stop, even after Martinez had declared himself satisfied with how things had gone.

The surgeon tried to browbeat her into silence. He appealed to the other three people in the theatre who would usually feel it incumbent on them to agree. But they knew Genoveva. She had a good reputation in the hospital, and two of those present had worked with her before and had reason to trust her judgement. They were trapped between the surgeon's status, his anger, and his insistence that he was right and Genoveva's apparent unshakeability.

They gave no opinion, but their reluctance to support Martinez was making it increasingly difficult for him to continue blustering much longer. He had tried to bully her out of her position. "You think I should listen to you? A nurse? Do you know how long I've been studying and learning my practice? And how long did *you* have to study? What gives you the right to question me?" All the resentment stemming from his treatment on the night of the concert, the day before the eruption, and the foreign volcano man's attack on him was present in his exasperation. By the time he had been forced, against his will, to reopen the wound, he was boiling with fury. Now they would see.

Apart from the anaesthetist who sat at the patient's head, they all saw. There in the abdominal cavity, partly hidden by a coil of intestine, was the missing blood-soaked swab.

For what seemed like an endless minute, nothing moved except the machines and the patient's heart. Martinez stared agape at the evidence. Genoveva stood expressionless. She was unsurprised, yet relieved. They waited. The surgeon moved the intestine out of the way and lifted the swab before dropping it into the stainless-steel bowl.

"Polydioxanone 6 and a curved needle," Martinez barked, but they were already in Genoveva's hand. He did not look at her as he took them.

When the patient was finally re-sutured and cleaned, the surgeon walked over to the bin, ripped off his mask, gown, and gloves. He chucked them in and stormed out of the theatre before anyone could say anything.

When he was gone, the doors swinging behind his outraged departure, Genoveva walked over to the wall phone and asked for a hospital porter. Then she accompanied him and the patient to the recovery room, where she handed over the notes to the nurse on station and waited for the patient to come round from the anaesthetic. As a result, by the time all that was accomplished, she realised that she and Dolores had missed the bus and wondered what they would do. She went to find her friend and colleague, who was working on the geriatric ward, but before she arrived, she heard her name called. Turning round, she saw the director of surgery coming towards her.

"Nurse Delgadillo, I need to talk to you."

"I couldn't refuse, could I?" she said to Dolores later as her friend drove out of San Miguel. She had offered to use her car to travel to Calixtlapan because, how else were they going to get there? The bus had left a long time before. "I mean, she's the director of surgery. She called me into her office, and I had to tell her everything that had happened in the theatre."

"How did she know anything had happened?"

"The anaesthetist, Aguirre, made a complaint. About Martinez screwing up, and mostly about the way he behaved. So unprofessional. And Aguirre, you know how fierce she is about male doctors bullying their female colleagues. The thing is, I didn't want to make too much of a fuss. The man hates us enough already! But I had to give my side of the story. Now we'll just have to see how it all turns out."

They drove on, out into the hills, wondering how the others were getting on. She had messaged them to say they were coming, but she heard nothing back. The atmosphere in the bus was probably too excited and excitable for that.

After about two hours, the land started to dip away, and they found themselves looking down into the valley, mountains shimmering in the distance. They passed the big trucks and buses.

Black cars with tinted windows whizzed past them, their thumping disco beats sounding blasts of noise as they sped by. Finally, they were levelling out, and they saw the twin towers of Clalixlapan's cathedral appear through the haze.

On the outskirts of the town, the dual carriageway ended at a large roundabout planted with flowers of many colours. They headed towards the centre where the cathedral, one of the most prized ecclesiastical buildings in the area, bordered one side of the plaza where the big meeting was to take place. They were excited now, wondering what the group were doing, ready to put on the white hoods they both carried in their bags. They were passing vehicles parked or abandoned on the dusty sides of the road. There were old trucks, cars on blocks with no tyres, and buses parked while their drivers went off for a snack at one of the roadside shacks or to visit a friend.

A crowd of people gathered around an empty bus, its windows missing except for shards of burnt glass, smoke-blackened sides, and naked wheel rims, all scorched from some kind of fire. Her heart was beating with excitement about what was to come, and perhaps that's why she didn't realise immediately what she was seeing. Later, she wondered if it would have made any difference if she had reacted more quickly or processed what she had seen more carefully. As they approached the square, her stomach churned with a mix of fear and excitement. The others would be there. Who knows what forces they would be facing and whether they were safe?

Dolores found a space and manoeuvred into it. Looking towards the cathedral, she could make out the crowd, the banners, and the stage. As far as she could see, things were peaceful. The two of them hurried along the pavement. There was no sign of their colleagues, but maybe they were out of their line of vision. Genoveva saw Dolores reach for her white hood, but she held her wrist, restraining her. "Not yet," she said, though she was not quite sure why. But something was not right. Now she was hurrying forward, Dolores right behind her. They squeezed their way between the people at the back of the crowd and gradually inched their way nearer the stage.

A woman was speaking. From this distance, she could see that she was blonde and smartly dressed. The watchers in the square were muttering their approbation. There was a mood of excitement and anticipation. She signalled to Dolores, and they made their way to the side of the square on their right. People in the crowd muttered crossly as they insinuated themselves through gaps and pushed past the banners. They were hanging on the speaker's every word.

"We need a strong hand to run this country. We need passion. And strength. We need law. And order." She spoke in short barks. "But above all, what we need is a nation that believes in marriage. And family. And God. None of the nonsense they are calling for." She had Genoveva's attention now. The nurse noted the black-clothed figures flanking her. They had large guns held against their chests. A man stood beside her. From this distance, she couldn't see him too well. But something about him reminded her of the old man spitting and spluttering in the theatre that night. Heredia, she thought, that's the old monster's son. She caught Dolores's puzzled, worried eyes. She shrugged her shoulders. There was no sign of the ESA gang anywhere.

As if reading her thoughts, the woman on the stage started talking of the 'enemy'. "And where are they?" before answering her question, "nowhere. Where are those hate-filled revolutionaries?" Some in the crowd had got the idea. "Nowhere," they shouted back. "Where are those cowardly fools who were going to come here today in their juvenile white masks?" The nurses exchanged glances. "Nowhere!" yelled the crowd, in answer. "And where do they deserve to be listened to or even heard, those irresponsible saboteurs?" "Nowhere," came the response. "And where will we allow them to make politics in this great country of ours?" "Nowhere, nowhere, nowhere, nowhere!" There was no stopping them. To Genoveva, they felt like a dark rolling cloud, a terrifying animal smothering wild beauty with their coiling poison. I must be imagining this, she told herself, but as the time passed and there was no sign of her comrades, she was beginning to feel more uneasy.

The woman on the platform waited until the shouting had begun to subside, and then she started again. "You need," she paused, "WE need someone to lead us, someone to say that you here have rights, that profit is not a dirty word, that prosperity is a God-given obligation, and that the forces ranged against you, against us, will be defeated. "Friends," her voice dropped, and now they were all listening intently. "My comrades, workers, colleagues, true patriots, I am that person." Here and now, I pledge myself to your service and the service of our great country. And to God."

"Service," yelled the crowd. "Country. God!"

Young Heredia, if that was indeed him, stepped forward. Lowering his arms, lifting them and lowering them again, he gradually quietened the excited listeners, "Here, before you, is the next president of our great country. Isabela. Isabela Gutierrez. With Isabela to lead us, the future is ours. Ladies and gentlemen, true believers, I give you Isabela Gutierrez."

"Isabela, Isabela!" The name echoed round the square. The man held the woman's hand high in the air. She was waving with her free arm, and the crowd kept on and on shouting her name.

Later, after the platform had emptied and the black-clad bodyguards had escorted the speakers down the steps at the side of the stage, the crowd started to disperse. Some carried their banners tall and proud. Others had shucked them onto their shoulders as they made their way back to cars and buses or the horses and carts that were waiting for them behind the covered market.

Genoveva bought soft drinks, and they stood in the colonnades to shelter from the fierce sun. They were both wrestling with their confusion about their absent friends. People were looking at them questioningly. "You two don't look like you're from here," a man said to them, and they saw other people taking interest in the conversation.

"No, umm, that's because we aren't," Genoveva said as light-heartedly as she could, "We came over from San Miguel."

"You did?" The voice did not sound friendly.

"Yes, but we'd better be on our way back now. "Dolores took over. We don't want to arrive late."

"You wouldn't be one of them protesters, the ones who didn't turn up?"

"Why would you think that?"

"We weren't going to let them anywhere near the square!" a voice proclaimed, and there was laughter.

"Come on, Dolores, we'd better be off."

They turned and started down the street where they had parked. "Don't run," Genoveva hissed, conscious of eyes boring into their backs as they made their retreat. She was terrified.

Why didn't her friends make it to the square? Where were they? And then, as they drove away from Claixtlapan, past the burnt-out bus, she realised, with a sickening lurch, that she thought she knew why they hadn't appeared and, overcome with a sudden sense of dread, she wondered what they could do about it and whether it was already too late.

Chapter 12
Martin

The moment they walked into the courtroom, Martin felt uneasy. On the raised curved bench in front of them stood three tall chairs. Behind them hung an old oil painting of some famous old judge, he imagined. There was a flag and the words 'Country and God'. Nearer them as they entered, there was a lectern facing the back wall and behind it four tables and chairs, and behind them rows of benches. On the right was a designated area for witnesses.

Black-robed officials organised papers and straightened chairs, placing water jugs and glasses on the high dais behind which the judge's chairs were positioned.

He didn't like it, this room where people had argued over life and death, where sad lives had been torn apart and bad lives had escaped justice. It didn't feel like the heroic scenes from his favourite TV programmes where right triumphed in final life-affirming conclusions. Here, Martin thought, he could hear tears.

Angelita held onto his hand as if he were saving her life. She had been dreading this day. She didn't want to speak in front of lawyers and judges, and especially not in front of her father. People would be listening and watching.

"But," he had protested, trying to calm her," that's what happens every time you perform!"

"Well, yes, Martin, but the violin is my voice. The composer has written the words, not me. I am a way of speaking for him or her — usually a him. The only thing I need to worry about with the violin is whether I am doing the music justice. I am content to be judged on that because I am good at it."

He smiled. She was very good at it. "But in that courtroom, I'm going to be judged as me."

"Angelita, mi amor, Angie." She loved the way he said that. "There is nothing to worry about, honestly." However, in truth, he wasn't looking forward to it either.

"We didn't do anything except climb a small volcano and see something and get nearly vapourised," he ruffled her hair play-fully, "and all we have to do is say that. And anyway, we may not even have to speak here. Remember what your father told us."

At the front of the room, where the tables were, there were groups of people. He saw Angelita's father talking to someone standing at a table to his left — another lawyer, he supposed. There was a stooped man with him who he thought was the music professor. Someone in a white coat accompanied two young men.

Federico looked round. He half waved and smiled at them. He indicated the bench behind him for them to sit on. The court-room was filling up. They walked to the front. Federico hugged his daughter and shook hands with his son-in-law. The professor, balancing himself with the help of his stick, turned around. He smiled weakly.

"Angelita," he said, "señor."

"Profesor," she muttered. He looked as if he were about to say something more, but at that moment an usher with a tall black staff asked people to take their seats. Two nearly identical faces turned round and stared at them as they were doing this. They were young, dressed in identical white T-shirts and extremely uneasy. There was something about them, though. A need. He wanted to give them a manly hug. Angelita was smiling at them.

"Hello," she said.

The identical twins looked at each other and seemed to come to some kind of agreement. They turned back.

"Hello," they said in unison.

The moment they had all sat down, the usher was there again, asking them to stand for the judges. Two men and a woman emerged from a door in the back wall. They bowed to the people in front of them and sat down; then everyone else followed suit.

The two lawyers set out their case. First, a man from the table on the left (from Martin's viewpoint) went to the lectern. He spoke powerfully and urgently. The judges had read the legal submissions, he was sure, and so there was no doubt about what had happened. Witnesses had described it. The two men on trial, he intoned with huge emphasis, in their evil twin-planned malice, had conspired to carry out a cold-blooded murder.

"You will no doubt hear again," he said, addressing the judges directly, "that the victim was not a good man. You have already been told that he was autocratic and headed an unpleasant so-called religious sect. And that may be true. But this courtroom is not the jungle. It is the pinnacle of civilisation. We do not countenance murder as a way of settling scores. Revenge is not justice, and we don't even know if it was justified! Justice is justice, and that is what we entreat you to offer us and the victim today."

It sounded convincing. Martin looked at his wife. She was

tense. He wondered how she would play tonight. And then Federico stood up.

Neither of them had seen him in court before. He was different. More present, but at the same time more distant. Martin watched Angelita's face and saw the wonder in her expression. Even from behind, they could sense her father's fierce attention. Invited by the judges to plead his case, he stood up, looked around the court, and started to speak.

"In my written submission, señores juezes, I indicated that these young men, the defendants here, are not suitable to stand trial. They have experienced a catastrophic mental breakdown. They are undergoing treatment. As you will see from the report, their psychiatric team say they are unfit to understand what they have done. Additionally, I now have a clearer understanding of what they were forced to endure. There was unimaginable psychological and physical cruelty. There was also a shattering of the beliefs they had been encouraged, nay, *bullied*, to hold. Their minds were altered by the experiences they were forced to endure.

"As you can see, *señores juezes*, this cruelty, this sadistic bullying, is not emphasised in my written submission. It is only since that submission that I have been made aware of the full facts of the case, and it is for that reason that I ask for your indulgence to be allowed to speak on these matters. They are fundamental to an understanding of what went on."

"My esteemed colleague talked of the importance of justice. My submission is that justice, in this case, can only be served by allowing me to bring to your attention the facts squarely and plainly. I earnestly ask you to allow this."

"Thank you, Licenciado Hernandez. What you are asking is most irregular. We will need time to consider your request. We will reconvene after lunch. Say, two o'clock? Will that suit both of you?"

It would.

The boys were led away. Federico and Jacinto Perez walked towards them, and Martin noticed again how precarious the ex-violinist's movements were. He looked at Angelita and saw that she was thinking the same thing.

"Come on," said his father-in-law, "let's go and get something to eat." Angelita brightened up at this. To his surprise, Martin heard himself say, "Profesor, maestro, will you join us?"

Jacinto Perez was about to reply when a large, imperious woman, her hair braided with ribbons, dressed in indigenous clothing and necklaces, strode toward them.

"My God, look at you," was the first thing she said to her husband, "they don't seem to have done a very good job, those doctors." He winced. "Well?" she demanded when he didn't reply, "where are they? Are they free? Have you done what you were supposed to do, Licenciado, or have you ducked the challenge and left my boys to rot in the corruption that surrounds us?

"Marisa," Jacinto Perez said meekly, "it is nice to see you." She snorted. "Señora," Federico said gently but firmly, "it is a pleasure to see you. Perhaps — and with your permission, *Profesor* — you would be kind enough to join us. We can then apprise you of what is going on, provided my client—" he indicated the professor — "agrees."

Maestro Perez nodded his head, and the small party made its way along the atrium to where a large sign announced a popular restaurant chain.

Chapter 13
Silverio

HE TRIED to calm her down. She was usually so enthusiastic, so practical, and so full of possible joy. But since she had returned from Calixtlapan, those qualities had been replaced by fear, outrage, unease, and a furious energy. He understood why. Her friends, her co-idealists — his friends — had quite simply disappeared off the face of the earth. They were not answering their phones, and it was clear that they had never made it to the meeting Genoveva and Dolores had attended. Something had happened to them.

"They might have been killed," she screamed in her anxiety. "Someone knows where they are, someone did — whatever they did — and I want, we want our friends and colleagues back. We have things to do; we have battles to fight. They are us. We are them."

He agreed with her completely, of course, and his heart was heavy with sadness and unease. He thought immediately that the fate of the protesters was unlikely to be good. More than that, whatever had happened could mark the beginning of something worse than even what he feared might have happened to the members of the EAS. He knew how brutal their enemies could be after the beating he had received on the night of the volcano concert. Drug wars had begun to spread tentacles to San Miguel, too, so God knows if that had something to do with this. He didn't want to be alarmist, but this could be very bad indeed.

Silverio was wondering how all this might affect Silvestre Ocampo's campaign, poised, as they were on the eve of his big launch, to secure the presidency. Then he cursed himself for thinking about that when he should be focusing on the fears for the woman in front of him. This might push her over the edge, he thought. She had still not fully accepted her brother's death, or the anger which had separated them before he had died, because she had protested in that concert at the moment of his most important public performance yet. Silverio had spent so much time since then trying to help her deal with feelings of anger, sadness, misery, and guilt that he didn't want anything to make her suffer more. But then he reprimanded himself for such a personal focus because, perhaps, he told himself, no one person is that important in the grand scheme of things. What had happened to the EAS campaigners, however serious or trivial, might be just one symptom of a much bigger problem, and that problem now threatened the Ocampo campaign, and maybe all of them.

Genoveva had rung the hospital and called in sick, and she was. Sick at heart. It was something she hardly ever did, but today was very different. Silverio suggested that she go to her parents' house for the day, but she hadn't wanted to. She was going to spend the day on the phone, on the computer and on any platform that she could think of. She had already rung the local TV news, which had expressed interest and promised to follow up. Then she started with all the other news media she could think of. Worried, he left her at home in her flat, frenetically hitting the keys and muttering to herself.

When he got to the Town Hall, the usual chaos reverberated around the old building. He could see all the functionaries toiling away at their screens, people walking from office to office, and the smell of coffee was everywhere. Once up on the mayor's floor, however, things got totally out of hand. The mixture of mayoral business and campaign activity was as disorganised as it had been on the previous days since Silvestre Ocampo had decided to launch himself into the toxic maelstrom of national politics. Everyone knew about that toxicity, of course, but hope surged around them too — the hope that things could be different and that they could all help make the world a better place.

He walked straight to the mayor's office. When Silvestre Ocampo saw him, he called him over. "Silvestre, amigo, I have come to a decision. It is time for me to stand aside from this position and devote myself one hundred percent to what we are about here. I feel the wind in our sails, the breath of justice at our back, and even though this may be the most considerable risk of my career, I say if we don't risk all, then we never gain it either. So what I've decided–"

"Señor Alacalde, Silvestre, I am so sorry to interrupt you, but something serious has happened and I think you need to–"

"They have broken cover, Silverio, the old order, and the corrupt elite. Finally, they have got their act together and I don't know how worried we should be—"

"Señor, yesterday—"

"Yes, yesterday. Did you hear? That woman. Poisonous snake. Isabela Gutierrez. Right wing. Links to gangs and drugs remain uncovered. She was over in Calixtlapan yesterday, a guest of some kind, I think, of that Heredia boy. She's put herself forward, and I know–" he held up his hand, seeing that Silverio was about to interrupt him again — "she has her followers with all that law and order and God stuff. So what we have to work out is how to stop her in her tracks."

"Señor Alcalde!" He had not meant his voice to be so loud. "Señor Alcalde!" At last, he had the man's attention. "Señor Alcalde. We have a situation. People have disappeared. Thirty-seven of them. Disappeared. Perhaps kidnapped or killed. Sir, it is dire. Something must be done about it."

"First I've heard of it." He was unhappy about the direction the conversation was taking. "Who's disappeared? What are you talking about?"

"The demonstrators from the EAS. They seem to have vanished into thin air."

"Oh, them!"

"Yes, them. This is serious. With all due respect, you need to listen to me."

"Come now, Silverio, you can take a bit of teasing?"

"Sir—" He was losing control. "Yesterday, thirty-seven members of the EAS were scheduled to go to Calixtlapan, but they didn't make it there. Or if they did, they didn't come back. Something has happened to them, and I don't think it is something good. And sir–" the mayor was about to interrupt — "this is going to affect the campaign." He had the other man's attention now.

"How so?"

"Well, sir, if something bad has happened, it could be a crime, a serious crime. And we have the landowners and the drugs gangs and now the Gutierrez woman, and from what I hear she is going to make law and order a big part of her campaign and if these poor EAS people have been harmed — they are good people Silverio, you know that, fighting for what is right, trying to make the world a better place, we don't have a response. We are handing Isabela Gutierrez a perfect opportunity to make an impact."

"I am sorry, Silverio. You are right, as so often. He picked up a phone on his desk and pressed a green button. "Aurora, can you find out where Rivendeira is? Get me the chief of police."

Silverio returned to the room where three of Ocampo's most trusted aides were digesting Isabela Gutierrez's announcement of her candidacy. They reviewed the Mayor's speech and attempted to identify which media outlets would be attending the event they were organising. But the conversation and the arguments, usually crisp and taut, were less urgent now, and he realised that he was primarily to blame. He was finding it almost impossible to concentrate, his mind full of the disappearance of his friends, and Genoveva was distressed. When he saw Rivendeira making his way to the mayor's office two hours later, he excused himself and followed. However, he couldn't hear every word of the conversation that ensued; he heard how it ended.

The police chief was making light of the mayor's concerns. "Disappeared?" he heard the police chief saying, "Señor Alcalde, I warned you about this. I warned you that something would happen. Now listen to yourself. *Disappeared?* Do you think that's what happened? Because I don't. It's just another of their crazy stunts. Mark my words, they'll turn up in their stupid white hoods and try to make something of this fake 'disappearance'. But what I don't understand, Señor Alcalde, is when I told you they were going to cause trouble in Calixtlapan, you didn't order me to stop them. Maybe, who knows, they did run into trouble. And then whose fault would that be?" There was a silence. 'Now, if you will forgive me, I have people who deserve our protection, and I need to direct that protection."

He turned round and marched past Silverio, giving him a contemptuous glance, and he strode past. But that wasn't what worried Silverio most. He had seen the self-satisfied look of triumph on the man's face before Rivendeira had seen him.

"*What caused the police chief's confidence?*" he asked himself. "*What did he know?*"

He looked back at the mayor. He was standing, his face flushed, thinking and thinking. He raised his eyes and saw Silverio. He walked up to him and paused before speaking.

"Silverio, I think you are right. We have a situation. I, too, am worried about those people, your friends. I may be wrong, and I very much hope I am, but I think we have forces ranged against us that will stop at nothing, perhaps, and unless we can work out how to deal with them, we are sunk."

Chapter 14
Angelita

"GENNY, what's the matter?

"I'm sorry I didn't come to your concert. How was it?"

"Lovely. My father came. Martin came, too—lots of people. We raised money. Genny, what's up?"

"I'm scared."

"Of what? Genny, for heaven's sake, what's going on? Tell me."

"The demonstration. The EAS. They've gone."

"What do you mean 'they've gone'?"

"They went to Calixtlapan to protest in a bus. Now, they've vanished. Gone. I think they've been killed."

"I thought you said you were going to that demonstration."

"I was, but I missed the bus. I was in the operating theatre. The operation went on for a long time. But, that's not the point."

"I'm having trouble understanding this, Genny. The bus you were supposed to be on has vanished?"

"Yes, that's it. But not me. I went later with Dolores, in her car. And that's when I saw a bus. I think it was our bus. Their bus."

"Genny, you're not making much sense."

"I'll try and make it clearer, Angelita," she sounded a bit irritated, "On the way to the demonstration, just outside the town, we saw a burnt-out bus by the side of the road. By the side of the road. I thought I saw bullet holes, but Dolores wasn't sure. But if that was the bus they were in — "she was beginning to lose control.

"Genny, where are you?"

"Home."

"Don't move. I'm coming over."

And now she was in a car with her friend, her increasingly distraught friend, watching the side of the road as they passed the roundabout. Martin was driving. Silverio had wanted to come, but the mayor had asked him, pleaded with him not to go. The sun beat down, there was dust everywhere, and there was only the merest hint of cloud.

"There, it was there."

"Where?"

"There, right there. But it's not there now. It was there." Genoveva was insistent.

Martin turned round and manoeuvred onto the dirt road edge where she had indicated. There were scorch marks in the earth. Shards of glass littered the ground near a mechanic's lean-to and a shack that served beer and coffee. Angelita could see a stall selling fruit, another selling peppers and chiles, and an array of different vegetables. People were watching them, two attractive young women and a foreigner. Genoveva had stopped and looked fixedly at the ground.

"Genny?"

Her friend didn't answer. Angelita followed her gaze, and though guns and weapons were utterly unknown to her, she was pretty sure those were shell casings on the ground. Genoveva was gulping, rocking back and forth.

"Genny."

"Guns. Someone's been firing guns. Here — where the bus was. I'm sure of it." Angelita hugged her. Her friend's body was rigid and unyielding.

Martin was walking purposefully towards the beer and coffee shack. "Genny, come on." They followed him.

The stallholder was viewing the foreigner suspiciously.

"Who are you?" she indicated the three of them, "another TV crew? You don't look much like TV people, but then again, what do I know?" She reached into the pocket of her apron and pulled out a pack of cigarettes and a lighter. She lit up, took a deep drag, and waited.

"We—" Genoveva began, but Martin interrupted. "We aren't from the TV. We are investigators, that's all. Trying to find out what happened here yesterday — that's if anything did happen."

"I'll say it did!"

"So, what was it? What happened?"

"Most of them survived. They were taken away. Well, they were all taken away."

"What do you mean by 'most of them survived'?" Genoveva's voice was strident and brittle.

"Means what it says, señorita."

Are you saying that someone kidnapped them? That people were killed? Oh my God. People were killed? Who did it?"

The stallholder didn't answer.

"Señora," Angelita said as calmly as she could, though her heart was beating wildly, "we just want to get an idea of what went on here. It's important, you see."

"Yes, maybe it is, but I can't tell you anything else."

"Can't or won't?" Genoveva barked.

The woman was about to answer when a man came from inside the shack. "Conchita!" he shouted, "enough. That's enough. And you," he said, indicating the others, "clear off, all of you. You want to get us killed, too? Just clear off and don't come back. We don't ask for much around here, just to be left alone. We keep our noses clean. We don't need folk like you. Stay here much longer and I'll set the dogs loose."

"We should leave," Angelita said, "Come on, Genny! We can talk about this in the car."

Angelita's mind was in turmoil as they headed back to San Miguel. She was sitting in the back to better comfort Genoveva, who was extremely upset. Martin was silent in the front.

They decided to go to the hacienda, it seemed best, so they called Silverio and told him to meet them there when he could tear himself away from the mayor's side.

Tiacuri, who looked after Marcela, watched them as they walked in at the entrance. They could hear the television from the rooms where she and Tia Rosario's daughter spent their time.

Angelita liked her, and she looked up to the violinist, even though she was only slightly older than Angelita. When Martin talked to her, however, she was often tongue-tied. Now she seemed nonplussed by the sight of the young couple leading in Angelita's friend, who was so obviously upset. They started up the stairs, but as they began to climb, the girl called out to her.

"¿Señora Angelita, Señora Angelita?"

She turned back. Tiacuri was standing there, her hands clasped together nervously. "Forgive me, Señora, but I couldn't help hearing you when you were leaving. You said you were going to Calixtlapan. I wasn't trying to listen, I wasn't, it's only because I'm from a village—"

"Yes, Tiacuri, and please stop calling me *señora*. Call me Angelita. If you don't mind?"

"Angelita," the girl was trying hard to say the name correctly, "Calixtlapan, it… people on a bus. Something I don't under-stand. It's on the news, on the television."

Angelita called the others to come down, and they all trooped

91

into Marcela's sitting room. She sat on the sofa, playing with a ball of twine. Her voice was barely audible, her vacant expression fixed on the television screen where Gaby Aguirre, the famous presenter, was speaking. It seemed she was from the same place from which they had just returned. She was speaking directly to the camera.

"I came to San Miguel a week ago to make a programme about Artemio's Fire, the name the locals have given to the volcano here, which, as you must know, erupted with such disastrous consequences, an event which, despite or because of the tragedies that occurred, has its own extraordinary stories to tell. But now it looks as if there's another story to add to the mix from just outside San Miguel de las Colinas.

"I'm standing at the roadside on the outskirts of the provincial town of Calixtlapan, where two days ago something took place which is causing great consternation among the locals and the people here.

"It appears that a bunch of protesters, part of a group called the Ejercito de Arturo Sanchez, named after one of our revolutionary heroes, came here to make a fuss at a big meeting of the landowners from around the region. The protesters, who disliked the landowners, intended to disrupt their meeting, but they never arrived. It appears that the bus carrying them was stopped where I am standing.

"A woman who saw what went down in this place is with me now."

Angelita gasped. It was the same stall owner they had talked to, and as if to echo what happened, just as she started to speak, the same man they had just seen walked up and, interrupting the interview, said no one knew anything and would they please go away.

"Hmm," said Gaby Aguirre, improvising, I wonder what went on here. Perhaps—"

She was interrupted by a man who had approached the camera. His hat was falling off the back of his head, and he appeared drunk.

"Happened? What happened? I'll tell you what happened," he was slurring his words, 'they pulled a bus over."

"Who pulled the bus over?"

"Police. Looked like the police. And then the others turned up. Guns. There was some shooting. A truck. They had a truck. Took them away."

"Who took whom away?"

"Except for the dead one, God rest their soul," he lurched. "Then they torched it?"

"Torched what? What are you talking about?"

"The bus. They burnt it. It was burning."

"So, you're saying there was a gun battle with the police? Why haven't we heard more of this?"

"I've seen you," the man said, confusedly, "on television." He wandered away, out of shot, muttering to himself.

"He does not appear to want to keep talking to us," Gaby Aguirre said, facing into the camera, one eye slightly arched, "but this is more important than one slightly disconnected guy. Something significant has occurred here, and questions need to be addressed. What happened to those protesters? Were the police attacked? Why were they here? And how come this story only surfaced twenty-four hours after it happened? None of it makes sense, but we will continue to look for answers. For Channel 8, this is Gaby Aguirre, outside Calixtlapan."

Martin switched off the television. Tiacuri looked surprised. Marcela swivelled round and seemed to look at him. Then she turned back and kept digging into her ball of wool.

Someone outside pulled the chain, and the bell started to ring. Angelita went to the gate and opened it. Silverio was standing there looking concerned. Angelita kissed him on the cheek and led him to the room where they had been watching the television, but before they got there, Genoveva came running out and flung her arms around his neck. He hugged her and caressed her hair.

Later, when they were sitting on the terrace staring miserably into the valley, Silverio suddenly blurted out," Something's not right." It seemed a strange thing to say because they all knew that. Angelita looked at him quizzically. He was conveying more than just the shock that they were all feeling. Silverio returned her look and spoke directly to her.

"The thing is, it doesn't quite add up. Why has this only just hit the news channels? Genoveva knew something was wrong when she returned from Calixtlapan yesterday afternoon. Why hadn't the people who saw it said anything? And what about the police, for God's sake? Normally, something this dramatic would be all over the airwaves in an hour or two after the event, especially these days. But there was nothing. Why are we hearing about it only now?"

Martin was looking puzzled. "What are you saying?"

Genoveva butted in. "What he's saying is that something criminal and disgusting has happened. My friends have gone. They've been kidnapped — the ones who weren't shot on the scene, apparently - and taken off and maybe killed. According to the person on the screen, at least one person. Probably their remains have been cremated or buried, or who knows what else? It wouldn't be the first time that something like that has happened. Well, would it?" They didn't answer. "It's this stinking country. The violence, the corruption. Everything."

"Maybe that is what happened," Silverio said, "and maybe something else. But what I do know is that Mayor Ocampo will find out where our friends are and what has happened to them. And if, God forbid, the worst has happened, he will not rest until we find out who is responsible."

Chapter 15
Rosario

SHE WAS PLEASED to have Angelita and her nephew Federico in the house. He was kind and solicitous, and she liked the young man — what was his name? She tried but couldn't remember — who seemed to be with her great niece, the musician, who played, what did she play? She remembered a concert that night with all the fuss. She tried to picture the scene. Ah, yes, Angelita was on the stage with a... No matter. She'd remember later, she was sure.

She forced herself back to the present and where she was — in the club. Yes, that was it. That nice man Arnulfo had collected her. She was beginning to enjoy these visits. She felt as if she was treated with respect and dignity here. People seemed interested in what she had to say, or at least they pretended to be, and that was nice, though she could never quite remember what they had talked about when she got home. Still, she enjoyed getting ready, making herself look presentable, and feeling just a little bit special. It hadn't felt that way in the years before.

Today's lunch was lovely. She had two bowls of the soup, a local speciality called *picante*, but not overly spicy. It brought back memories of her childhood and made her feel comfortable. Conversation flowed around her at the table, and occasionally people would come and squeeze into the chair beside her, asking questions and listening with flattering attention to what she had to say. She did like Arnulfo, although she sometimes had to fight to remember his name.

He was more attentive than any of the others and made her laugh. He was very handsome, she thought, not unlike that young rogue who had kissed her on the square when she was just a teenager. The thought of him, the memory of that moment! She could almost smell the night air of her childhood. Arnulfo was older, of course — they all were — and he didn't have that kind of swagger. Anyway, she wasn't a teenager anymore. On the other hand, he was kind and told her how amazing she was, which, if anyone else had said it, might have sounded patronising. But coming from him, it was strangely pleasing.

She ordered another glass of wine from one of the waiters. She was already feeling slightly light-headed, but now that Arnulfo had returned to his seat, she thought she should try to pay attention to what was being said. Mercifully, her hearing was still functioning quite well, even if less efficiently than before. For example, she sometimes found it difficult to differentiate one voice from another, which could be pretty problematic. She had to admit that if people weren't addressing her directly, she occasionally struggled to follow what they were saying. Still, she wasn't overly worried. Many people even younger than her had far greater problems, and anyway, from what she'd heard, they were inventing better and better devices to help with all that. She'd get one of those if she lived long enough.

"I am quite optimistic," the old man who wore jewelled waistcoats was saying, "I think Isabela has made a good start. I don't know who advised her to go to Calixtlapan for her announcement, but that was a good call."

Tia Rosario wondered whether the man was younger or older than she was. She could never tell. All the old people were her age or younger, and all the young ones were just children. They didn't know anything. If only they would listen to her, she could teach them a thing or two. But then she forgot about that. A woman she knew vaguely, wearing more jewellery than necessary — her gold bracelets clanking as she gesticulated — was holding forth.

"We mustn't forget that our side still has a long way to go. This is just the start. That wretched Ocampo fellow has got a head of steam," Tia Rosario nearly laughed at the image this brought to her mind, "and have you noticed? Some of the smaller parties have begun to rally around him. He's going to be difficult to beat," there were murmurs of agreement, "but beat him we must. His weak permissiveness threatens us all, everyone here. Everything we have fought for, our land, our way of life. If he and his followers win, and believe me," she gestured to the group, "your houses, your haciendas, your wonderful companies — none of them will be safe. They'll impose new labour laws to stifle productivity, introduce workers' rights, and increase taxes," there were murmurs of agreement, "so we must do everything to support Isabela. After all, she's one of us. She understands."

Who is Isabela? Tia Rosario wondered. She couldn't remember anyone with that name. Did that matter?

"I was talking to one of her *people*," someone else said, "Apparently, she's going to be much more visible in the days ahead. She says it's time to take the battle to all who stand against us. For are we not the ones who built the prosperity of this great country, do we not deserve to continue with our lives as they have always been?"

There were noises of approval. A brief silence followed as they all processed her words. Then someone restarted the conversation.

"Have you heard about this business with the demonstrators, the missing demonstrators?" they asked, "I saw something on the evening news."

"Nothing to worry our heads about," Arnulfo was saying, "no one cares about them. Just a bunch of misdirected lefties if you ask me. Probably all fake news."

"Demonstrators?" another person said. "They don't represent anyone but themselves."

"That's a nice thought," the woman who had spoken before said, "but I'm not so sure. Remember, most of them are sons and daughters, brothers and sisters, and cousins of the people here. They're not going to let this go. Think about it — if those protesters had been killed, there would be a lot of understandable anger about that. Who knows who people would blame? I'm worried it could be turned against us."

"That's all speculation, the old man protested."

"Hold on," Arnulfo interjected, looking around the gathering, "I don't think you have any need to worry. It's all in hand. In fact, I can assure you it will work out to our advantage. I know what I am talking about."

Tia Rosario was starting to feel sleepy. She didn't want to doze off at the dinner table. But it was warm, and she had to struggle to keep her eyes open.

"How can you know that, Arnulfo? I agree with Doña Margarita. This could play out very badly. And how can you be so sure?"

"Look, I can't say any more right now. However, I can assure you that things are happening as they should. That's all I can offer at this moment."

Tia Rosario could feel her eyelids beginning to close, but a loud voice made her lift her head. It was a younger lawyer who had been there yesterday, a hotshot from the city far away (too fancy for me, Federico had said). How could that suddenly flash through her mind?

"Señoras y señores, have you forgotten where we are? Have you forgotten that San Miguel is just a provincial city, nothing more? I am grateful for the welcome I have received here, so thank you all. However, I must say that all your plans and the impact you think you might have are not decided here. It's what happens in the capital, what happens all over this republic; that's where opinions are formed. San Miguel had its moment in the sun — I am sorry, that was a terrible way of putting it — but it only became famous after your volcano erupted, and then you had that terrible earthquake. Indeed, the whole republic was transfixed by stories of suffering, heroism, and the like, which has given your mayor a platform.

The people around him have been astute in spreading his message across the country. He is talked about everywhere; the media love him and will continue to do so unless something can be found to damage him, or unless people forget him, which is unlikely while he's running for president. But he's only in the running because he's been brought to the nation's attention. Otherwise, nothing important is happening here, so if Isabela Gutierrez is to go anywhere, she has to leave San Miguel behind. And yes, the gentleman is correct, a few local protesters in this backwater? Will the nation as a whole care about that?"

"You know nothing, Licenciado," Arnulfo said as he rose to his feet. "Nothing. You people from the capital with your airs and graces. But just you wait. We will surprise you."

The lawyer put his hand into his pocket and took out his phone.

I am sure you have a hectic schedule, Licenciado," Arnulfo continued, and Tia Rosario thought he was not being very nice or polite now, "and much more important things to attend to than concerning yourself with our 'provincial' reality, so please do not let us keep you from your business."

'You could cut the atmosphere with a knife' was the saying that suddenly occurred to Tia Rosario, no longer quite so sleepy. The prominent city lawyer said nothing. Everyone was watching him. Deliberately, he finished his wine and wiped his lips with his napkin. He placed the napkin on the table and slowly stood up.

"Ladies. Gentlemen. With your permission," he said, leaving the table and strolling nonchalantly to the entrance of the dining room while quietly speaking into his phone.

Honestly, Tia Rosario thought, these children. Nothing has changed since the playground. So ridiculous. Quite funny. And it was funny, and perhaps it was the wine, but she started to laugh, a dry cackle that, once it had started, she couldn't stop.

Later, Arnulfo dropped her off at the hacienda as usual. Was it her imagination, or was he slightly less attentive than before? "Silly fools," she muttered to herself as she walked towards the stairs. Tiacuri was crossing the hall from a room on the right. "What did they mean, those people, about the protesters in that place — what's it called?"

"Protesters?" she asked, unprepared for this contextless question. "Perhaps you mean Calixtlapan?"

"That sounds about right, I don't know. But do you see what they meant by saying that things were working out as they should? Answer me that!" She was addressing Marcela's carer as if they had been talking for some time.

"Señora?"

"I can't work it out in my head. I do get a bit confused. But they know something about whatever happened to... to who? I can't remember now." She was becoming agitated. She turned to look at the girl. "What are you standing around for?" she barked. Tiacuri was about to reply, but Rosario was already striding unsteadily towards the staircase.

Chapter 16
Maria

SHE DOESN'T THINK of him every day anymore, but when she does, her husband Juan is much less ridiculous than he was when he was alive. At some level, she recognises this, but it doesn't matter. She prefers a better version of him than the man he had become. She still does not understand why he got so angry with her or why he assaulted her more and more frequently as he sank deeper into his sense of failure. That he had died in a ridiculous car crash on his way, it was clear, to find her, had made her feel guilty. Perhaps it always would.

But that was the past. Her life had undergone significant changes in many ways. Now she lived with the lawyer, the one who liked Señora Bicky so much. It was he who had persuaded her to try this class, and to her surprise, she was enjoying it a lot. That was partly because of the other students. They ranged from teenagers who hadn't got on well at school to people much older than herself. There were drivers and porters, mechanics, street sellers and domestic servants like her.

Initially, no one had spoken to each other. They all looked nervous. She was nervous too. She had nearly turned back when she reached the building where the classes would be. But then she thought of how grateful she should be to Señor Federico. She knew she would feel guilty if she disappointed him, and so, head down and heart beating fast, she went inside.

It was a surprise to her that she had enjoyed that first session so much. Their teacher was a middle-aged man with a cheerful smile and an encouraging manner. He told jokes. True, some of them weren't that good, but she liked the fact that he tried. And there was something else. At the front of the classroom was someone she knew she had seen somewhere before. Throughout the lesson, she was trying to figure out who it was.

He hadn't seen her when she arrived late because she had ended up sitting near the back. It was only when he turned round to say something to a person behind him that she had recognised him, and as yet, he clearly hadn't seen her, or even if he had, he probably wouldn't recognise her. After all, she still couldn't quite place him. He had a lovely face, she thought. Gentle. Kind.

They were looking at a picture of a house and its surroundings, learning the shape of the words that described everything. They didn't make sense to her yet. They looked strange, especially the one for garde- and then it came to her. He was the man who worked at the house just next to Señora Bicky's. The moment she realised this, she felt relaxed and comfortable, which was strange. She didn't know him at all. It was just that he had always greeted her kindly when she had arrived or had been leaving her employer's house.

The class finished, and people started to leave. That's when he saw her as he was making his way to the door. He stopped and looked quizzically at her. Then his face lit up.

"Señora? I think we know each other. If I'm not mistaken, you used to work for the gringa?" he named the street where Alex and Vicky Kassonaliki had lived.

"Yes. Yes, I did." She was a bit hesitant.

"Are you keeping well, señora? I heard about your husband, the taxi driver. I am sorry."

"Thank you. It was a shock." Now she remembered. His name was Santiago.

"And how are you?"

"Older, ha ha. But I am still doing the same job. And you? What are you doing now that your employers have moved away? If you don't mind me asking."

"I do not mind at all." She smiled. "I work for a licenciado, a lawyer. He is a perfect gentleman. I am lucky." There was something about the gardener that made her trust him. Somehow, after they had left the building, she found herself accompanying him to a café where they sat at a little tin table and ordered soft drinks. For a moment, they sat in companionable silence.

"I'm not finding the classes easy," he said, smiling.

"It's difficult, yes." She paused. "But I am excited. When Licenciado Federico told me about it and said I had to come, I didn't want to do it. But I think I'm going to like it. He arranged everything. Did your employer do that for you?"

"Do you think you're going to be able to do it? Read and write?"

"I don't know. I hope so. I think so."

Santiago pulled out a crumpled packet of cigarettes. "Tonio wanted me to come."

"Tonio?"

"My friend."

"Oh."

"I didn't want to. But he kept on at me."

She felt content being here with him. It seemed normal. Most of her interactions these days were with Federico. Anyone who came to visit, like his daughter and her husband. She enjoyed chatting when she went to the shops or stalls to buy groceries, cleaning supplies, and her favourite face cream. However, all of those conversations were polite, superficial, or necessarily formal, despite her employer's efforts to bridge the distance between them. Now sitting there in the café, she allowed herself to think, for a moment, how much more enjoyable her classes would be now that she had seen Santiago here.

It had not occurred to her to think of men at all, like that, since Juan. She had spent too much time trying to get used to being a widow and to her new life, and anyway, she told herself, at my age! It was all very strange, and Señora Bicky had gone, along with the two children. She realised she had gone silent and that Santiago was looking at her expectantly.

"I always thought you looked after the garden, "she said, 'and the grass outside the house, where you work. Is that right?"

"Yes. And I sometimes help the servants carry things and take out the rubbish. Lots of odd jobs. I like it, I think."

"And your employer? Is she okay?"

"I suppose. Always polite, to me at least. She seems to be some kind of businesswoman, I think. Those people. So much money!"

"Not for the likes of us!"

"You're telling me. The world isn't fair. Never will be." He laughed.

"Never was. Never will be. But my licenciado is a good man."

"Well, my señora, she's—" he paused as if searching for the right words — "something has changed. Suddenly, the house is full of big people, those people who drive big cars and have bodyguards. Scary! And yesterday they had a whole film crew there. Can you believe it? And you know what?"

"All right!" she laughed. "What?"

"One of the many carrying the camera equipment says she might be the next president. Can you imagine? My employer, a woman, is our president!"

"What's wrong with her being a woman?" Now she was laughing at him.

"Don't make fun of me!" he was smiling, "there would be nothing wrong, and everything right. Maybe you women could start to make the world a better place."

"Now you're mocking *me*." She looked at him, and he was grinning. She felt comfortable. It was unfamiliar.

When she headed back to her room in Federico's flat, she found that she was smiling and, unusually, she hardly noticed the crowds and the roar of traffic around her. She thought that life was beginning to seem better.

Chapter 17
Jacinto

He was back in what had become his favourite spot, sitting on his favourite bench, the sun warming him as usual. He felt stronger every day. True, he had to keep his burn-ravaged face out of direct sunlight; they told him so, and he had taken to wearing a large sombrero, almost like the vaqueros from the north. Coupled with his sunglasses and the stick he used, it gave him a slightly sinister appearance. But he was a familiar sight now, and people greeted him, often with affection. He had taken to having long chats with the shoeshine guy, whom he visited frequently, because, hell, he might look a bit of a fright. Still, a man has his pride, and well-looked-after shiny shoes displayed a kind of elegance, didn't they?

Camilo, the shoeshine man, held strong opinions on politics and had no qualms about sharing them as he polished the maestro's shoes. "We should have a bit more law and order, señor! Things are going downhill. And food, we have the best food in the world here in our beautiful town. Cannot get anything like it anywhere." Sometimes he nearly tempted the ex-musician into everyday schoolboy antics, "see that one over there, maestro? She's a bit of all right. Look at those... look at that...."

He had views on everything and seemed completely confident, something Jacinto greatly envied. He was a big fan, it appeared, of Isabela Gutierrez. "She'll be my kind of president," he said, "even if, you know..." Jacinto had noticed the woman's name coming up in conversations quite often in recent weeks.

What does it matter? he thought. There'll be time for all that rubbish later once I have the twins back in my care. He couldn't, of course, be sure that it would ever happen, but he clung to the hope that it might. And when they were released, he wasn't going to let them go to that wife of his. She was as crazy as a parrot with all the mystical nonsense she was involved in. Fine, that was her business, but he wanted nothing to do with it or her.

She belonged to the past. She had taken one of his sons away already, he reminded himself angrily, and he was damned if she was getting the twins too. But she still had the power to get under his skin like that last time outside court, when they'd looked for somewhere to have a bite in a break during proceedings. Marisa had swanned in and tried to take over the whole thing as if she were the one in charge, as if she were the one who had found Federico Hernandez Placencia, not him, as if, he told himself indignantly, she was footing the legal bill. It was ridiculous.

He and the lawyer had built an uneasy but mostly productive relationship regarding this case. He had to acknowledge the lawyer for managing to establish some kind of small connection with his sons, one that had begun, in infinitesimal steps, to open the door to the possibility that he might one day communicate with them more openly himself. Marisa seemed oblivious to all this as she proceeded to dominate the conversation around the restaurant table that day.

She subjected Federico to an almost hostile cross-examination, questioning his approach, asserting, with no evidence whatsoever, that her boys were incapable of murdering anyone and that the witnesses must be lying. He looked over at Angelita and her new husband at that point. There were bright spots on her cheeks, and she seemed about to reply, but her father calmed things down before she had a chance to erupt. Watching him, Jacinto admired his extraordinary self-control even as he was nearly overwhelmed by her haughty condescension.

It worsened when they returned to the courtroom. Marisa insisted that she should sit at the table with the lawyer, Jacinto, and the twins. She tried to speak to them in a piercing whisper as the court reassembled, but they merely looked straight ahead. Jacinto was acutely aware of the danger she posed. She could easily cause a scene, and the judges would not like that one bit. And, as he had feared ever since she had appeared, she would create a scene. First, though, the judges addressed the court.

We have had an initial review of the written evidence you submitted, Licenciado Hernandez Placencia. Although the situation is most irregular, we are nonetheless inclined to give it our full consideration.

The prosecution lawyer rose to his feet to protest.

"Please sit down again, Licenciado. We recognise the unusual nature of our decision, but, as always, we are guided in these cases by a concern for natural and lasting justice." Jacinto heard a snort of almost laughter behind him. "In this case, it is clear that the two accused did carry out the unlawful killing of the victim.''

"That's rubbish," shrieked Marisa in her most formidable soprano, "that is an impossibility. My sons, my sons would never do something like that."

"Licenciado, could you please restrain your client?"

Señores jueces, la señora is not my client, it is her husband, Maestro Jacinto—''

"Be that as it may, Licenciado," please tell the woman to be quiet."

Jacinto looked over at his wife, her face red and shaking slightly. Her eyes were blazing.

To return to our ruling," the judge's foreman said," I repeat that we are of one mind that the evidence pointing towards the accused's guilt is overwhelming. However, the exonerating circumstances in this case—"

Marisa was back on her feet, berating the bench, shaking her fists, her jewellery rattling as she gestured wildly.

"Madam, we have warned you to desist from these interruptions. Please resume your seat."

"Justice? You call this justice? The ancient book of the sacred gods—"

"One last chance, madam. Sit down."

She wouldn't stop. She was causing a massive scene. Finally, the foreman snapped.

"Guards, remove that woman from the court, by force if necessary. Do it, now."

Two guards moved in to apprehend Jacinto's wife. After signalling that Jacinto, the lawyer, and Francisco should step aside, they approached Marisa. They began to forcibly remove her from her seat. It took quite some time, and throughout, she was shouting at the top of her voice, as if she believed she could influence the outcome through sheer outrage. Even after the door was slammed behind her, her protesting voice could still be faintly heard.

The silence in the courtroom was thick with a mixture of awe and embarrassment. As for Jacinto, all he could think about was that his wife's outbursts had jeopardised his sons' chances of anything even remotely positive. As the judge resumed speaking, it seemed as if he might be right.

"Licenciado Placencia, the appalling behaviour we have just witnessed, from one of your party, is not something we are used to in this courtroom. Indeed, we would venture to say that we have never seen anything quite like it. Furthermore, it makes us doubt the wisdom of the decision we were about to announce."

Without thinking, Jacinto stretched out his arms in supplication, but now the lawyer was standing. "Señores jueces, I can only humbly apologise for what has just occurred. La Señora Perez has not contributed to the preparation of this case. She and her husband," Jacinto found himself looking at the floor as if to make himself invisible, "have been separated for some time now. I am as shocked by her disrespectful behaviour as you are on the bench. I can only, once again, and with absolute sincerity, apologise for this unbecoming conduct." He sat down, refusing to meet Jacinto's gaze. The twins, meanwhile, stared fixedly ahead as if unaware of everything that had transpired.

"Thank you, Licenciado. We will confer. You may remain in the courtroom." The judges leaned in towards each other and spoke in hushed tones, making it impossible for the observers to hear them. Finally, after a few minutes, they seemed to reach some sort of agreement.

Licenciado Hernandez Placencia, members of the court. Despite the absurd display we have all witnessed, we will not reverse our decision, which is as follows: the two accused will almost certainly face some form of custodial sentence." Jacinto felt tears welling up in his eyes. "The law permits no other possibility. However, considering the written submissions we have received, we will need to reassess the terms of that sentence, which we will do and return our final verdict in three weeks." The prosecuting lawyer began to rise to his feet but, perhaps reconsidering, sat down again. "The court is adjourned."

The judges left the court, and the twins were led away. The room emptied.

Outside, there was no sign of Marisa or her youngest son.

Chapter 18
Vicky

SHE HAD BEEN SITTING in the waiting area for more than twenty minutes before they called her through, time enough to get used to the ramshackle art on the walls — large, bold swathes of colour that, she gradually realised, had been created by primary-school-aged children. Perhaps that was intended to make people feel more comfortable and less uneasy. A hospital for people in serious mental difficulty is not an especially happy place, she reasoned.

A man came from the door to her right. He was dressed casually, not like a doctor at all. "Mrs Kassoloniki?"

"Yes?"

"I am Mr Chambers. Would you like to come with me?"

She followed him back the way he had come, swiping a card that hung from a lanyard round his neck to open the door. They walked along a corridor to a door to the left. "Do come in," he said.

It didn't seem like a hospital room at all. There was a nice carpet and comfortable-looking armchairs grouped around a low table, which contained magazines and some books. Two of the chairs were occupied. From one of them, a smart-suited woman stood up and came towards her.

"Welcome, Mrs Kassoliniki. It is a pleasure to meet you." She didn't look pleased at all. "My name is Molly Bright. I am the director of the facility, and this," she pointed at a young man who had been sitting next to her, "is Senior Nurse O'Leary. Would you like a cup of tea? Or coffee?"

"No, thanks." She was thinking, *Why is the director here?*

"Water?"

"No." She sounded more aggressive than she had intended.

Mr Chambers sat down and indicated the seat next to him.

She sat down. "How is my husband?" she asked. Alexei had been here for a few weeks now. Initially, her visits had been refused, but they were only recently occasionally allowed. She had been told she could not come as often as she wanted. He was heavily sedated, for one thing, and her visits did not help. Frankly, they had said, not in so many words, the visits might be holding him back.

She didn't believe that; she didn't want to. She was the one who loved him most, she told herself, although she had begun wondering about that. Everything about him scared her now. The gloomy drama of their recent lives had turned their relationship monochrome with occasional flashes of flame and terror, unlike her contact with Federico.

She knew she shouldn't make that comparison, but he had become her lifeline. He was caring and quiet with her, and she loved his deep empathetic eyes staring at her from the screen in their frequent online exchanges. She didn't seriously misinterpret that increasingly special connection as a viable alternative to her present situation, though. She was married to Alexei for better or worse. He was the father of her children. He was her strange visionary, and that meant something. No, it meant everything. But it was getting complicated. All the awe she had once felt had been dissipated from the moment that she saw him in San Miguel, behaving weirdly and disconnected even before he'd been broken in that fetid jail. But she was married to Alexei Kassoloniki, and she knew the meaning of duty.

It was, for example, her duty today to be here. They had messaged her and asked her to come in, presumably for another meeting with the psychiatrist in charge of Alexei's care. But instead, she found herself with three people she had never met before.

"Mrs Kassoloniki," said the man called Chambers, "we have asked you here because we have some news." He stopped as if he didn't know what to say. She waited.

"The thing is," Molly Bright took over, "there's been a development."

"You have to understand," Chambers said, taking over again, "your husband was not progressing as we'd hoped. The psychotic episodes that led him to be brought here were not so severe, perhaps, but he was delusional and presented a danger to himself. That is why, regrettably, we had to prescribe, that is, his medical team had to prescribe, quite a strict regime of medication."

"Yes, I know all this. Doctor Mordecai told me all this. Will he be coming to this meeting?" she asked hopefully.

"Sadly, no," Molly Bright answered, "he is not available. He has been called away on another case."

"I think," the nurse interjected," we should stop beating about the bush and tell Mrs Kassoloniki why we called her in. I must get back to the ward soon."

"Very well," Chambers said. "The thing is, your husband has gone."

"Gone? What do you mean, gone?"

"He has absconded. After attacking one of the staff, he managed to escape. We believe he exited through a lounge located at the end of the corridor he was in. Somehow, he managed to get through the window. We thought it was secure, but he seemed to have prised it open. And now he has quite simply disappeared."

"But surely it is supposed to be safe here. That's why Alexei was brought here. You're supposed to be protecting him, caring for him, helping him to get better. Isn't that the whole point of his being detained here?" She witnessed the woman and Chambers exchange glances that she couldn't interpret.

The nurse started to speak again. "We take the patients' care very seriously, Mrs Kassoloniki. My staff are all highly experienced and highly trained. But this has stumped them. It's not just how he did it, it's how he had the idea of doing it."

"How did he do it? You said one of the nurses was attacked."

"Yes, I'm afraid so. He's got a nasty bruise and a sore head, but as far as we can tell, it's not much worse than that. "

"Has he been aggressive before? No one told me he was violent, except to himself."

"Well, that's just it, Mrs Kassoloniki, he never was. Recently, though, something was different about him. He started becoming a bit more manic again. The doctors were considering a review of his medication since his last prescription didn't seem to be working as well anymore. That concerned us to be sure, but we had not anticipated that he would attack a member of staff."

"Let me try and get this straight," Vicky said, "my husband has walked out of a secure facility that was supposed to keep him safe and protected from himself."

"That, unfortunately, is an accurate summary of the situation," Molly Bright said.

"So what happens now?"

"Well, we have alerted the relevant authorities. The police are on the lookout. In particular, they will be keeping a watch on your home."

"My home?"

"Yes. We are concerned that if he returns, he could pose a danger to you, your family, and himself as well. He needs to be here."

Vicky felt all the frustration and anxiety she had been holding back for months now starting to well up. Before she could help herself, she shouted, "And here is where he was, but your sheer incompetence and lack of care mean he is somewhere else. Do you have any idea, any inkling of where that might be?"

There was silence. No one was looking at her.

"No, of course you don't. Is he safe? You don't know that either. Am I safe? You don't even know that. And the children? What of the children? Dear God, we should never have come here. And he should never have been brought to this place."

"Mrs Kassoloniki, we can understand that you are upset, but I assure you—"

"Assure me what? What exactly?" She got up. The director stood up too.

"Out of my way!" she said and stormed out of the room and into the corridor.

She had to come back, of course.

"Will someone let me out. For God's sake!"

Chambers came with her to release the door. "Mrs Kassono-liki, when you have had time to absorb the news, we should talk again. We have to make plans."

She ignored him and walked away past the reception and out to the car park. It was only when she was sitting behind the wheel that she started to calm down. She recalled a moment on her radio show when she'd snapped at a caller, letting her emotions get the better of her. Why had she done that? Alex, Alex of course. Always Alex. *Not anymore*, she thought. *I'm done with this.*

As she turned the key in the ignition, she knew it wasn't true.

Chapter 19
Silvestre

"ARE YOU READY? Do you have the speech? Where is it? Good. Is everything alright?"

Silverio fussed over him, which was slightly irritating. Out of the corner of his eye, he saw the rest of his team watching the young man with concern. They all knew how he had been shocked by the events at Calixtlapan, whatever had happened there. Silvestre had tried to persuade him not to come to the capital because of this.

"Go and look after that lovely girlfriend of yours," he had said, "she needs you." The younger man had just looked at him sadly and then, as if deliberately controlling himself, replied, "She understands Silvestre. This, this," indicating the large crowd in the square, "is more important. If we have success this evening, we can change the world. I mean, of course, you can change the world, and then what happened back home will not happen again. Señor Alacalde, you can build a better future for Genoveva, for me, for everyone. Good luck, good luck."

Now he was waiting to be introduced, feeling incredibly nervous. He was accustomed to speaking at public events; after all, he had been the Mayor of San Miguel. But this was a large crowd, the biggest he had ever faced. Suddenly, he felt unequal to the task ahead, yet his team and supporters were all relying on him. The people around him had worked so hard for this moment — his first major campaign speech in the capital — that he felt he owed them something, that he owed them everything. It was a big event. The press and TV were everywhere. The leaders of the parties lending their support were on the platform with him; the event manager had everything ready, and he could feel a great wave of anticipation from the square surging up towards where he stood.

Oh God, he asked himself, *why am I here?* I should not be here. I am not worthy of all this. I just want to go home. His mouth was dry. He was crumpling up the speech in his nervous hands.

A great roar swelled up from the crowd as the leader of the Workers' Party approached the podium. He stood there until the cheering had started to subside, and then he made a short, impassioned speech about rights and freedoms and the future before he said, "And the future, my friends, is here with us — a bright future of peace and prosperity, freedom and justice. Ladies and gentlemen, it is my proud honour to introduce you to the next president of our great republic, Silvestre Ocampo."

No escape now. He looked at the floor, cleared his throat, stood up, squared his shoulders, and looked out over the square and the multitude of faces turned towards the stage. It's now or never, he thought, and strode up to the podium.

The noise was deafening. It nearly lifted him off his feet. The Workers' Party leader gave him a great bear hug. He smelled of Blanquita Silvestre, though before letting the man go. The crowd had started chanting a shortened version of his name. "Silve, Silve, Silve." When had that started? He had no idea. He straightened out the papers of his speech and tried to stop his hands from shaking. His legs felt as if they might not hold him up. He placed the text on the lectern in front of him. He looked out. He waved. The crowd went wild. He kept waving, and it might have gone on for hours, but he thought, 'I have to start this'. He indicated that the crowd should be still, and gradually the noise died away.

"My friends," he began, his voice ringing around the square. They cheered again. "My friends, it is so good to see you all here. It is a great honour to stand before you in this wonderful city, the heart of our great republic. And with your permission, I would like to share a story with you— a story of change and renewal, a story of revelation, and a story of truth. I know this story well because, you see, it is my story." He paused. There was absolute silence. This is what they had come for. His nerves had evaporated. Possibility flowed through his veins like adrenaline.

You know, my friends, that I was once the mayor of San Miguel de las Colinas, my beautiful home. I was responsible for city administration, but I was unhappy with my job and felt I was not performing well, as I was not serving the people as I should have. Worse still, my plans and ideas were constantly being thwarted — snuffed out like candle flames — by powerful individuals who cared more for their entrenched power and themselves, yes, for themselves, than for the people who worked for them, the people who helped keep them rich. I do not mean, of course, that it is wrong to be successful, that wanting to achieve more or to better ourselves is bad. No, no, my friends. That is the dream we all share. We believe that hard work and decent lives will help us realise that dream. My friends, we must never stop dreaming. We must never stop dreaming. *We must. Never. Stop. Dreaming.*

The cheers nearly overwhelmed him.

Thank you, my friends. But those forces — the forces of reaction and entrenched power — were crushing people's dreams everywhere. And for me, they were doing their best to obstruct any reforms I wished to implement. Whatever direction we took in my administration, they were there, trying to block progress and attempting to ensure that nothing we planned threatened their wealth or positions. And that was wrong. It was wrong. It was unjust. It was immoral."

He looked out over the crowd and raised his hand. "My friends, we must never again allow those backwards forces to stand in the way of our dreams — for if our dreams are taken away, what will become of us? Look, my friends, I know this is not easy. Life is not easy. Sometimes terrible things happen, but even then, we need hope to keep us on the right path and to keep us moving forward.

"You know, all of you standing there, what happened in my lovely town. You are aware of the suffering and pain we endured. I mourn the people of San Miguel who lost their lives in that terrible time, and I know you will want me to convey your love, respect, and support to the families who are still grieving for what is to come in the sad years they must face. But the dawn comes after every darkness, and the dawn is called hope. That is what I have discovered in my own life.

"My friends, ladies and gentlemen, comrades, you know what happened to me after the earthquake in San Miguel, and it is because of those events that I am standing here today. What happened when I stood shoulder to shoulder with my comrades, trying to move concrete and stone with our bare hands, was hope, pure and simple. And what is that hope based on? It is based on the absolute conviction that every human life, every single one of us, is equally important. In that dreadful situation, amid all that suffering, we all, every one of us, knew that we were one, that no one is more than anyone else, and that unless we all worked together, no one would ever be saved and pulled from that wreckage. And I learned more. I realised that every tragedy that day and in the days that followed was not just a tragedy for an individual or a family; it was a tragedy for all of us, for the whole community, for the country, for the world. But from that great sorrow, new hope was born. A dream was formed. And what is that dream? What is that hope?" He was reaching his peroration, and the crowd was loving it.

"We must respect each other equally. We must ensure that the lives of every man, woman, and child are as important as those of everyone else. And that is my dream, my friends. We will build a new society; a new community will rise from the ruins of the old, and a new city will be constructed from the ashes of past destruction. Will you share my dream? Will you share my dream? Will you share my dream?"

"Yes, yes, yes!" the crowd roared every time he asked the question. The air rippled with fervent ecstasy. He waited.

"My friends, I hear your hope. I hear your dreams. I hear you all, and I am with you. But my friends, it will not be easy. There are forces against us—the same forces I have spoken of. And be warned: those forces have their champion, and she is a formidable rival. Yet I tell you, she will not win. Entrenched power and backwardness will not win, cannot win. They must not win. They must not win if we are to keep our dreams alive. Do you understand me, my friends? The battle lines are drawn. We know our enemy, and the question is: are you with me, my friends? Because if you are, we can dream further, and when our dreams become reality, we will change the world. That is the hope I live by. Thank you, and God bless you."

Part Two
Mountains to Climb

Chapter 20
Alexei

HE WAS RUNNING out of breath, but he was used to that. Reaching the top required a great deal of effort. All his years on the mountains had taught him that.

It was so good to get out of that place. They all seemed nice enough, but they seemed to want to stop him from doing his important work. And if he couldn't get out to where the fumaroles leaked their fetid breath into the open air, what was the point of anything? Besides, he was never, never ever, he told himself, going to be locked away again. That jail had been the worst of the worst times in his life. The hard concrete floor, the smell of urine, the stink of frightened men, the snores, the curses, and all the while the bruises where he had been beaten throbbed to some malevolent rhythm. At least the place he had just slipped out of wasn't like that. It was soft, gentle, and antiseptic. Deadening.

The people in cars passing by as they climbed to higher floors to find a space saw a spindly, wild-looking bearded man weaving his way uncertainly along the parking lanes where pedestrians were not supposed to be. They must have realised that he was in an unsettled state, but no one stopped to ask if he was all right. In their defence, they were hemmed in by cars behind and in front of them, climbing too and anyway, who knew how dangerous this strange figure might turn out to be. They continued upward, hoping they could reach the lifts without worrying about him. Hopefully, when they came back from their shopping trip or restaurant visit, he would be gone. Homeless people are like that, they told themselves. You see them, you don't see them. No problem.

Alexei carried on upwards. He could feel a light wind coming in from the sides of the mountain. He ran his fingers through his hair. This was the life, he told himself. Wait till I get home and tell Vicky all about it. I hope I'm in time for the eruption, because it's expected to occur. He was sure about that. Something big was going to happen. He swayed, almost stumbling as he climbed. The old excitement was back. *This is my life,* he shouted — or he thought he shouted — *this is what I do. This is what I am.* He had a sudden thought of that lovely girl in San Miguel. Where was San Miguel? This wasn't like that at all. Strange. The air smelt different too. Fumes. Fumes. Fumeroles. They didn't usually smell like this. Like burnt petrol, squealing rubber. Still, every mountain was different. He knew that.

Look, Vicky, he said. *This is why I couldn't stay cooped up in that house. You know me. I have to be here, here where the crater edges scrape the sky.*

He had reached the top floor of the multi-storey car park, open to the elements. Cars were parked in serried ranks. There were some spaces. He breathed in the night air and the city's pollution. He went to the edge and looked over. The city was spread beneath him. Lights. Traffic crawled along congested streets, the occasional squeal of a siren, the thump of music from a passing car way beneath him. For the life of him, he could not understand why people chose to live so close to brooding mountains when the danger was so obvious — their choice.

It was sweet to be up here at last and to be able to wander on the crater's edge. To look down and see life going on, people unaware of the wonder of nature in all its majestic glory. Silly little people. Look how ridiculous they were. If they could only feel what he felt, wandering here, free as a bird in the night air. But they were too bound, too trapped in their landed lives. What could they know of the majestic beauty of the angry gods in the grumbling earth? What could they know of the grace of this celestial earth?

It was 'down there', however, that a young boy, about nine or ten years old, grabbed his mother's sleeve. "Look, mummy," he said, tugging at her sleeve and pointing upwards, "look at that man up there. What's he doing?" When she saw the figure of Alexei balancing precariously on the edge of the multi-storey car park, the boy's mother knew at once that something was wrong. Drugged, mad or suicidal, or all three, he, whoever he might be, was in imminent danger of falling, and so she called the emergency services.

The first that Alexei knew of this in his confused, altered state was the sight of blue flashing lights and a bright beam spotlighting him against the evening sky. He found himself laughing uncontrollably at the prettiness of it all. What a lovely way to celebrate the volcano's birthday, he thought. Lights and sirens and people looking upwards in awe.

"Hello there," a voice behind him said. He turned round and, for a second, he almost lost his balance. "Woo!" he shrieked. You have to be careful on the mountains. The slightest slip can land you in trouble. Remember that poor girlfriend of Martin's! Look what happened to her poor thing. That was not my fault. Was it?

"Hello," the voice said again. "Are you okay? You okay up

there? Do you fancy coming down for a second so we could have a chat?"

The person speaking was a woman, about his age, dressed up like a police officer. She looked nice, he thought. He liked the hat she was wearing. It suited her.

"Hello," he said. "You've come all the way up here dressed like that. I am very impressed. I like the costume." He was having trouble getting his words out for some reason. Maybe it was those wretched pills they had made him take. He had managed not to take them all, he reminded himself triumphantly, but he couldn't help swallowing some of the dosage.

"Could we have a chat?" the woman said again. "Maybe you could come down here and we could talk about things — about anything that's worrying you?"

"I'm not worried about anything," he laughed at her. Suddenly, he realised she *was* a policewoman. Maybe she was going to take him back to that stinking jail. No. No. He couldn't stand that. He'd rather—

"Are you okay, sir? What's your name?"

"*I. Am. Not. Going. Back. There. Ever.*" He waved his arms around in panicked alarm.

"No one's going to take you back, sir. Just come down here and we can sort everything out."

He knew he could not trust her. He had to get away from her. He could do it, too, because he knew his way around mountains. I bet she doesn't, he thought to himself. He turned around to get away from her. Down below, something was being blown up.

"Honestly, sir, you'll be all right. I promise. Things will be okay, you'll see. Just tell me your name and we can talk." He could hear the urgency in her voice. The deceptive friendliness wasn't going to fool him. No. Not ever. He was Alexei Kassoliniki, a vulcanologist, an adventurer. He was free.

He started to run away from her, along the wall. He would

never be taken, not by her, not by anyone. He was laughing out loud now, happy, sure of his own power.

He didn't see the cabling which snaked over the rim of the parapet. Inevitably, he tripped, spinning around and flailing desperately with his arms to keep his balance. But it was no good. For a second, he teetered precariously on the edge, and then he fell.

It started to rain.

Chapter 21
Angelita

"I HAVE HAD A THOUGHT."

"A thought?"

"More like a decision."

"Go on, then." It was difficult to hear her above the city noise and the shouts and drumbeats coming from the marchers.

"I want to change my name."

"Change your name?"

"Martin!"

"Okay," he said. Try me."

"I want to be called Angela, not Angelita."

To their right, people were walking past, beating drums and blasting ear-splitting tunes on trumpets.

"Angelita is a girl's name" She seemed very serious.

"Well, but I like it. You are Angelita."

"Am I? Am I really?"

"To me, yes."

"So I'm just going to have to live with it?"

"You've managed pretty well so far."

"Creep."

They were walking down a main street of the capital with a large crowd of people. There were chants and drumming, banners and signs. *'Justicia para los heroes del EAS'* — Justice for the EAS heroes they read — and 'Where are the heroes?' Carried aloft, they swayed as the enormous wave of humanity rolled onwards. There were, of course, counter-protesters, too. They lined the streets. *'Fuera los comunistas'* — communists get out of here — and, perhaps more ominously, Martin thought, large banners showing the face of Isabel Gutierrez. 'For president,' they proclaimed in loud lettering. Along the side of the street, and more reassuringly, he thought, were large banners which proclaimed "Silvestre Ocampo. From the troubled past to a better future."

This was the second demonstration in the big city about the missing EAS members from Calixtlapan, and public protests were beginning to take place all over the country. They had started, of course, in San Miguel. Genoveva, her family (entirely on board), her friend Dolores, and the families of the disappeared had quickly organised a big gathering in the square opposite the cathedral. There had been speeches, most notably from Silvestre Ocampo himself.

"My friends," he had said, "something has gone wrong. Something disgraceful happened in the valley of Calixtlapan. I promise you that, if we are elected, my administration will not rest until we get to the bottom of what took place on that fateful day and until we have returned those people to the loving arms of their families. My future administration," he continued, "will always — *always* — defend the rights of peaceful protest. It is the foundation on which any democracy must be built, the right of every person, man, woman and child to gather and show the world how they feel. The right of every citizen to have their voices heard."

"Whatever other people call you, can I still call you 'Angie'?"

She turned to face him and lifted her head to kiss him. "Guapo," she said, "you can call me whatever you want. I am not particular. It's just that somehow things — I don't know, the world is not quite so cheerful as it was perhaps? No, that's not it. I think I just feel different, that's all. More grown up. Do you think I am more grown up?"

"What? I didn't hear that." The noise around them made it almost impossible to hear anything except for the chants and the trumpets.

She smiled to herself. Her life with Martin was going well. Exciting sometimes, but mostly, and especially, comfortable. Her music was becoming more fulfilling every day, and she was securing more work, which in turn meant camera sessions for both her and her quartet, providing them with valuable publicity material. She had been interviewed on an arts programme, and thanks to the work of her agent, she had her first foreign trip planned out. Maybe that would give her time to visit her sister-in-law and get to know her better.

When Martin and Angelita got together, everything had been very chaotic, even before the eruption and the earthquake. She hadn't had a chance to bond with her new sister-in-law amidst all the chaos, which included getting Victoria and her children and the strange husband out of the country as quickly as possible — and it then felt as if she might never really know her at all. A trip abroad would give her a chance to rectify that, and she looked forward to it.

Her life with Martin was a daily demonstration of their genuine affection for each other, but sometimes — and she did this without complaint — it felt as if she wasn't just her husband's lover; she was also being asked to fill the space that Martin's sister had left behind. She knew, too, that Vicky's troubles were preoccupying him more than he was letting on.

The crowd moved forward. They were obliged to go with it.

She decided to stop focusing on her own life and concentrate instead on why they were here.

There was growing national confusion about the exact circumstances of the events on the road to Calixtlapan. What was beyond question was that shots were fired, the bus carrying the ESA protesters had been burnt out, and there had been injuries and maybe deaths. Beyond that, things got murky. Some rumours suggested that local thugs — essentially the Heredia private army, with the help of gangs from other landowners — had carried out the attack and whatever it had led to.

Other reports suggested that the attackers were the state police in disguise. Someone claimed to have seen a uniform under a black jacket. Still others suggested that it was all a put-up job, all fake. It was, as indicated by some of the growing number of Gutierrez supporters, all a plot by the protesters themselves (in reality, it was claimed, old-style communists) to bring attention to their exaggerated claims and accusations. As each day passed, new theories emerged, each one more outlandish than the last. Aliens were even touted as a possible cause, but surely no one took them seriously. Or perhaps they did, Angelita thought. We live in such a crazy world. That was part of the problem in a presidential campaign year. People become overexcited, claims become increasingly extreme, and promises become more outrageous.

But it was no joke. She only had to talk to her friend Genoveva to understand that. Real people might have been killed in an increasingly lawless state — not the only one of its kind in the republic — and the population was getting angrier. As far as Angelita could tell, Genoveva was desperately worried and unhappy. Silverio was always on the go, working for the Ocampo campaign, so her friend often felt alone and, it has to be said, somewhat afraid of who might be out there searching for any more members of the EAS.

They had reached a big square. Music was blaring out from a line of loudspeakers on either side of a temporary stage, which was ringed by people in yellow and red. They looked more like an army or a crowd of football supporters than the protesters who were pouring into the square to stand in front of them.

"Who are those guys?"

"I don't know," Martin said, "but it doesn't quite feel right to me."

"Maybe we should go?"

"Might as well stay and see what this is all about. I'm not sure if anyone will speak or anything. Hopefully, someone's going to give us some news."

"I've just had a thought," she shouted back, "about those colours."

"Colours?"

"Yeah, the colours those people are wearing," she pointed to the groups standing near the stage. "They're the colours on the posters for that woman, Isabela Gutierrez."

"Yeah, I think you are right."

And a few seconds later, there could be no doubt about it as a man came out onto the stage and started addressing the crowd. "Friends, my friends, it is good to see you all here raising your voices in defence of our freedoms, our freedoms that are being eaten away by the evil messages of people who wish to destroy our country with their attempts to rewrite the sacred truths that have made us great. These disappeared people — that is, if they *are* indeed disappeared — what were they trying to achieve? Why were they going to Calixtlapan in the first place? Something bad has happened, but what exactly? And who profits from it?"

The crowd was getting restless. They hadn't expected this.

The speaker's words echoed from the buildings around the square. Still, he stopped speaking when someone, wearing the blue T-shirt of the march organisers, rushed up and tried to pull him away from the microphone. Then it all became very confused. Three more people wearing Gutierrez colours rushed onto the stage, and march organisers joined in, sparking a scuffle.

On the ground, it was no better. The people standing around the stage had started to chant. At first, their words were indecipherable, especially as people around Angelita and Martin were shouting in protest. Above them, a police helicopter hovered, and approaching sirens meant the police were about to join in.

More blue-T-shirted people had crowded onto the stage. A man Angelita recognised from the publicity that had circulated about the march approached the microphone.

"Friends," he shouted. "Friends. We are here for the same thing. We are here to demand that the members of Ejercito Arturo Sanchez be returned unharmed to their families. We are here for justice, for peaceful protest, for democracy."

On the ground, the yellow and red groups had unfurled some banners. 'Truth, not lies,' they read and 'Down with communist lies'. For a second, their chants could be heard. "Truth, not lies," they called, "Defend our values."

Some of the crowd surged forward and began trying to take the banners from the chanters' hands. And then the fighting started. The situation quickly escalated as fists were thrown, poles were used, people fell, and they were kicked.

From a side street, helmeted riot police with shields were running into the melee, hitting their shields with their batons. There was the crack and fizz of tear gas, and the air became thick with its stinging clouds.

"Come on," Martin yelled, clutching her hand. They fought their way out of the crowds and the fighting, eyes stinging, their breath coming in shallow gasps, until they were suddenly on the sidewalk with the crowd behind them.

Angelita wiped her eyes. Martin took his water bottle and poured some water on her face. She blinked, her vision all blurry as tears and water poured down her cheeks. Through her sniffles, she said, "That was weird. It was like a setup. Who were those people?"

Martin was in the process of pouring water on his own eyes now and didn't answer for a bit. They were walking towards a metro station where they could catch a train back to their neighbourhood.

"I think they were kind of paid thugs for the Gutierrez camp or something like that. I don't really know. But I just don't get how they could mess up something like today. All we are asking is to know what happened to those people and to get them back safe and sound. But those guys seem to have other ideas. Almost as if they were using us—"

"Us?"

"The demonstrators. Using us to stir things up. God help us if the election campaign is going to be like this."

"Looks like it will. How bad would it be if that Gutierrez person won?"

"Well, it would break Silverio's heart, apart from anything else!"

"No."

"Your guess is as good as mine, but if what happened just now is anything to go on, it might get very ugly indeed. Hold on." He reached into his pocket to get his phone.

"Vicky. How are you? What now? But can't we talk when Angelita and I get back to the flat? Federico? Why Federico? Well, okay, if it is that important. But I still don't understand. Vicky?" He looked confused. "She hung up on me!"

"Why were you talking about, Papa?"

"She wants us to go round there."

"To his place?"

"Yes. Apparently."

"But why?" She needed to get home, clean up her face, and feel safe.

"I don't know. I'm sorry. I know it's weird. But that's what she said, and Angie sounded desperate."

Again? She thought. But she didn't say anything. She just kissed him, and hand in hand they went towards her father's flat.

Chapter 22
Maria

THEY WERE SITTING in the café, which had become a familiar place for their after-class conversations — that is, if three times could be considered familiar. Maria was happier than she had been for a long time. She was enjoying the lessons now, and the strange letters that she had never understood were beginning to be recognisable, and she had even, in today's session, been able to identify a whole word. *Manzana*, she thought, *apple*. I know those letters together mean a *manzana*, an apple. It was a heady feeling, and she was longing to tell Señor Federico all about it. She knew how pleased he would be. He was a good man.

"Are you listening to anything I'm saying?"

"What? Oh, sorry. I was just thinking about what Señor Federico would—" She stopped and blushed. "I'm sorry. You're right. Start again. I promise to give you my full attention!"

Santiago was a good man, too. She was sure about that. She had suspected that in what she now thought of as the 'before time', but now she had good reason to actually believe it. He had lovely eyes and was an excellent listener. He was a bit unlike anyone she had met before — or rather, anyone she had spent a bit of time talking one-to-one with! It was almost as if they were getting close.

Of course, that door was closed for her after everything that had happened, and this, whatever this was, didn't feel quite like that kind of thing. But she did feel a little less hopeless in his presence; she had found herself thinking more carefully about what to wear in the morning, and when she considered this, she had to admit that it did have something to do with the fact that she was going to meet him later in the day.

Yet, there was something slightly off about the picture. It looked as if Santiago enjoyed her company — why else, she asked herself, would he have been the one to suggest going to their coffee place each time? But, she didn't sense that his enjoyment was suggestive. On the other hand, how would she know? Apart from the lewdness you encountered on the street from bored men, no one had expressed that kind of interest in her for years now. I am too respectable, she thought to herself. Despite that marriage, my marriage, I was too respectable.

She was unused to complex introspection, and the effort it was costing her right now was perplexing. It almost hurt!

"Maria, forgive me. I don't know what you are thinking about, but your coffee is getting cold, and I am just sitting here while you worry about whatever it is that is going on in that head of yours!" Now he was laughing at her.

"Sorry. Sorry. I was just thinking—" She stopped.

"Well, now that I have your attention, I'll tell you my story. Okay?"

"Okay."

"I told you — except you weren't listening — about having to stay late for work yesterday. I had too much to do. It was almost dark as I put things away in the shed in the señora's garden. Someone was knocking on the door of the back garden wall. It was unusual. No one usually comes that way. But whoever it was kept on knocking."

He stopped to take a breath.

"I suppose I should go and unlock the door and see who it was when the señora came out of the house with a couple of the men who seem to spend a lot of time there now, something to do with her wanting to be president, I suppose, and they almost ran to the door. One of the men said something, but I couldn't hear what it was. There was some kind of response, and then he opened the door. Two men came into the garden. One of them was a young guy, and the other was someone much bigger, one of those security guard types. The younger guy, I saw his face for just a bit; there was something about it that reminded me of someone I'd seen somewhere, but I couldn't remember where. Probably someone important in politics or something, so I wouldn't know who it was anyway!"

"You do live an exciting life!"

"No, but there was something strange about this."

"Santiago," it was her turn to laugh, "someone comes in through the garden door? That's strange?"

"That's what Tonio said, too. But it was strange," emphatically, "the big one took off his coat and put it over the other guy's head like the police do when they take some bad guy to court."

"Not always bad!"

"And then they ran into the house. Then one of those helicopters roared over the house, its lights on. Tonio says—"

"Maybe they didn't want the people in that helicopter to see him?"

"Yes, but why?"

"If you're trying to be president, you must have secrets, I suppose. And anyway, all those people…"

"S'pose so."

After a minute, he said, "What are you doing over the holiday? Do you have to work?"

"Señor Federico said I could have the day off. I think I'll just rest."

"You should join us in the park. A little picnic?"

"Umm. I'm not sure."

"Come on. I'm sure you deserve a day out after everything that's happened to you."

He had such warmth in his eyes. "Why not"?

As she walked to the metro station, she found herself smiling. Would she go? Why? Why not? It made her feel a bit nervous.

But when she got back to the lawyer's flat, all thoughts of picnics and parks left her completely. Her employer and the young couple were sitting round the dining table. Something had happened. Señor Federico lit another cigarette, but Angelita did not tell him off. They all looked a bit shocked.

She had tried to let herself in quietly, and the moment she saw their faces, she tried even harder to make her way past the kitchen and into her room without disturbing whatever was going on. But they looked round. Angelita and Martin turned away. Her employer sucked on his cigarette and blew out smoke.

"Maria," he said, and started to cough. She waited.

"Maria, come and sit down."

"Señor?"

"Come and sit down. There's something we should probably tell you."

Chapter 23
Silverio

IT WAS LATE when he returned to the flat to find Genoveva asleep on the sofa. He tried to wake her up gently, but she still gasped when her eyes fluttered open and she saw him there.

"Sorry," he said, "I didn't mean to startle you. Are you okay?"

The television was on with the sound muted. He reached for the control to switch it off, but a picture of Isabela Gutierrez appeared on the screen. He hit the unmute button.

".... just released a new statement about the missing protesters from San Miguel de las Colinas…"

He would have switched off for Genoveva's sake; anything to take her mind off her fixation with what had happened to her friends, which he understood, of course, and anyway, he was obsessed with the dark mystery of it himself. Not only was it an open sore on the body politic, but it also worried him that it was taking attention away from Silvestre Ocampo's campaign. Everything they were doing had to be about more than just the EAS disappearances.

He hated himself for his disloyalty when he thought like this, and yet unless they could find some way of deflecting the media's attention, irrespective of the genuine need to find out what had actually happened, their presidential campaign was seriously threatened. And what he was hearing and seeing on the TV only underlined this."...shows a serious dereliction of duty by the authorities in San Miguel," the Gutierrez statement went on, "and the valley beyond. Not only should whatever has happened not have been allowed to take place, but nothing seems to have been done about it. Not one of these so-called protesters has been found. No one has been arrested. There have been no leads in this frustrating case.

And who was in charge when this took place? None other than the mayor, Silvestre Ocampo, the same man who is asking for your support to be president of this great republic. Who in their right minds would want someone like that to lead us when he couldn't even organise his own backyard? And I ask you to wonder why there has been no progress in this baffling case. Is it because Ocampo has something to hide? Perhaps he knows where these people are and is withholding this information for a reason.

Perhaps it is all part of a political game, one that shouldn't be played with the fate of so many people at stake. Everyone will know that the aims of this so-called movement are not the same as the vast majority of patriotic citizens, but that is no reason to treat them any differently from anyone else in this great country. If they have done wrong, it is for the law to take charge; if they have not, they have the same rights and the same need for safety as anyone else.

Of your candidates, I am the only one who can promise you an honest and just investigation into this case. You can expect nothing but lies and obfuscation from Ocampo's team. Silvestre Ocampo must never be allowed anywhere near the seat of power."

Gutierrez's words were read out, appearing on the screen as

they were spoken. They were followed by pictures of the candidate travelling around the country, shaking hands with people, inspecting a herd of cattle, and visiting one of the country's largest oil refineries.

'Is it true?" Genoveva asked sleepily, her voice a pale imitation of the bubbling personality she once displayed.

"Is what true?"

"What is she saying about Silvestre? Is he hiding something? Maybe he doesn't care?"

"You know that's not true, Genny. Silvestre, we are all doing everything we can. It's a major issue with Silvestre in particular — and me, of course — and it's a real headache for us. If we are not careful, the press will turn against us and all the goodwill Silvestre earned after the earthquake will be wiped away by that woman's poisonous insinuations."

"Who cares! Who cares about the campaign? Damn the campaign. What about us? What about the EAS? Thirty-seven of us. Thirty-seven. You were us before you got seduced by all this presidential nonsense. But which is more important? Silverio, what is happening to you?" Her voice had risen dramatically. He noticed the empty bottle of wine on the table in front of her.

"Genoveva. My love." She looked away. "I love you, you know that?" There was a silence. After a pause, she nodded. She did not look happy, but he was growing accustomed to it. It was as if the burnt bus and the disappearances had switched off a light inside her, and she now existed in subdued twilight. "You know I care about the EAS, you know I have always cared. I will never stop caring until they all return safely. They are your people, but they are also my people. And look, Silvestre has accomplished a great deal. Before he stopped being mayor, he questioned Riveira endlessly, but that corrupt bastard of a cop hasn't helped at all. True, we do know some things. Those store holders have been forced to tell us what they saw, at least."

The bus was pulled over by a police motorcycle cop, who the police denied any knowledge of. The moment it had left the road, a group of men turned up on more motorcycles and started firing guns. No, the stall holders didn't know what kind of guns. No, they didn't recognise any of the men. The people on the bus scrambled out. There was screaming, and then a truck turned up. They were herded into that before it sped off down the road, quickly followed by the motorcycles, but not before the supposed policeman had poured gasoline all over the original bus and then set light to it.

Silvestre Ocampo was sure Rivendeira knew a lot more than he was saying, and kept trying to talk to him, question him, challenge him about what, if anything, he had found out about the people involved in the whole episode. The disadvantage, of course, is that he was no longer the mayor. Although he was potentially even more important and influential as a possible president, he had not yet achieved that status and might never do so. So the policeman could afford to be difficult to get hold of and even more evasive than usual when they did speak.

No one had found the truck that the EAS members were taken away in, no one knew anything about the men on bikes, and no one knew anything at all. Despite all the noise in the media, no one had come forward with any more information. It was as if the missing had been spirited away by a bunch of wraiths.

"Look, Genny," Silverio went on, and even to himself, his voice sounded strangely pleading. "However cold-hearted this sounds, there are other priorities as well — a whole world of them. And the most important thing, the very most important thing, is to get Silvestre elected. Only then can we truly make a meaningful difference. Only then can we start to change the culture of this place - though God knows it will not be easy. We've had too many long years of doing things the way they've always been done. But we need to escape from that, leap from our little familiar cages into a bright new dawn for the people, for the country, for the future. Unless—"

"Stop! I am not a crowd at one of your rallies."

She was not laughing at him. She looked fed up and showed no sympathy. It stopped him in his tracks. He realised that yes, he had been sloganeering. And to Genoveva. In their own house! What was happening to them? It had all seemed so reasonable such a short time ago, and now suddenly their relationship seemed to be under strain. He felt as if his heart would break if anything went wrong, but he couldn't seem to find a way through.

"Genny, I am sorry. I am so sorry. I just can't help myself. I'm breathing this campaign, dreaming this campaign. I'm so tired. But I can't stop. I mustn't stop. It's everything. For me, for us, for our friends, for everyone."

"Is it?"

"Yes, it is, Genny. Surely you can see that. If that woman wins? What then? She'll go into battle against workers, trade unions, opposition parties, and the intelligentsia. God help the doctors and the teachers, the artists, the writers — and yes, the workers in factories and on farms. It matters, Genny. It matters."

She stood up. "I'm going to bed."

Silverio stood there looking at nothing. The television was still on, but they were talking about something else now. He switched it off. He sat down on his side of the sofa, his head slumped, an overwhelming tiredness threatening to overwhelm him. The two things he cared about most in the world were his campaign and his partner, no, make that three, he thought guiltily, the disappeared EAS members, he cared about them too, of course he did — and his family, of course, and the music he loved and the sight of light clouds on the mountains. But it was Genoveva, the

146

miracle that had come into his life, who mattered the most, didn't she? And then the campaign and the EAS.

Everything seemed to be in opposition to everything else, and the atmosphere outside was becoming ugly. What was he going to do? He sank into a hopeless misery and must have dozed off, his half dreams populated by unfamiliar people in vaguely familiar landscapes. When he half-regained consciousness about twenty minutes later, he felt terrible. It was a struggle to get up and make his way to the bedroom.

It was dark, but there was enough light coming in from the bathroom, which he was about to visit, for him to take off his clothes and find a T-shirt and shorts to replace them. He made his way to the bathroom and brushed his teeth half-heartedly. He switched off the light and stumbled to the bedroom. He sat down on the bed. Genoveva moved, and a light sleep-infused groan escaped her. Silverio's head sank down, and his shoulders slumped. He was in danger of falling asleep and tumbling forward — whichever came first. He forced himself to turn and slither down the sheets. *God, I am so tired,* he thought. He put his head down on the pillow and stretched down to the bottom of the bed.

Sensing his presence, Genoveva turned over and sleepily laid her arm across him and snuggled into his back. He felt a wave of sweet sadness sweep through him as sleep enveloped him. But, he thought, surely Gutierrez knows there's nothing underhanded about the fate of the EAS. Unless she knows something different, could it be that…

He didn't get any further. He slept.

Chapter 24
Rosario

SHE COULDN'T FIND her shoes. Where were they? Where did she keep her shoes? They must be somewhere. Why were things so complicated? She decided to sit down and have a think about it. When her maid came in a few moments later and asked her what she was doing, she wasn't sure.

"You're not wearing shoes," the maid said, and she looked down at her feet. Sure enough, her feet were shoeless. She went over to her cupboard and chose a pair she was especially fond of. Or was she? Maybe she should wear something else. This was all so difficult. She stuffed her feet into anything she could find and walked downstairs. She wondered how Marcela was. In the room where she lived all the time, she was playing with her ball of wool — was it a different colour? She couldn't remember. The girl came towards her. What was her name? She knew that, surely.

Tiacuri looked up and said, "Good morning."

She said good morning back because it seemed the right thing to do. "Señora, forgive me, but your shoes?"

Her shoes? She looked down. Yes, she was wearing shoes.

"My shoes?"

"Yes, señora, but forgive me, they are not the same. You are wearing odd shoes."

What was the girl talking about?

"If you will permit me, Señora, I will get you a pair. Is that all right, señora?"

Tia Rosario looked at her and tried to work out what she was saying. But she had gone. She returned later. "Señora, would you mind sitting down?"

She sat down and watched Tiacuri — yes, that was her name — take off her shoes and put on a new pair. She wondered why. No matter! She looked at the girl's face — such a pretty face, such a sweet expression.

"Are you ready now, Señora?"

"Ready? Ready?" Then she remembered something about today. Ah yes. The club. That club. She liked the club. Didn't she?

Rosario knew something was wrong. Whereas before she tended to forget things and could at times be somewhat absent-minded, now she recognised — when she remembered — that things were a bit different. It wasn't just the names. She'd always had trouble with those. It wasn't today's shoes, was it? She was finding things more difficult, having trouble with simple tasks, such as what she had just done, where time went, where she was supposed to be, and what she was supposed to do.

Maybe I've got an infection or something, she thought. She would have also considered calling the doctor, but she forgot what she was thinking about. With Tiacuri's help, she stood up.

"You look fine, Señora. I'm sure you will have a lovely time."

"Why, thank you. You are such a pretty girl, you know?"

"Thank you, Señora."

"What I don't understand is that those people...." She stopped, trying to remember. Then she got it. "In the club. My friends," she smiled. "Those people seemed to know all about the people who disappeared. But how could they?"

"How could they?" Tiacuri prompted.

"What are you standing about for? Take me to the car." A car was driving up and stopped outside the main entrance. Tiacuri noticed that the usual driver, the man who usually drove her employer, had been replaced by a younger man. Maybe he was a private hire driver, she thought.

Tia Rosario made her way to the car. She greeted the driver and immediately engaged him in animated conversation, as if she knew him.

The girl watched them go and wondered what she should do.

Chapter 25
Tiacuri

"¿Señora Angelita?"

"Who's this?"

"It's me, Tiacuri, the one who cares for the Señorita Marcela. I'm from your aunt's house, from San Miguel."

"Tiacuri." The maid sensed the surprise in the violinist's voice and, for a moment, she faltered. Maybe she shouldn't be ringing. But then she thought about the reasons for her call, and that helped her gain the courage she needed.

"Señora Angelita, I am sorry to ring you. I got your name from the list we keep, you see. I thought I should call you because I do not know the licenciado well, and I don't know you well — I am sorry I am not doing this right."

"Tiacuri, it's all right. Please go on. Tell me why you are ringing. It's okay."

"Thank you, Señora. It's just that I am worried."

"What about?"

"It is about your aunt, Señora. She is, she is forgetting things."

"She always has. Is something different now?"

"Yes, I think it is. She forgets what she is doing or what she has done. Today she put on odd shoes. Her mood seems to change from one minute to the next. I think, señora Angelita, she may be suffering from some kind of decline, some mental decline."

"What do the others think?"

"I have talked to Lupe and Claudia, and they say, yes, something is different, but I shouldn't worry, so where's the harm? But I think she might be a danger to herself, and what happens when she goes out? Will she be safe? And I have probably said too much, but I didn't know who to talk to."

"You did right to call me, Tiacuri. I am not sure what to do either. I suppose I will need to talk to my father. I will come up as soon as I can. Or maybe he will. I am not sure. But Tiacuri, thank you for calling."

She could sense that Angelita was drawing the call to an end. "Señora, there is something else."

"What? More about my aunt? About Marcela?"

"No, Señora. This is about something different. Well, it's something your aunt has said, and I know — or at least I have heard you and your friends talk about it — you will want to know. It's about the disappearance."

"The disappearance?" Now, she could tell that Angelita was surprised.

"Señora, yes. I know I shouldn't say anything, but it's just strange, and I know it's not my business, but Calixtlapan is near my village, and anyway, it's on television and everyone is talking about it and your friend, it's her friends, and so I thought—"

"Tiacuri! What? What has my aunt said?"

"Well, she forgets that she's said it, and then she repeats it. She may just be confused. It may be nothing. It may not even be true, I suppose."

"Go on, Tiacuri."

"She says—" She sensed Angelita's impatience on the other end of the line. "She says the people in the club, the ones who collect her and bring her back, she says they know all about those people — she means the disappeared — they know what happened to those people. She's sure of it, she says. I can't tell, and of course it may all be your aunt's imagination, or she might have got it wrong, or maybe I have, but it's been worrying me, you see, and I don't know who else to talk to about it. Señora...."

She gave up at that point. Maybe she shouldn't have called.

There was a silence on the line. Tiacuri felt miserable and stupid. But then Angelita started to speak again.

"Tiacuri, thank you again for calling. I'll talk to my father about Tia Rosario, though he's very busy with something else now. We all are. I'm not sure I can do anything, it's just too... sorry, Tiacuri. I'll think about all this. Leave it with me."

"Señora."

"And the other thing? I'm unsure what Tia Rosario meant, and I'm not even sure I believe her. I don't know what I can do about that either. But I'll probably mention it to my friends. I think I will. Tiacuri, I am so sorry, but I must go. I will see you soon. Give my love to Marcela."

The phone line went down. Tiacuri started to shake. She had had to summon up the courage to make the call. Now she was amazed that she had.

Chapter 26
Vicky

"I WILL NOT CRY," she said to herself. "I will not let the children see me crying again. I don't want the sympathy of the other mums and dads. What would I do with it? Please leave me alone, everyone. Please don't come up and talk to me, saying how sorry you are — that's if you have heard. If you haven't heard anything, I don't have the heart to pretend everything is okay. If someone offers me pity, I don't think I can take that. I shouldn't have come. I can't stay here. I'm going. I can't go. Oh, God. What are we going to do?"

She stood by herself, a forlorn figure at the school gates. A man she recognised, one of the fathers from her daughter Sarah's class, approached her.

"Victoria, how are you?" he asked kindly, just as he had been kind on the two occasions they had talked before.

"I'm fine," she said, more sternly than she had meant to.

He scowled and walked away.

How could she tell him what had happened? He'd be shocked. Then, he'd start offering sympathy — if he was able to think of anything to say, that is. Then what? How could she explain what had gone on? Where would she start if she were going to tell him about Alexei, her rock, her mysterious God-like husband, her lover who had turned into a trembling, withdrawn shadow of the hero he had once been? She couldn't even think about him falling and hitting the ground. She could almost hear it. Yes, they had told her, the inflated mat had partly broken his descent, but it hadn't been enough. It wasn't fully inflated, and anyway, he had hit the side of it and bounced off before smashing into the road and cracking his head so savagely that now — her mind skated off into inattention, a sort of grey limbo — she dragged it back. But why? What was there that was worth being dragged back for? What was she going to do?

It had taken the hospital a bit of time yesterday to find her, since Alexei did not have any identification on him. She only got the call as she was taking the children to school. The voice on the other end of the phone wanted to check that she was Alexei's wife. When they were satisfied with her answers, they informed her that they were calling from the hospital and then explained the reason for their call.

Once the kids had gone through the school gates, she got to the hospital and found him. He was deeply unconscious. His smashed-up face was red and raw despite the efforts they had made to clean him up. There were tubes everywhere, monitors, a screen with graph lines moving across it, and the rhythmic sound of a machine that was breathing for him. She spoke with the doctors and nurses. She got in touch with one of the other mothers and asked them to collect the children; she'd pick them up from her house.

Once reassured that nothing about Alexei's condition was going to change and that he was almost certainly not going to regain consciousness during the night — and if he did, they would call her, but it was doubtful — and that they would do some tests first thing in the morning, she collected the children and made her way home. Then she told them that Daddy had an accident. He fell off a building. We're not quite sure how it happened, but we'll find out soon, I'm sure. Then, with her heart pounding and a terrible band of tightness around her skull, everywhere, she had made them supper.

For once, she had let them watch more than an hour of TV on the screen they had bought for the one that Alex had thrown out of the window. It was only later, when they had gone to bed, that she had opened a bottle of wine, drunk two glasses almost at once, and called Federico and told him what had happened, and to get Martin to come to his, Federico's flat, so that when she told him he would be there next to her brother. He was going to need support, she thought. She and Martin had had to survive their parents' double suicide all those years ago. Then Martin's girl-friend had fallen off that cursed mountain outside San Miguel, and that was long before the eruption had cut across everyone's life. Now this. It was too much. It would be too much for her brother. It was too much for her, especially since she was alone.

She called Federico. He was so safe, so secure. She cried. She thought it must be mainly the shock. She began to mourn the Alexei she had known before this. She had shared her feelings with Federico and herself, but now, there he was in the hospital, and it was overwhelming, bigger than anything. Except that last time, of course, but that was a long time ago. She talked and talked, and Federico just listened, offering occasional words of support. She felt shivery and untethered.

Then she spoke with Martin, and something about that conversation helped her. She seemed to snap back into her elder sister role and felt it her duty to comfort him. The two glasses of wine helped, she supposed. And Martin's shock was palpable. He kept asking if she was okay, and so, being the older sister, she told him she was, treating him a little bit like Daniel and Sarah.

"What are you going to do?" he kept asking her, but she had no idea and told him that.

"I'm going to try to sleep," she said. "The kids are going to need me." She suddenly felt very weary, so when she could, she finished the call and finished the bottle.

She slept for two or three hours and then woke up. She was instantly sure there was no chance of any more rest, so she crawled out of bed, turned on the immersion heater, and in the middle of the night had a long bath — something she hadn't done in a long time. At one stage, she dozed off and was in danger of sinking into oblivion below the surface, but the cold woke her up.

She dried herself vigorously, punishingly. Somehow, she managed to get through the next few hours until it was time to take the children to school. She called the radio station to say she wasn't coming in because of a family emergency, which was true, and bundled the kids into the car. When, twenty minutes later, the school gates closed behind them as they lined up by class, she made her way back to the hospital and was taken to see a senior consultant, a neurologist, she said, and that's when it got worse and worse.

Brain dead. Two words. Brain dead. That's what the woman said — no possible chance of recovery. In almost every sense, he's no longer with us. She was sorry to be the bearer of such bad news, but unfortunately, it was bad news, she said. Then, "We — that is, the team and everyone who has worked with your husband since his admittance — we think we should switch off his life support system and let him go."

Vicky sat there looking at the woman stupidly, trying to absorb what she was being told. She couldn't think of anything to say. "The thing is, Mrs Kassoniliki," she was very matter of fact, this woman, Vicky thought idly, "we would need your permission, your authorisation to do that, so the ball is very much in your court. Mrs Kassoniliki?"

Vicky's usual decisiveness completely deserted her. She was paralysed. *Why can't I focus?* she asked herself. *Am I in shock?*

"I know this is difficult to take in. I'll leave you to think about it."

There she was in the relatives' room, taking it in. Except she couldn't. Switch off Alex's life support? She was his life support. He was hers. He wouldn't be very pleased if she just switched him off forever, would he? But he'd be dead, so he wouldn't know. She started to laugh, and then she laughed some more. Now, she was laughing hysterically, her laugh turning into a scream that became a howl. She was weeping, weeping, and weeping. A nurse who was passing must have looked in and seen her. The next thing Vicky knew, someone was standing there with a large box of tissues and a cup of sugary tea.

"Drink this love. It won't solve anything, but it will help, I promise you." Then the woman sat next to her and held her, and she was momentarily comforted.

Later, the woman said, "I'm sorry, I have to go, but I'll be back to see how you are getting on." Vicky finished her tea, stood up, straightened her clothes, wiped her eyes with her hand, stretched, and went back to Alexei's bedside and looked at him. Brain dead? But that's Alexei. Big brain. Mountain conqueror. Brain dead? She held his hand, but it was lifeless. She watched his chest rise and fall, but it wasn't him who was breathing. It was that horrible machine. She wondered if he would show any signs of life. Maybe he would make one of those miraculous recoveries. Perhaps he'd surprise everyone again. She knew that was not true, but how could one be sure?

Someone coughed, obviously behind her. There was a policeman there. He wanted to ask her some questions. She nearly said no, but why not? Nothing made sense anymore, so she let him start asking questions. She knew little, though. She told him about Alex being sectioned, about the mental institution, and about how they had managed to let her husband abscond when he was clearly in no fit state to do so. In turn, she learnt more details of the car park and what people had seen.

His colleague, PC Smythe, said he didn't jump. He tripped over a wire, but he was behaving strangely. "I'm so sorry, Mrs Kassoniliki. PC Smythe did her best to make him safe, but he was going through something, so he just tried to run away from her, and PC Smythe is distraught." She said nothing. The policeman left.

The consultant came back, and Vicky said, "How can you be sure?"

The consultant said, "We're going to run one more set of tests. One of my colleagues will administer it. But I must warn you, I don't expect anything different. It was, it is a catastrophic brain injury. It would be impossible to come back from this. I am so sorry."

"I can't—"

"We suggest you have a bit of time to think about this. We know how hard it must be."

"You don't."

"Well, yes. No. I mean…."

She told them they would have to wait. Then she told them she had to pick her kids up from school. Then she left the hospital. She made her way back to the school to collect Daniel and Sara.

When the gates opened, all the children streamed through. Daniel came running, but stopped short of a hug. When Sarah turned up, running towards her a few minutes later, there was no such reserve. Overruling Daniel's reluctance, learnt so quickly at this school, Vicky then hugged them both, and in reply to their enquiries, she told them that they shouldn't worry about Daddy anymore. He wasn't suffering at all, and she'd tell them all about it when they got home. She tried to gather her thoughts for something else to say, but her children had stopped paying attention. They were staring at something behind her in absolute surprise and disbelief. Sarah broke first, and then Daniel charged past her, dropping his satchel. "Uncle Martin, Uncle Martin, Uncle Martin."

She turned round and there he was, a bag thrown over his shoulder and the two children hanging on to him. She found that she, too, was running.

Now she was hugging him too, crying, and all she could say was, "Martin, Martin, Martin."

Chapter 27
Silvestre

"COME IN, COME IN!" he said as Silverio arrived at the house. It was a fine morning. "Is your lovely girlfriend not with you?"

"No, I am afraid not. She's staying at home — so sorry. She thanks you for inviting her."

"Silverio, is something the matter? You don't sound like your usual self. I hope you two aren't having difficulties." Silverio was about to say something, but he stopped himself.

"Silverio?"

"It's about the disappeared. The EAS. She's obsessed, fixated even. We all are. They are my friends, too, at least most of them. We have campaigned together, faced danger together, and now they have vanished into thin air."

"I know. I know. It's a huge worry. But for Heaven's sake, don't just stand there. Come into the office and we'll see what we can do."

They walked through the house. He waved at his wife, who was sitting out on the terrace working at a table. They entered his study. Papers everywhere, posters, two TV screens on, and a couple of the campaign workers whom the candidate observed contentedly were getting close to and whom he trusted. They were doing a fantastic job as well.

They greeted each other, and Silverio took a seat around the table across the room from his desk. They looked at the man they were supporting expectantly. He turned away for a bit, then switched on the TV, selected a channel, and pointed at the screen. There she was again. Isabela Gutierrez. Hardly a surprise. It was a station that was notoriously populist and right-wing. Still.

"Friends." He paused. "Friends, we are facing a real threat. That woman there – "he pointed at the screen – "that woman is doing well. Her numbers are up. She's getting more and more airtime, and I think she's having a real effect. We've always had a mountain to climb, of course, but seeing the way things are going, it's beginning to get a great deal steeper, I think." There was silence. He was rather pleased with his metaphor.

"Sir," the young woman on Silverio's right interrupted, "it's the disappeared members of the EAS. That's the biggest problem. She's milking that for all she's got and — forgive me — trashing your reputation. By coming up with completely unfounded lies about your time as mayor."

His principal opponent had launched a few well-placed criticisms since she began her campaign, and, in the case of the protesters who had disappeared, she had tried to pin the blame squarely on his shoulders. She was able to say, correctly, that he had not taken measures to have the demonstrators stopped, even though the police chief had suggested it. But how could he, in all conscience, have prevented people from performing their democratic rights? It went against everything his post-earthquake conversion had convinced him of. That damned Riveira. He knew what he was doing. In retrospect, it felt as if he was setting up the mayor to fail, though he couldn't quite work out how or why. His smirk of triumph as their conversation had ended that day was one of pure scorn.

Well, he was not going to give him the satisfaction of caving in on this. Whatever had happened was not his fault, and somehow he would get to the bottom of it, wherever the truth led him. The trouble was, of course, that he no longer had the power to order things. Now he was just a candidate for the presidency, not an elected official. What he did have, however, was the weight of public opinion and support. Still, in the light of that woman's relentless attacks and her campaign's ferocious advertising, he could not be sure how that might be sustained. She had branded him as weak and ineffective, and unfair as that was, it seemed to be having an effect.

"Sir," the young woman continued, echoing his thoughts," the disappeared. It is hurting you, this situation."

"Yes," her companion said, "she's making the most of this, and unless we are cautious, the public will go with her. There's a lot of anger out there, and she's turning that into a weapon against us."

"It's almost as if," Silverio thought out loud, "she had been waiting for this. It's just kind of fallen into her lap. But I don't get it. The ESA represents everything she hates, everything she's fighting against. Where did she announce her campaign? Calixt-lapan. I ask you. But she's relishing this almost as if she were expecting it. It doesn't feel right."

Silvestre interrupted. "In case you think I'm just another cynical politician, a charge I will sometimes admit to, obviously—."

He smiled and continued. "Quite apart from our campaign, be in no doubt that I am desperate, desperate to find these young people, as desperate as you all are. What has happened to them? Where are they? All I know is that they have to get back home, irrespective of our campaign."

"Silvestre, señor, I wasn't going to mention it because it is just gossip."

"Mention what?"

"But what you just said… We knew from the beginning that something was wrong with this. Not just that people had disappeared, that's the worst part of what has happened, but the events surrounding it — the demonstrators being spirited away, vanishing into thin air. It stinks."

There was a silence as everyone contemplated the situation they were in yet again.

"I wasn't going to mention this," Silverio started again, "and it's only hearsay and gossip, kind of third-hand, so I'm not sure if we should listen."

He was urged to continue.

"There is a woman, the great aunt of a good friend of my partner's." This didn't sound promising. Silvestre saw the same suspicion on the others' faces that he felt. This was Silverio. He was usually more succinct than this.

"I know this sounds ridiculous, and if you think it is, I'll shut up about it, but this woman, she's probably suffering a little bit from dementia, I know, I know this doesn't sound important, just gossip, and I usually wouldn't dream of wasting your time, but—"

"Get on with it, Silverio. It sounds very unconvincing so far."

"I know, I'm sorry, but this woman, she has started to go to a club here in San Miguel, and it's stuffed full of people who aren't necessarily our natural supporters. Indeed, from what I understand, Isabela Gutierrez was there shortly before her campaign launch. So what this old woman has expressed on more than one occasion is her confusion. Yes, it may be her dementia. Still, there's something about it because she seems to be saying," his voice was rising to stop them from interrupting. "Is that the people there, in the club, know about the disappearances? '*We've got this in hand'* is a phrase she has repeated more than once, because she doesn't understand what it means."

"You can't take that seriously! I'm sure Señor Ocampo doesn't take it seriously, do you, sir?"

"No, but look, and I know this is just completely fanciful, and please forgive me if I'm wasting all of our time, your time but, how do I put this, it's that I just can't help wondering, what if this old lady, Tia Rosario they call her, what if Tia Rosario has, in fact overheard something important. Just suppose—"

He paused as if needing time to decide whether to go on. "Just suppose that those people, Gutierrez's supporters, just imagine if they organised all this themselves. Which could mean that the disappeared aren't 'disappeared' as such, but instead kidnapped and held for some purpose, maybe so that they have something to attack us about, and—"

"And at the right time," Silvestre took over, "they miraculously find these people and 'rescue' them, showing how much better they are than us. They can taunt me, telling everyone that I was hopeless and couldn't do anything about it. They, being the 'law and order' party, could get away with it. We wouldn't stand a chance."

No one said anything. The idea was sinking in.

"But it would be against the law!" the young woman burst out.

"When has that ever stopped those people? I mean, she has allied herself with all those caciques and patrones over there with their mistreatment of their workforce, and now, God help us, the drug gangs. It's like the truth has been inverted. The ones I am fighting against should be renamed the 'no laws' party, like something from those old Western films. They represent everything I am against, and we are against it too. I want this republic to have as much integrity in practice as it does in theory, and that means controlling all those people and keeping that woman and her cronies away from power. We need to clean up the place. We need to make this country somewhere to be proud of, so we can hold our heads up with anyone on the planet. We need…"

He stopped and saw the look on the three faces before him.

"Sorry, you've heard all this before, hell, you even wrote some of those words! I just got a bit carried away. I tell you what, why don't we walk down to the end of the pasture as we keep talking?" Silvestre's house bordered a large field, which ended in a few scrubby trees and a mostly dry riverbed.

They trooped out of the house and wandered over the dry, sparse grass, yellowing in the sun. The heat was building, but it had not yet reached a comfortable level. Everyone was lost in thought.

Silvestre dropped back to walk side by side with Silverio. "Tell me, what does your girlfriend, er, Genoveva, say about what this lady heard?"

"I haven't told her."

"Why on earth not? Surely she has as much right to know about it as any of us do. More, in fact. And she might have a better take on it than we do?"

"Yes, I know, but she is going through it now, and I don't want to do anything that would make her feel more upset than she is at the moment. She'd find it difficult not to tell people about it, and we can't risk that, I think."

"You're having a bad time?"

"Yes, but that's for another day. Silvestre, do you remember the concert and the wedding? You remember Angelita, the violinist?"

"Of course I do. A beautiful girl and a wonderful player. An absolute joy, although the first time I saw her, I found it difficult to concentrate. There was a lot else going on."

"Sorry about that!"

"Water under the bridge. What of that lovely girl?"

"Well, Tia Rosario is her great aunt, and she was told all of this by a maid who works in the house, and that makes it all even more implausible, except for the fact that the moment she told me, I was convinced that her great aunt HAD heard something of interest."

"Let's not run before we walk!"

"But look, I saw that statement the Gutierrez campaign put out, suggesting that we knew more than we were telling, that maybe the whole disappearance event was some kind of political game we were playing, and I couldn't work out why she would say that. She can't seriously believe we would be that manipulative, that we would jeopardise lives like that."

"They don't believe it. I am sure of it. But following your thought through, how would it be if they are saying this because they are talking about themselves? What's that expression, 'hiding in plain sight'?"

"You think?"

"It's possible." All four of them were now standing in a little huddle as the sun rose in the sky.

"The thing is," Silverio said, screwing up his eyes against the increasing glare, "if we are right, how could we resolve it all without it seeming that we were doing exactly what they are accusing us of doing?"

"Well, if they do have the disappeared, we have to find them and then make it impossible for them to deny that they were involved."

"This is all a bit fanciful. Based on the words of a deranged old lady?"

"I know. I'm sorry."

They reached the end of the pasture and turned back to look at the house. Silvestre held his face up to the sun for a moment and felt the healing warmth on his skin. Why can't things be more straightforward? Why is everything partial and riddled with duplicity? For a minute, he felt empty and distressed. He lowered his head and appeared to be closing his eyes. The others waited.

"Come on," he said, rousing himself. "We have speeches to prepare and a campaign to run. We can get on with that in earnest tomorrow, but why don't we at least make a start on it today?"

Chapter 28
Federico

HE WAS GETTING USED to the airport. All through his youth, and when he had first moved to the city far away, he had travelled to and from San Miguel by bus or car, braving the Mil Curvas section of the road and marvelling, as the years went by, at the amount of time the new section of motorway (when it was new) saved compared to when he first made the journey. But now, as his life got busier and he oversaw the hacienda and his aunt's situation, he found himself flying more often. It was easier, there wasn't any danger of falling asleep at the wheel, and, despite the airport queues and waiting, it was quicker.

Today was different, though. Unlike during other trips, he couldn't switch his mind off in the no-future-no-past atmosphere of the plane. All he could think of, like a recording playing repeatedly in his head, was her. What was he going to do? What would she do?

And yet, Alexei, who he hadn't known except as the paranoid prisoner he got out of jail and then encouraged to leave the country, was as good as dead (he had not spoken to her for a day or two, so he didn't know quite how dead he was). Poor Vicky. How did that affect him?

He had nearly flown to see her the moment he had heard, so great was his absolute conviction that she needed his help, but Martin had gone in a rush because he had no other choice, he said, and reluctantly, he supposed that it was Martin who would be most important for Victoria now. They were so close, and her children, apparently, adored him, and anyway, he was family. And so instead of running to support her himself, he'd had to accompany his son-in-law and Angelita as they went to the airport the moment that call had finished. He'd watched him finding a flight, buying a last-minute ticket and disappearing through the security barrier.

Angelita hadn't wanted Martin to go, she told her father, but she knew he had to. Federico, of course, wished with all his heart that he had gone with him or instead of him. Next best thing? He could ring her now, but maybe that wasn't such a good thing. Perhaps he should wait till he reached the hacienda, or maybe longer. He should wait longer. Martin would have arrived by now, which meant that she wouldn't have time to talk to him. But this was agony. As he walked off the plane, he realised, with a shock, that he was jealous, jealous of his son-in-law.

This is ridiculous, he told himself. There is nothing for you here. She is a recently bereaved widow, in shock at the terrifying nature of her husband's disintegration and death, brain death probably. The decent thing would be to leave her in peace. She must be in such a mess that I would just make things worse. But then he told himself that simply wasn't true. She had started contacting him all the time — or he got in touch with her. They had almost come to depend on each other, hadn't they? So why wasn't he there now? Well, because Martin was. He and Martin got on so well that it would have been fine. Perhaps, but then again, she needed space to work out what was going on. Or maybe he would have been able to help her.

It was in this state of confused chaos that he realised, beyond any doubt, now, that he was in love with her. He was also as sure as he could be that she felt very strongly about him. But they had never said anything out loud. He would just have to wait, even though he thought about Vicky more often than he did not.

The reasons for this trip back to San Miguel seemed unimportant in comparison. But he was a dutiful nephew, and what the girl Tiacuri had told Angelita about his aunt's mental state was worrying. It was simply fortuitous that he was coming back to work on the case of the music professor's sons. The summons to everyone involved in that case had come quickly and had surprised him as it must have done to all the others. Nor had they been told why they were being recalled so quickly. Federico supposed it was because some decision had been made about what should happen to the Perez twins.

They had arrived at the hacienda. He paid the driver and went in. He greeted Tiacuri and went in to see Marcela. She was standing by the window, but she turned when he came in and called her name. She fixed him with her vacant stare and, maybe it was his imagination, almost smiled. He talked to her for a moment and then asked Tiacuri where his aunt was, and as a result, he headed upstairs.

He found her in the first floor *sala*. She was drinking tea. There was a plate of little cakes on a table next to her chair. She had a magazine in her hands, which she may have been reading. The TV was on. As he came in, she heard him, and her face broke into a wide grin when she saw who it was. "Sobrino, nephew! How lovely to see you!"

He went over and kissed her. "You're looking well," she said, "he will be pleased to see you too." She reached for a cake. "Delicious. Why don't you try one yourself?"

171

"Thank you, Tia." He leant down, picked one up and took a bite. "Very good," he said, his mouth full. "Who will be pleased to see me?"

"Why, your father, of course." She paused. Then she frowned in confusion. "That is, I think. Where is he? He should be back soon." She paused again. Federico wondered how to react. He hadn't received any training for this.

"Oh! Of course, he won't be back. He's not here anymore, is he?"

"No, Tia."

"Well, don't just stand there. It's not polite. Sit down." She sounded a bit cross. He sat.

"How have you been, Tia? How is everything here?"

"How have I been? What's that to you?"

"It's everything to me, Tia. You're my aunt." He was wondering how to negotiate this strange conversation. He noticed that Tia Rosario's voice was a bit slurred.

"I expect you are busy. You can go now if you want to."

"Tia, I don't want to go. I've only just arrived."

"Have you?"

"How is everything up here, Tia? Is everyone keeping well?"

"Everything is fine. These cakes are good."

"Are you still going to the club you have joined?"

"Club? Oh yes, the club. I go to that club, but it's not so diverting as it once was. All these people getting angry about things, talking about winning, criticising, talking, talking." She stopped and looked at him as if trying to size up his reaction.

"That doesn't sound too good. But Tia, honestly, you don't have to keep on going if you don't want to."

"Go where?"

"To the club."

"Ah. Yes."

He thought, so it is true. Whatever is wrong, Tia Rosario

seems to have deteriorated since he was last here. She seemed confused about her mood and what was happening around her. Was she beginning to lose her mind? Maybe something had happened to her, a minor stroke perhaps? Maybe it was her medication? Or possibly her quirkiness had become increasingly exaggerated, and only now was he noticing it.

They talked in a stilted way about the weather and the crops. At one stage, she asked about the horses, and he had to remind her that they didn't have horses anymore, that they hadn't had horses for a long time. "We don't?" she exclaimed, and then, "Of course, you are right. We got rid of them years ago."

Later, he went to find the two maids who looked after her. They agreed that their employer had become erratic. "Surely, sir, that was only to be expected at her age."

"Is it?" he asked them. "Old people do forget things more easily and lose energy and all that, but this seems different. You know what? For a short time, she was convinced my father was still alive."

"Yes, sir, it is true things like that do happen."

"Has she seen a doctor?" he asked. It was clear she had not. "In which case," he continued, "I'll get Dr Gonzalez to come out and see her, maybe tomorrow, well as soon as he can. But in the meantime, are you both able to look after her?"

"I don't know what that girl has told you," the older one said.

"That girl?"

"Tiacuri. She thinks she knows everything, but she's only just arrived here. Her job is with that girl, not with our señora."

"Yes," he said. He had run out of words. "I have to go. I'll be back later this evening."

He looked at his watch. Time to go. He returned to his aunt. He was relieved to see she was more lucid now. He said goodbye, summoned a cab, and headed to the courthouse.

The professor was waiting for him when he got there. He

explained that he didn't know why they had all been called back to the court. "We will soon, I hope, find out," he added.

When they were called in, the courtroom was empty apart from court officials, the prosecutor, and his assistant. The twins entered with their guards. A short time later, the judges returned. They all stood and then sat again.

Once the court had been called to order, the senior judge began to speak.

"Counsel, you may be surprised that we have called you back so soon. In truth, it is not something we had contemplated. But this case raises several issues, both legal and humanitarian. Or should I say it is both an issue of law and of natural justice? Usually, these are the same thing, but perhaps, occasionally, they come into conflict.

"While this case is not so clear-cut, still, there is the danger that the situation in front of us is somewhat ambiguous. I know," he said, looking at the prosecutor, "that you may find this all highly irregular and of course, there is always the option of an appeal to a higher court. However, after reading the report submitted by Licenciado Placencia, we find ourselves swayed by some of his arguments. So much so that we have decided to delay our decision, and accordingly, we will conduct more enquiries and acquaint ourselves with more precedents. We will reconvene at a time when we can announce our decision. However, we must emphasise that the obvious sentence will involve some kind of custodial sentence."

Federico was relieved. He had to admit that he was also surprised. He trusted in the submission he had made to the court. It was far from legal trickery. On the contrary, the stumbling conversations he had with the twins, coupled with the meeting with other surviving members of that cult, made their actions, if not justifiable, at the very least more straightforward to comprehend. People can't go around killing each other. But, in a case like this, there had to be mitigation. He looked over and saw the confusion on the professor's face and smiled encouragingly.

A short time later, they were in the corridor outside the court-room, and Federico was trying to explain what the judges' decision might mean. It was possible it would change nothing. At the very least, there would be a consideration of the Perez boys' state of mind and how they got there — facts that might have contributed to their actions.

"It doesn't mean they'll get off. The judges made it clear that they will be detained. However, it might mean the sentence is lighter and the conditions are less severe. I can't tell," Federico said.

Jacinto Perez looked like a man with hope, the lawyer thought, the first time he had seen this on that scarred face.

He started to speak. "I don't know how to thank you, Licenci-ado. I am grateful. Thank you."

"Just doing my job, professor," Federico replied. "Let's hope for the best. I'll be in touch the moment I hear anything from the court."

On the way back to the hacienda, he thought about how life seemed to be taking all sorts of unexpected turns. He worried about Vicky — about him and Vicky, to be more precise. His life had never felt so empty.

But come on, he told himself, *you haven't spoken to her for three days. That's only seventy-two hours.*

He dozed off in the back of the taxi.

Chapter 29
Vicky

POOR MARTIN, she thought. He looked utterly exhausted, a mix of jet lag and the children's excessive excitement about his presence. Staying up too late drinking wine didn't help either, but that's what they had done. She wouldn't have slept well anyway. She wondered if she ever would again.

She had known instantly that what the doctors were saying yesterday was true. Alexei's brain no longer functioned. But she had found it almost impossible to think quickly or sensibly. Lying there on the bed was someone who, despite his injured face, was her husband. It was Alexei. How could she believe that the figure that she was looking down at was as dead as any dead person? He still had his face, his beard, his once-strong stomach, his wandering feet, and full-striding legs. If she agreed to what the doctors were suggesting, then all of him, all that gaunt wonderfulness of him and the memories would disappear forever.

On any typical day, her practical, rational mind had been able to face up to the situation she had been presented with and take charge of it. But yesterday was not an ordinary day, and today was no better. She was finding it difficult to stop crying, and she couldn't talk to Alexei about it. She was alone even though Martin was here. His presence comforted her, of course, but he was in shock too, confused by the time shift and distance. He seemed unable to articulate his true thoughts. There was no getting around it; this was her decision and hers alone.

When the children were finally asleep, excited that Martin was there but unsettled by whatever was happening, which they didn't understand and hadn't been told about, Vicky and Martin discussed her dilemma. Still, neither of them knew quite what to say, and after a bit they sat there in silent misery and incomprehension. She poured another glass of wine. Then they talked about Angelita and Federico, but that conversation withered and died too. Then they listened to some music they liked, and he played her a recording his wife had made.

They then talked about topics such as politics. They drank more, until finally Martin pretty much fell asleep right in front of her, so she left him there, slumped in an armchair and went upstairs unsteadily to make up his bed, which she did inexpertly, and then she came back to the sitting room and managed to rouse him just enough to get him into his bedroom. He was barely conscious and just for one horrifying moment she imagined she was going to have to undress him, but he roused himself just enough to kick her out and close the door behind her as she left.

In the sitting room, she drank some more until she became too stupefied to continue. Dragging herself to bed, she fell into an immediate coma. Then, when that was over, far too quickly for it to have done her any good, she wriggled in an endless discomfort of mental torment and dehydration. At about five in the morning, she got up, drank about a pint of water and tried to sleep again. That caused her to have to get up and go to the toilet after a brief forty-five minutes of troubled restlessness. She gave up some time later. She contemplated another bath but didn't have the enthusiasm for it. She lay in the darkness, eyes wide open, while the horror of her situation pressed in on her and, despite her efforts, she couldn't drag her mind away from it.

Nor was dawn much of a relief, even though the pressing weight of the blackness around her was dissipated by the grey light which slipped in under the blind. She ached all over.

Eventually, she managed to drag herself off the bed. She turned on the shower and got in, still wearing her pyjamas. Then they got too sodden and heavy, so she sloughed them off and stood there vacantly as the water splashed off her shoulders. Then Sarah woke up, and she reacted as a mother does. She dried herself and let her daughter get into her bed beside her after quickly finding something to wear, and watched Sarah fall instantly back to sleep while she lay outwardly warm as toast but frozen cold inside.

When Martin finally surfaced, they had coffee while the children held onto him, one on either side. Once Daniel asked, 'What's the matter, Mummy, ¿que pasa?' and when she told him she was 'worried about Daddy because he's not very well' he looked relieved as if that was something he could understand. She saw Martin staring at her, mouth open.

"Martin," she said, "now that you are here, do you mind making yourself useful?" She seemed to be teasing him.

"Oh God, must I?" he was joining in.

"Well, could you take the children to school?"

"Yes, yes," they chorused.

"And maybe collect them this afternoon and, depending, give them supper."

"You don't want much!"

"I'm sure you can handle it." She sent Daniel and Sarah to get ready.

"Are you going to call Federico?" he asked.

Not now, she thought. This was not something to be discussed, not with Federico. It wouldn't be right, not now. It wasn't like talking about Alexei's mental state and the facility he'd ended up in. This was more personal, more private. This was for her alone. It had nothing to do with him. Did it?

"Maybe."

"But I thought–"

"I have to go, Martin."

"Shall I come with you?"

"You're in charge of the children."

"Oh yes." He looked uncertain.

She was back in the same relatives' room with the same consultant, two other doctors, and the same nurse — Sue Atkins, she now knew — who had comforted her the day before. She felt terrible, and she knew she looked even worse. The medical team, on the other hand, was attentive, professional, solicitous, and doing their best to make her feel at ease, which was as silly, of course, as it was impossible.

"I know this is distressing, Mrs Kassonilki, and you must believe us when we say we have every sympathy for you having to make an almost impossible decision." They all nodded sympathetically. She felt like a laboratory subject as they all watched expectantly. "We have to tell you, however, that the tests are, sadly, absolutely unequivocal. They show that there is no chance of your husband's brain coming back from the catastrophic damage it has suffered. We ran two sets of exhaustive tests yesterday and this morning; before you arrived, we ran even more. Your husband is to all intents and purposes — please excuse me for being so blunt — completely dead, and but for the machines he is being supported by, he would leave us very, very quickly."

They waited.

"But you hear of times when people seem to survive? I mean

miracles?" Even to herself, her voice sounded weak and insubstantial. What was wrong with her?

"Yes, you do," another doctor took over, "but they happen incredibly rarely, and even when they do, the quality of life is completely unsustainable in the long term."

"But at least he'd be—"

She stopped.

"Mrs Kassoniliki, I do understand the need to hang on to hope even in the most hopeless times. We understand your desire to find some way out of this horrible situation. We do, but now we must ask you to understand that if there was anything, anything at all that we could think of to try and reverse this situation, we would tell you about it. But I'm afraid there's no way getting away from it, there just isn't."

She looked away. Through the window, she could see a long crane arm lazily traversing the skyline. The silence in the room grew louder.

"Mrs Kassoniliki?"

"If you 'switch off', how long?" She turned back.

"It's impossible to say. It could be fairly immediate, but sometimes it takes up to 24 hours."

"And then?"

"Then he would cease to function in any way at all, and it would be over."

"I can't, I mean, I—"

"We'll leave you now, Mrs Kassoniliki, but Nurse Atkins here will stay with you if you would like that."

Time passed. There were more cups of sugary tea. The doctors came back again. She felt as if she was not even there, even though in the background, her mind was struggling to come to some rational decision about what they were asking her. Then Martin arrived, surprising her. "Well, I couldn't let you go through all this on your own, could I?" Nurse Atkins was nowhere to be seen. They looked at each other and, recognising how shattered they both appeared, they laughed. Then she hugged him. "Hey, steady on!" he joked, and for a moment the fog in her brain cleared and she knew, now, what she was going to do.

"Would you like to sit down?" the consultant asked some time later. Martin said, "Do you want me to stay?" She thought about it and then said yes.

"Shall we go ahead then? Mrs Kassoloniki?"

"No, wait." She leant down and put her face next to his damaged head. "Alexei," she whispered so quietly that the others probably could not hear above the noise of the machines keeping him almost alive, "I think it is time for you to go. I am sorry, but I do not know what else to do, so I think it is the right time now. I have never loved anyone as much as I love you. You have been everything to me. We will keep you in our lives. Goodbye."

She was crying softly and continuously now. She straightened up and nodded at the consultant. Then she took Alexei's hand and held it against her chest.

There was a click as a nurse pressed a switch, and a moment later, the pumping mechanism that had been keeping Alexei alive stopped, and the room was quiet. No one moved. They waited. She looked at her husband. Nothing happened. He did not move. His eyes were still closed. There was nothing to indicate that anything was happening except for the fact that his chest had stopped its gentle motion. A long, continuous beep sounded from the monitor above Alexei's bed. The nurse switched it off, and the screen went blank. An awed silence hovered around them at the majesty of death. And then the consultant cleared her throat. "He has gone," she said gently. "We'll leave you now to be alone."

As they left the room quietly, Vicky's phone went off, and apparently without thinking, she pulled it from her coat pocket, looked at it, and screamed something that sounded to Martin like "not now," before throwing it across the room, where it kept ringing until it stopped. She looked once more at her husband's corpse and marched out of the room without saying a word before Martin had a chance to do anything.

He turned to follow her, but remembering the phone, he reached for it. He couldn't help checking who had rung her. It was Federico. He started to leave. That seemed wrong. He looked back at the figure on the bed — Alexei, his brother-in-law. Should he say goodbye?

Alexei was no longer there, so he didn't.

Chapter 30
Angelita

SHE WASN'T keen on this trip. It was inconvenient. She was insanely busy with the classes she was teaching, the music she had to learn for upcoming concerts, and her administrative duties at the conservatoire, but her father had asked her, almost pleaded with her, to go with him. On the other hand, she felt lonely without Martin and hopeless too, because she was unable to be with him when he seemed to need her most. As for her father, she wasn't used to the note of supplication in his voice, and it unnerved her.

They met, as arranged, in the departure lounge. There were still forty-five minutes before the flight was due to leave. He bought them both coffees. "How are you, Papa?" she asked, and when he replied, as if surprised by the question, "me? Fine. Never better", she knew instantly that something was bothering him. "Papa?"

"Yes?" he had always been unable to hide his feelings.

"What is it?

"What's what?"

"You know, Papa. I can always tell. You're worried about

183

something. You don't look happy. You're looking tired. What's going on?" She leant over and kissed him on the cheek.

"Haven't been sleeping well."

"Why? What's the matter?"

"Nothing."

"Papa! Stop it!"

"All right. I suppose you have a right to know. It's Vicky."

"Oh, her."

"Don't say it like that."

"Sorry. What about Vicky?"

"She hasn't answered my calls or my messages. I don't know what's happened."

"Papa! Her husband, he's, she had to turn off his life support machine. That's what's happened. She's in pieces, Papa. Martin's in the pieces. The children. It's a mess."

He looked instantly contrite. "I'm sorry. Here I am thinking about me all the time when you are going through it too, my lovely child."

"It's all right, Papa. I'm not having a great time myself, it's true, but I have work, music, and colleagues to keep me busy. Martin's far away, and now, I like having him around; I need him around. But poor man, he's right in the middle of it."

"I know. I feel sorry for him, for all of them." He paused. "But why isn't she answering my calls? We get on so well, I thought — oh, it doesn't matter what I thought, if she is all right. She almost certainly isn't, though."

"Are you in love with her?" She hadn't thought about it before now. It made her feel incredibly grown-up to ask.

"No. Maybe yes. Would you mind? But maybe I'm just a silly old fool. I don't want you to think badly of me."

"I'll never do that."

They stood up to join the queue to board. They had booked their flights separately, so they found themselves in different parts

184

of the plane. "See you when we get there," she said and sat down in her seat.

She drifted in and out of consciousness on the journey. She wasn't sleeping that well either. After getting so happily and quickly used to being with Martin as if he had always been there, she was already feeling as if, without him, she was missing one of her limbs.

They found a taxi and headed for the hacienda. They discussed how to handle Tia Rosario. She already knew the bare outlines of it all; the doctor had confirmed that yes, Tia Rosario seemed to be in the earlyish stages of some kind of dementia. However, he couldn't say precisely what it was without further tests. She needed a scan to see whether she had suffered some type of stroke, even a minor one. The doctor's opinion was that she would increasingly require more care.

Of course, she had people working in the house. Still, they should prepare for the possibility that in the near future, she may struggle to care for herself. It was difficult to know exactly what lay in store or how quickly it would progress or, for that matter, how long she might be around for. To Angelita, this all sounded clinical and heartless. Still, in truth, there wasn't much she could do to help, not while her career was taking off and she and Martin, when he returned, would have so much to do.

Despite being forewarned, she was unprepared for the change in her great aunt. She seemed confused and unsure, even mistaking Angelita herself for someone else entirely, someone she couldn't quite 'put my finger on'. It was only a momentary lapse, but for Angelita, it was alarming.

They passed the time talking about nothing very much. Sometimes, Tia Rosario would ask them the same question repeatedly, apparently forgetting she had already asked the same question more than once. It was dispiriting and, for Angelita, who was not very much used to this kind of thing, depressing.

She had assumed that Tia Rosario would always be there, shepherding Marcela round the hacienda. It was just one of life's certainties, but now it was no longer.

In the evening, her father surprised her by suggesting they go out for dinner. They found themselves in a restaurant that they had always liked. They had some beers, and he talked to her about Vicky again, which made Angelita uncomfortable.

"Why won't she talk to me?" he asked more than once. "She has always called me and asked for support when things have been tough for her, and we get along so well. It felt as if I had known her all my life. Not really, but you know what I mean. Angelita sort of did because that's exactly how she felt about Martin, although that was completely different, of course."

"I just don't get it," she said.

Her father continued. "Do you have a clue? Has Martin said anything?"

"No, Papa." She hated the neediness in his voice. "Only that she's depressed and confused, and he is trying to support her and the children as much as she can."

She couldn't tell him about the scene Martin had described in which Vicky threw the phone across the room when Alexei had just died. Or that she didn't want anything to do with him now that he had — in her words - intruded on the most private and emotional moment of her life.

"She's not being rational," Martin had said. "She's all over the place. One minute she's laughing, then she cries, then she gets angry. Daniel and Sarah are also in shock. They can't cope with the chaos all around them. I'm just doing my best to make things as normal as I can, but it isn't easy, *mi amor*. I wish you were here."

She let her father continue expressing his uncertainty and unhappiness, and did her best to convince him to be patient.

"People behave differently at times like this, don't they?"

"How come you have suddenly got so wise?" he laughed.

Then they discussed Tia Rosario again, and they agreed she should be persuaded to give him legal power over her affairs.

"Will she agree to that?" Angelita asked. "I don't know. She might resist. Still, I dread to think what kind of trouble she might get into otherwise."

When they got home, they talked in the sala at the hacienda. He had his regular glass of late-night whisky while she opted for a tea that she particularly liked.

"You want to know something interesting?" he asked.

"Of course."

"You know how I told you about Maria and her classes?"

Angelita nodded.

"Well, she's excited about them, and I'm thrilled about that, and she's met a guy there she seems to get on very well with. She's meeting up with him in the park on Sunday."

"Good for her." She wasn't enormously interested.

"Yes, *hija mia*, I understand that's not the most exciting news in the world, but there is something more. The man she's met, or rather re-met, Kassoniliki, was someone she knew before. Not well, obviously, but he was — still is — a gardener, an odd-job man at a house just near where Vicky used to live."

"Papa, dear Papa, why are you telling me this?" She smiled at him.

"Because, listen, he works for that terrible Isabela Gutierrez."

"The one trying to be president?" She was interested now.

"Yes, and according to Maria's friend, he saw one of those kidnapped people at her house."

"That can't be true."

"He stayed late one evening, and this young man came in through the garden gate in back. Maria's friend said he thought he looked familiar, but it wasn't until he saw something on TV that he realised he was the so-called leader of your friend Genoveva's group. Guillermo something."

"Papa, that's, that can't be true."

"You said that before, *querida*. But I have no reason to doubt Maria. She's the most decent person I know, and from what she says, this gardener is straight as an arrow, too."

"I must tell Genoveva about this. It doesn't make sense to me."

"Me neither, though it sounds suspicious, even corrupt. I suppose that shouldn't be much of a surprise. They're all as bad as each other. Still, it makes you wonder what on earth is going on."

"Wow! Yes, it does. But what does it mean?"

"I don't know."

"Maybe Genny can work it out when I tell her tomorrow."

Chapter 31
Genoveva

WHERE WAS SILVERIO? She wanted him here.

She needed him, but he wasn't always there. Instead, he was away with Silvestre Ocampo — *Silvestre Ocampo!* She liked him well enough, and she desperately wanted him to win the presidency. She just wished the campaign hadn't taken over her partner's life completely. She understood why it was like this, and her boyfriend's commitment and hope for a better future were some of the qualities that had drawn her to him in the first place.

Right now, though, she needed him more than ever, and she desperately wanted to hang on to him, but she was afraid she might not. There hadn't been anything special, but he seemed a bit distant, and the more miserable she became, the more that distance seemed to increase. She knew it might be her fault. She was finding it difficult to be cheerful. A savage dread oppressed her, and she felt guilty about her friends. She should have been there when it happened too, but she wasn't, and now the family, friends and lovers of the ones who had disappeared wouldn't leave her alone. It was almost as if they blamed her for not having disappeared herself, which was completely unfair, even though she kind of understood it.

They held marches. They had demonstrations in the town centre and spent all their time trying to get on the radio and the TV. As someone who was scheduled to be there, she was frequently interviewed, but she had recently refused and would continue to do so. She found it too painful, too stressful.

During all this, she had her work, and if anything, it was almost a relief to have at least part of her mind occupied with looking after patients, checking medicines, liaising with doctors and colleagues, and writing things up. It had always been high-pressure work, but now it was almost a relief for her despite the life-and-death struggles that played out every day on the wards. She still loved her job. Amid everything that was going on, it was her one safe haven. At least that's what it felt like. But as soon as her shifts were over, there it was again, the bleak reality she was facing. Home was less comforting, too. How was it possible that the excitement she and Silverio had felt had evaporated so quickly? Why were they only occasional lovers now? How could she make it better?

"You all right?" a colleague said one day. "You look terrible."

"Thanks a lot!"

"Sorry, but seriously, are you okay?"

She was saved from having to answer by one of the new nurses calling her and asking for help. At the bedside of a young man recovering from surgery, she listened to her young colleague express concerns, and indeed, there was something not quite right about the patient's appearance and his charts. She didn't even feel the time passing or the sense of impending doom enveloping her as she talked to the man and tried to find out what was going on. She was good, she was useful, and this was her place.

Later, she took a break and checked her phone. A message

from Angelita. Were they still meeting later on? She'd completely forgotten about that. Did she want to see her? Wouldn't it be better just to go home and wait for Silverio? But he might be late. He was always late these days, and tomorrow he was off on the campaign in a northern state. Damn the wretched campaign. No, I didn't mean that, honestly, she said to the imaginary Silverio in her head. But she did mean it too. She hated this. Maybe Angelita would cheer her up.

If the musician was shocked by how she looked when they met, she didn't say anything. They were in the hospital atrium.

"I admire what you do, Genny," her friend said when they had stopped hugging each other.

"Well, I admire what you do," she replied, and they both laughed, the first proper laugh she'd had for a few days.

They agreed to go to a bar they knew, one that was famous because it had sustained hardly any damage in the earthquake and, as a result, had been renamed *El Milagro*, the Miracle. It was very popular in the town, and it was already packed and noisy by the time they arrived. They bought drinks and went back outside in the balmy evening air. They told each other about their lives; absent boyfriends, absent husbands. It was liberating to let go and tell her friend how she felt about the presidential campaign, about how it had taken Silverio away from her, how worried she was about their relationship, and how she didn't know what to do. It was the first time she'd had a chance to unload and say what she wanted, knowing she would be heard. So, she didn't hold back. There were tears. Angelita bought more drinks. She talked about Martin being away, about families, and about the awful death of Alexei.

"Alexei died? But how? Why? I liked him even if he was a bit weird. He and volcanoes. But he was a gentle soul, I think. But he was kind. And what he did for us...."

She was shocked.

"Music wrecker!" Angelita teased her, an almost joke. They had long since got over the fact that Genoveva had disrupted Angelita's first big performance. In the context of everything that happened, that seemed less critical. She pressed her friend to tell her everything about it, and so she learnt that after he had left the country, the state he was in after being put in jail, if only for a short time, just got worse, and then the escape from a psychiatric hospital and the fall.

"He was nice to me," Genoveva repeated, "even if he was a bit, well, old! He's dead? Oh dear." She felt the dread coming back.

"Genny?"

"Sorry. I don't want to ruin the evening."

"So, what is it?"

"What it always is. The EAS. The mystery. Where the hell are they?"

"Wait! That's something I was going to tell you?"

"What? What about?"

She repeated the story that Maria's friend had devised. Genoveva listened intently. A light had come back into her eyes.

"Guillermo," she said, "that must be Guillermo Vargas. I never quite–"

She stopped. Angelita could almost see her brain machinery whirring around." I knew there was something that wasn't quite right about him." She stopped again. She was thinking. Angelita did not interrupt her.

"If he was there in her house," she said as if she was talking to herself, "then he wasn't kidnapped at all. He wasn't killed or burnt or worse. It doesn't make sense."

"I agree. Provided that Maria's friend saw what he thought he saw."

"But if he did see Guillermo, that means…it can't be… it has to mean…"

"Genny, that means what? What are you talking about? I don't follow you."

"Sorry, Angelita, hold on a minute." She reached into her back pocket and retrieved her phone. "I have to ring Silverio. This is big, Angelita, this is big."

She looked at her friend's transformation, amazed at the energy that was suddenly flowing from her. She had loved Genoveva's effervescent personality. Even in her sadness after Julio's death, it hadn't been entirely extinguished, but this evening, until just now, she had been alarmed by the despondent cloud that had seemed to hover over her.

Now she was talking into her phone, "Silverio, no, listen, it seems the pieces are falling into place. You said that first day that something wasn't right, and this just goes to show that…." She listened for a bit. "No, no, come and join us. I don't care about the campaign, not right now. That campaign has you all the time. Right now, I want you here, me, I want you. We're at El Milagro. Come and join us." She listened for a bit, and then she erupted, "Silverio, you don't get it. If you want anyone at the flat when you get back, come here now. If that doesn't matter to you, don't." She hung up.

"That felt so good!" She was almost laughing. "Want another one?"

Silverio finally appeared, looking sheepish, a rare expression for him.

"Genoveva," he said, and kissed her. Then they hugged each other for a long time. She wondered if she should slip away, but instead, she asked him if he would like a drink and went off to get him a beer.

When she got back, she was having a go at him. "Why didn't you tell me?"

"Because I was worried about you," Silverio said. "I couldn't be sure of how important or true it was. And I didn't want to burden you with something you wouldn't be able to tell anyone about."

"Have you told Ocampo?"

He paused. "Yes."

"But you didn't tell me?"

"Come on, Genoveva, I was waiting until I saw you."

"And you told him before you told me?" She looked at her friend, one eyebrow raised.

"You didn't answer your phone. I didn't want to put it in a message."

"But you didn't tell when you knew?" She had turned back to Silverio.

"I explained that to Genoveva. One thing at a time." He was trying to placate her

Genoveva swivelled back to her friend. "But you told Silverio, not me."

"I told you. You didn't answer."

"Whatever. Sometimes I wonder—"

"Genny, for heaven's sake," Angelita said.

"Genoveva finished the contents of her glass. She started to stand up, but sat down again quickly. "My God," she shouted. "This is unbelievable, unbelievable!" Her voice was getting louder. People at the next table turned to see what was happening. "This means they're not dead. Not all of them, anyway. But look, if what your aunt heard is accurate, and if the gardener in the city saw Guillermo Vargas, then all of this is a disgusting ploy — a fake. We've got to tell people. I'll contact the TV. Silvestre Ocampo can make a speech. Silverio, don't you see, we're going to get them back." She looked at them triumphantly.

"God, I love you when you are on fire," Silverio said and then blushed and coughed. "Genoveva, hold on. As it happens, you may be right about all of this. But we can't go to the media, not unless we can prove it, not unless we know where they are and how we can get them back. If we reveal our suspicions about the Gutierrez woman's involvement and can't prove them, we are sunk. She and her lot can go back on the attack and — I wouldn't put this past her — claim that we are the ones who faked this, and if she can get enough people to believe that we are finished, *fracasados*. We must have more. We have to be able to prove beyond any doubt what we think has been going on."

"How on earth are you going to do that?"

"I don't know, Angelita, I just don't know. Where on earth has Genoveva got to?"

It turned out that she had gone to the bar. She came back with three more drinks, one of which she attacked with enthusiasm.

"God, I hate you sometimes, Silverio." She burped. "Oops, sorry."

"Genoveva!"

"What? Sorry, am I being a bit too–"

She laughed and then plunked herself on her boyfriend's lap and threw her arms around him.

It was at this point that Angelita decided to leave. She walked unsteadily out of the bar without having the drink Genova had just bought for her and wondered briefly if miracles do occur.

Chapter 32
Silvestre

THE STEWARD BROUGHT A FRESHLY SQUEEZED orange juice, slightly chilled, and a plate with eggs and beans. He spread the napkin on his knees. He sipped the delicious, sweet juice and speared some eggs on his fork.

Outside, the sun shone through the oval window as Earth gently turned. *Let's hope it's a good omen,* he thought to himself, that beautiful light.

He wondered how long he could go on like this, surviving on little sleep, crisscrossing the country, one private jet after another paid for by the wealthy backers with liberal tendencies who had flocked to his cause. Not many coal and oil men, though, and he didn't get much support from the agribusiness sectors either. You couldn't have everything.

He looked across the aisle to where Silverio was sleeping, his mouth half open. I envy him, he thought. He looks so young and carefree. I couldn't sleep even if I tried. I have too much to do, too much to worry about. If I lose this election, what then? What would I do? I can't think that far ahead. So I'd better win. He told himself, I must win, and that's all there is to it. But he was worried. The Gutierrez woman was sucking up the air, filling the airwaves. She knew how to capture the media's attention, which increasingly flocked to her as she made more and more exaggerated accusations and claims.

It was evident that she was lying most of the time, but that only seemed to make her more fascinating to everyone. Silvestre knew that one lie about the ESA disappearances was cutting through. He and his team were struggling to fight it, as how do you prove something is not true when you don't know what is true? Gutierrez was having considerable success by suggesting that he either knew more than he was saying or that he had been hopelessly incompetent and had allowed the incident to take place.

Of course, he talked about this in speeches and interviews, and sometimes he sounded convincing. Still, if the interviewer was excellent, or, more obviously, partisan in the wrong way, he would end up protesting ineffectually about how unfair the accusations against him were. But what if the gossip Silverio had reported to him about the old lady at the club meant something? His young assistant's theorising was temptingly persuasive, and they were all now embarked on trying to find evidence to support it. So far, however, they had nothing.

It was clear, though, that something had to be done. Even the man who had lent him today's plane had started to ask questions. Silverio had organised a meeting at a moment's notice. The whole team was there, and their benefactor seemed, in the end, to have been convinced that Isabel Gutierrez's claims were preposterous. How long would that last, though? If I lose his backing, Silvestre thought, will others follow suit? He could feel pessimism begin to take hold, but another sip of his orange juice and a forkful of egg and beans revived him. The steward approached with a coffee, which, he knew from two earlier flights, was good. Behind him, he could hear the team talking animatedly. It was time to bring Silverio back to life.

"Wake him up and give him some coffee," he told the steward and watched, amused, as Silverio opened his eyes. It is evident that for a second, he couldn't quite work out where he was. He had fallen deeply asleep as soon as the plane started down the runway. Tired, yes, but he seemed happy, and just before he closed his eyes, he said something about the pieces falling into place. It was time to find out what he meant.

"I'm sorry Silvestre. I didn't mean to. I couldn't help it."

"Good rest?"

"Well, yes," he started to smile and then stopped himself, "I mean, not enough sleep, but..." he stopped. He's embarrassed about something Silvestre thought.

"Yes, well, anyway, have a stretch, get up and walk around. I know there's not much room. Then let's get to it."

"No, it's all right. I'm awake now."

"So what was it you wanted to tell me?" When Silverio told him about the man in Gutierrez's garden, almost certainly the EAS leader, and went on to suggest that if you added that to the things the old lady had said about the club, well, it all fitted together. "It is clear to me, I mean, I don't think there can be any doubt, that the Gutierrez campaign or the Heredia clan from the valley, or both together, planned and executed this whole disappearance thing. And if it was Guillermo Vargas in that garden in the city, then that proves that we might get them back, the EAS people, and that would be a bit of a triumph."

"I know, Silverio, but we've thought that before. It doesn't get us anywhere if we can't prove it, I mean, if we can't show it to be true."

"Well, as to that, Señor Presidente—"

"I like that!"

"I thought you would. But anyway, I've been talking with the others." He indicated the people behind them. "We think we should get a bit more active about this and bring in some outside help."

"What do you mean?"

"One of the guys, Pablo there," Silvestre nodded. He liked Pablo, an intelligent young man, "his cousin runs a private investigation company."

"You're not serious."

"No, but listen. It's a big company. They have branches everywhere. They work with some influential people. They even have bodyguards."

"A private militia? You can't be serious."

But he was and continued with his idea. Silvestre was not sure what to think. On the one hand, the campaign would be annihilated if it got out that they were using a private force. Still, on the other hand, they had to counteract Gutierrez's poison quickly. He found himself listening to concepts like 'plausible deniability' and 'arm's length'.

He agreed that doing something might be better than doing nothing. He'd have to think about it. But not now. They were descending, and it was time to prepare himself for the media crowd he hoped would be there — and hoped they wouldn't at the same time — when they got out of the plane.

He need not have had any doubts. In the terminal building, a jostling crowd of microphone wielders and cameramen clamoured for his attention. His small team stood back as he advanced on the crowd.

"Señor Ocampo, why are you here? What will you tell the people of this town? Why should they believe you?" A thousand different questions were shouted at him.

He held up his arms. "Hello, everyone. Thank you for meeting me. So much nicer than having no one at arrivals, don't you think?" He was rewarded with a few chuckles. People started shouting again. He went on quickly.

"I am here to offer hope to your community, to the community of the whole country — a hope for fairness, for justice, for progress, for equality. Far too many groups are marginalised in this great republic. Still, we want to bring them all into our beautiful family to play a part in the life of this incredible society."

In reply to the first question, he replied that yes, their message was getting through and that people were flocking to the campaign in increasing numbers. When questioned about the exact number, he referred the journalists to the small team that accompanied him. "They know all the details," he said, "I am the vision and ideas leader of all of this." Maybe that's not a great line, he thought. I hope they can deal with that. I hope it's true.

A man he vaguely recognised from earlier encounters had pushed himself to the front, a camera operator behind him, "Señor Ocampo, Señor Ocampo, why should anyone trust you? Anyone at all?"

"Because I am here for the people and the future. What you see here is what you get. I am a man of the people, someone the people can trust."

There were shouted questions from the media scrum, but the man at the front hadn't finished.

"But the people can't trust you at all, can they?"

He looked for another questioner to answer, someone who wasn't so hostile, perhaps.

"Did you organise the disappearances in Calixtlan, or did you just let them happen?"

There it was again.

"Let me be clear. I fervently reject such a disgusting suggestion. Of course, I did not organise those disappearances. The ones who disappeared are exactly 'the people' I have mentioned." Keep it all under control, he told himself. Be firm. Don't go over the top. "And as for your other idea that I somehow let it happen, I utterly refute that ridiculous smear. Suppose you want to know the truth of this — and let me tell you. In that case, our police forces are doing their best to get to the bottom of what has happened. Perhaps you should ask Isabel Gutierrez, whose slanderous and baseless insinuations you have so slavishly parroted. "

"And now," he shouted to the assembled journalists, "I hope you will forgive me. I have a rally to get to and a speech to make!" With his team close behind him, he forced his way through the crowd, braving a forest of microphone booms and shouting reporters. I don't know how pop stars and other celebrities learn to live with this, he thought to himself. If I become president, I will find a way to make it all more efficient. I'm sure it can be done.

In the small bus that was waiting for them, he turned to his 'gang' as he sometimes called them, "Pablo?"

"Sí, Señor?"

"Silverio here was telling me about your cousin."

"Sí, Señor."

"Well, I tell you what. When you have time, I would like you to contact your cousin, the one who does investigations. I don't want to know anything about it, and I want as few of you as possible to be involved, just you and Silverio. We need to find out something, anything we can about any possible connection between what happened in Calixtlan and Isabela Gutierrez. How much would it cost? How much of our budget would it absorb, and how could we make any expenditure as discrete as possible? And the rest of you, forget you ever heard this conversation. All right? Pablo?"

"Yes, sir."

Silverio was watching him, a smile on his face.

Chapter 33
Rosario

THE LIGHTS WERE STRUNG across the square. Music was coming from the colonnades. She was wearing her very best new white dress with a beautiful blue sash at her waist. Something was exciting about the air, the lights, the moon, the laughter, and the voices. There was singing. Now everyone was joining in. She had never felt so alive. She hugged her body. She felt pretty, and the future dangled in front of her like a shiny bauble reflecting the silver and gold all around her.

Her heart sang in time with the music. The future, all that future stretching out ahead of her. Who knew what was going to happen? Excitement, fresh and glorious, pulsed through her. She had never felt this well before. She twirled around. And then there he was - oh, and he was mysterious, beautiful. She could sense his strength, his power. She looked at him as he pushed his hat back, took a drag on his cigarillo and smiled at her. She was suddenly aflame. And then he kissed her.

There was music all around her. The night sang. He was tall and beautiful. A force surged through her, a kind of craziness. Could anything be this glorious? I will dance for him, I will dance, and then I will give myself to him, and he will take me. She twirled and swirled around, the music faded, and the lights went out. She heard the crack as she hit the floor. The lights went black.

"Tia Rosario. Tia Rosario, are you all right? Let me help you."

Hands grabbed her and pulled her upright. How it hurt. Who was the man? Who was the woman? What were they doing with her? She was suddenly frightened.

"Let go of me," she tried to shout, but she couldn't make them listen.

"Here, Tia, let us help you sit."

But it hurt so badly. Who was that girl? She was just a girl.

"Get away from me!" She lashed out with all her strength and hit her full in the face.

"Ow, Tia! What are you doing? That hurt!"

Good — so it should. Who are these people? It still hurt.

Someone was on the phone. It sounded like someone she knew. Was that Federico? Yes, that was Federico. An ambulance? Who wants an ambulance?

And then they arrived, and now she was in this ambulance and people were taking her pulse and saying things like, "you'll just feel a scratch", and she did, and things were much calmer and nothing hurt so much, and that was good. They seemed to be going very fast.

Now she was in a hospital.

"Rosario? May I call you Rosario? Do you know where you are?" Well, of course, she knew where she was. Did they think she was stupid? This was a hospital.

"You're in the hospital, all right? You seem to have had a bit of a fall, so we'd better check you out and see if there's any damage. I hope that's okay." It wasn't okay, as it happens, but there didn't seem to be much she could do about it.

Later, Angelita turned up at her bedside.

"Angelita? Hello child. What are you doing here?"

"Not so much of a child, Tia!"

"What happened to you? Is that a black eye?"

"Looks like it."

"How did it happen? Did someone hit you? Did you bump into something? Have a fall?"

"Something like that." She was smiling at her. Where had she seen her recently?

"Is your father here?"

"He's working. He's away on court business."

"Whatever for?" She was so tired. Maybe she would sleep now.

When she woke up, there was a man at the end of her bed. What was he doing?

"What are you doing?"

"Don't worry, my dear. Just taking you off for a quick look in the scanner."

"Scanner? What? Where?" She didn't like this at all. "Why did he say 'my dear'?"

"It'll be all right. The nurses will explain when we get there."

Corridors. Tubes were coming from her arm. People. Lights in the ceiling. She lay back and closed her eyes. That was better. When she opened them again, there was a nurse and someone else — a doctor? — telling her what was going to happen, and it would be all right. It might seem a bit uncomfortable, but not to worry. They put something on her ears. Now all the sound around her was muffled. Then she found herself in a tiny tunnel, and she had no idea what was happening. Things were getting very frightening. She wanted to leave, but she couldn't think straight. She tried to get up, but it seemed she was strapped in. She tried to move her head, but something was holding her in place. She wanted to scream, ask for help, please get me out of here, but she couldn't.

And then it was over, and they were back in the corridor. Well, that was something. Better than that terrible tube she'd just been in.

They got back to her room, only to find it wasn't hers at all, but it was a lot nicer than where she had been. Two nurses came.

"Hello, Rosario. I'm Catarina, and this is Genoveva."

"Tia Rosario, what are you doing here?"

Did she know the nurse? She didn't think so. But she looked vaguely familiar. She tried. But then she gave up.

"Would you like something to drink? A juice? A tea or something?" The one called Catarina was speaking. "I'll bring you something."

The other one was speaking. "Tia Rosario! I'm Angelita's friend. We met at your house. Good to see you again, though this isn't the ideal place, is it?"

She had a lovely, friendly smile.

"Is there anything I can help you with?"

"She wanted to trust this nurse. Something about her made her feel safe. "What's going on? I don't know what's going on." It was such a relief to say it.

"Nothing to worry about. You've had a bit of a fall, that's all. They brought you in so we can have a good look and see what's going on. Once they know more, they'll see if you can go home."

"Go home?"

"Yes, go home. You'd like that, I expect."

Would she? She supposed she would. It sounded right. She liked this nurse.

"Sometimes nurse…" she paused. She had to get this right. "Sometimes I get a bit confused."

"You do?"

"Yes. I can't remember things. I don't know what" What was she trying to say?

Another person came into the room.

"How are you, Tia?"

She flung her arms around the nurse.

"Genny, what are you doing here?"

"It's the hospital. I work here."

"Yes, I know. But I mean, *here*."

"They were short-staffed, so I volunteered to work an extra shift. Silverio's away on the campaign, so I might as well."

"Nurse. Nurse." What was going on?

"Yes?"

"Who's that person?"

"Tia, it's me, Angelita."

"But Angelita's… I couldn't see you. The light's not very good in here."

The other nurse, the one whose name she couldn't remember, came in with a cup of tea. "Excuse me, just a minute," Genoveva said. I'll be back in a minute." She walked out with Angelita.

"Come on, then, let's sit you up. I'm Catarina, remember."

She felt the bed moving, and it almost felt as if she was sitting up.

"Would you like me to help you with the drink?" How nice to be looked after in this way.

"Nurse," she said as Catarina brought the cup closer to her mouth, "How long is this going on for? When is it going to end?"

Chapter 34
Martin

"WHERE DO dead people go when they die?"

Where indeed? He had to get this right.

"I don't know."

"You don't know. You said Daddy would always be here."

"Well, he is here. He's here." He pointed at his head, "And here and here." He touched the heads of his niece and nephew.

"But you said you didn't know where people go."

"That's right. I don't."

"Then how do you know he is in our heads?"

"Because we carry him here in our heads, in our hearts."

"But doesn't anybody know where people go?"

"Some people think they do, but I don't. That's all."

"Who knows? Who says they know? I want to speak to them. I want to know where Daddy is."

"Sarah." What could he say? He wasn't very good at this death thing himself either, especially when it was this close to home. Two people in his life fell to their end. His parents didn't count. He tried not to think about them at all. What are the odds?

He forced himself to concentrate.

"Look. Everyone dies in the end. That's just the way it is. But it's okay."

"Will you die?"

"Well, yes, but I'm not planning on it anytime soon!"

"Neither was Daddy."

"Well, no. But that's the thing, you see. You never quite know when or anything like that. It just happens. And sometimes it's an accident, sometimes it's a bit of a surprise, and sometimes it's just because you get very old," he pretended to be ancient, "and well, you just kind of switch off."

They laughed.

"But how do you know you aren't going to die, like today?"

"Well, I don't. But it's very, very, very unlikely. I tell you what, let's make a bet. I bet you that I won't die tomorrow."

"What do we get if you do?"

"All the chocolate you can eat for two whole days. But if I don't die, you have to give me all the chocolate I can eat for two days."

"But Uncle Martin, we haven't got any chocolate of our own and Mummy doesn't give us enough money to buy you enough chocolate."

"That's just too bad. Either we have a deal or we don't. What do you say?"

Daniel picked up a cushion and threw it at him, so he threw it back and then both of them were on him, thumping him, screeching as if the conversation they had just had never taken place.

"Children!" Martin thought she sounded too sharp. "Children, leave your poor uncle alone. Go and watch TV or something.

"Can we?"

She didn't say anything, so Daniel went over and picked up

the remote control, and soon they had settled down, their attention completely fixed on the screen.

"I heard that conversation."

"Didn't know you were listening."

"I didn't mean to."

"Vicky?" He wanted to say something to her, to help her, to move them forward somehow. Everything seemed to have stopped since Alexei's death. The children were back at school. Vicky had told their teachers what had happened, and they were sympathetic but were held back from expressing this too volubly by the look on her face, an absence of expression. And now they were stuck in the house. He wished Angelita were here. He wished he were there. "I'm going to sue those bastards," she said with no warning.

"Those bastards?"

"Yes. That home, that hospital, that whatever-it-is. He was there. He was sectioned. They had a responsibility to look after him and keep him safe. He escaped. But they should have been able to prevent that. They were negligent. I'll make them pay."

"You'll need a good lawyer."

"Yes, I will. Some kind of pro bono outfit that I don't have to pay too much for."

"It's a pity Federico isn't here. He'd be able to help you."

"That's ridiculous. He doesn't know anything about how things work here at all. He'd be no use at all."

"You'd feel better having him here, surely."

"I would not, I would not." Martin was shocked by her vehemence.

"I don't understand."

"There's nothing to understand. He interrupted the most sacred — he had no right, no right."

"How was he to know?"

"He interrupted me just when—,"

"Vicky, you answered."

"Martin, if you're going to say things like that," she was screaming at him now. The children looked around, alarmed. "If you're going to go on like that, you may as well go home, go home. Go on. Get out now."

"Mummy," Daniel wailed.

He stood there, stock still, wondering what to do. He was utterly perplexed.

"Mummy," Daniel wailed again, and as if obeying some invisible command, she went over to him and sat down on the sofa. The next thing he knew, she was hugging both of them, one on the other side, so tightly that it looked as if they would not be able to breathe.

He crept out of the room and went into the kitchen. He was confused, depressed, and uncertain of what he should do. Listlessly, he went to the fridge and took out a bottle of milk. He poured himself a glass and felt the cold consoling liquid go down his throat. What was happening? So much tragedy. So much joy. He, for example, had never felt so secure, at least since their mother and father had left in such a cruel and precipitate way, as he did now with Angelita, the most beautiful person he had ever known, let alone been able to give himself to unconditionally. Trying to be a support to his sister and the kids right now was one of the hardest things he had ever done, and coming to terms with what had happened to Alexei was grotesquely difficult, but Angelita had chosen him, and he was doing his best to hold on to that.

Later, when the children were in bed and Vicky had gone to her room with a bottle of wine, he called his wife even though it would be the middle of the night for her. She answered after a few rings, struggling to drag herself from sleep. The sound of her voice was far better than the milk he had drunk earlier. It calmed him and excited him all at the same time. It made him feel warm and desired, which he liked. He told her about the children and their conversation, marvelling at her empathetic understanding of how difficult that must have been. Shall we have kids? he asked her, half-jokingly, and she laughed a sleepy laugh. Can we wait a bit? I have a career to make, to which he said we could do anything we want, though he felt the idea slowly taking hold in his bloodstream.

They discussed what was going on with Vicky, including her mood swings, her drinking, and how she was still in shock. They also talked about what he could do about it.

Angelita said, "What about Papa? He's like a lovesick puppy! It's pathetic. I've never seen him like this."

He told her about the incident that had occurred earlier in the day and tried to convey some of the character of her outburst. "I mean, I don't get it. They were so close before this. I was even a bit uneasy about it, my father-in-law, my sister, and my brother-in-law. I was almost a bit scandalised if I'm honest."

"I was uneasy, too. But you couldn't deny the connection they had. It was lovely to see. He's been so supportive, so kind to her and always there when she needed him — and she did need him, didn't she?"

He felt aggrieved, as if his sister was being criticised, even though he knew she was right. He told himself that, yes, blood is thicker than water, and he genuinely loved and had always relied on his sister. But he couldn't deny what Angelita was saying, and anyway, it was Angelita who was saying it. God, he ached for her right then and there. Then he felt guilty. The situation here was too desperate for that kind of thing. He said, "I don't get it about your father. It was just so bizarre. I mean, when she threw away her phone, when he rang her. It was as if some switch had been clicked, some anti-matter reaction, and she flipped completely. We've had our moments before, she and I, but I've never seen anything like that."

"Anything like what?" Vicky had come into the room. She was holding the wine bottle, now half empty. She looked slightly unsteady. "Sorry, Angelita, I have to go," he said, and then he hung up, hoping to make it better later. He turned to his sister.

"Martin," she said, her voice fuzzy, "you are my best brother. My only brother, who needed me so much, and I was probably cruel and horrible to you."

"You weren't. At least not often."

She didn't flinch at that, but he couldn't be sure that she had picked up on the humorous intent of his comment. "But now it's my turn," she said. "Martin, now I need you. I don't know what to do. I don't know what to feel, and I can't even face what has happened. Oh God, I'm all over the place. But you! I heard you with the children. You were amazing." He waited. "Want some wine?"

"I'm drinking beer."

"Hmm." She seemed to be thinking about that. Then she went to a cupboard, got a glass, and poured more wine. "Help me, Martin."

Of course, he said, "Vicky, my darling sister, of course I'll help you. I'll do anything I can. This is terrible. What's happening? What happened? But I'm here." They hugged and stood there for a long time.

Then she drained her glass and said, "I'm going to bed. Let's see if I can sleep. Probably not. This is all so..." and her voice drifted away as she headed out of the room, not objecting when he rescued the nearly empty bottle from her loosening grip. He stood there finishing his beer, feeling suddenly that he had a role, something he had to do, and that for the first time, he was the strong one of the two.

Later, as he lay in bed, he heard her asking for his help again, and 'I will,' he told himself as sleep claimed him, but how, how?

Chapter 35
Jacinto

"I'm grateful, I really am."

"Don't be silly, you old rogue." Marisol Cardova patted his knee with one hand as she drove them out of San Miguel. "I'm happy to help."

"You're very kind, my dear."

"And you are a smooth talker, you old Fox." She paused, staring at the road ahead. When she spoke again, her tone was wistful. "We did have fun all those years ago, didn't we?"

He remembered their two nights together that time, picturing her warm flesh and the lascivious groans that erupted from her as they reached their peak together in a riot of sweaty exertion. Some things you don't forget.

"Yes, we did. I suppose I treated you poorly, didn't I? I usually do. I think."

"Course you did, but you didn't do it alone. It wasn't like you forced yourself on me. You had that magnetism. I was hot for you, kind of desperate for it. I think I threw myself at your feet!"

"That was then, Marisol. You wouldn't do that again. Look at me. I'm a monster."

"You're just fishing, you flirt."

"That obvious?"

They drove on in silence for some minutes.

"The thing I don't understand, maestro, is why."

"Why what?"

"Why do you want to go and see this place? It's just going to be a horrible reminder of what went on there."

"But that's it. You know, ever since they left, ever since they vanished into the clutches of that monstrous group, that cult—"

"The Sons of Perpetual Light?"

"Yes, yes, them. Ever since, I have done nothing for those poor boys. I probably wasn't much of a father for them anyway, even when they were children."

"Fatherhood was not something you were especially suited for."

"Maybe not, but now's my chance to make up for that. Everything I've done since, well, since a day back in the city when I went too far, I think, has been an attempt to…"

"Feel better about yourself?"

"Maybe. Do something decent, I suppose, apart from the music. So I determined to find those boys — that's why I agreed to conduct your festival concert."

"I thought it was to see me again."

"Yes, of course, Marisol, of course."

"I'm teasing you."

"Oh."

"Why do you want to see this place? Isn't that where your boys were?"

"Yes, that's where unspeakable things happened. That's where, at least from what I understand, they had a breakdown due to what they witnessed and what was done to them. If I'm going to fully embrace those poor lost souls, I have to travel the path with them."

"I don't understand all that. But I can see that it's important for you."

Artemio's Fire, the importunate newcomer, loomed up on their right-hand side. Jacinto looked up at it and felt a heavy emptiness in his stomach, where the fear had taken hold. He remembered his long, phantasmagorical, nighttime walk and the strenuous climbing, climbing, climbing, the hurt in his legs, the rasping ache in his lungs as he reached the rim of the crater. He gulped at the hideous memory of a great searing horror that had burnt him and damaged his body almost beyond repair. Today, though, as if to mock him, the mountain looked pathetically rocky and benign, its jagged peak outlined against a refreshing blue sky decorated with a few fluffy white clouds.

"I think we turn here," Marisol said, indicating right. The road they now started on was uneven, and she slowed down to navigate the bumps and potholes.

He loved this kind of scenery, with its raw beauty, and tried to imagine what it must have been like for his two sons when they were brought here, already in thrall to the weird gang they had joined. However, it was impossible. By the time they had arrived, they were already, he assumed, so completely changed from the boys he had once known that trying to get inside their heads was beyond him.

"We're getting close, I think," his companion said, "how do you feel?"

"I am not sure. I'll tell you when we've seen the place!"

They turned off again, and now they were following a track across a pitted, desolate landscape which would almost certainly have been more inviting before the eruption. In front of them was a circle of trees to which they were headed. The track led them into a large crescent, and there it was: a large building, typical of the kind of landowner hacienda which had once dotted this landscape.

Outside, to the professor and Marisol's complete surprise, stood three men armed to the teeth with what looked like submachine guns and pistols. They wore black balaclavas, which made them look even more menacing than they might have otherwise appeared. They shifted ominously as the car came to a halt, and then one of them came up to the door, his right index finger inside the trigger guard of his weapon. He indicated that Jacinto should wind down his window.

"What do you want? What are you doing here?"

"Good morning," Jacinto said politely, unnerved by the guard's threatening attitude. "My name is Jacinto Perez, Professor Jacinto Perez."

"Never heard of you," the man said. "I'll ask you again. What are you doing here?"

"I want to visit the hacienda." The man's two companions had come up to the car.

"Have you been invited?"

"No. But you see—"

"Excuse me, maestro," Marisol said, and then, addressing the guard, "We're here because the maestro wishes to see the place where his sons were once living. They were part of a religious sect here, you see, and now they're in trouble with the law, because—"

"My heart bleeds for them, but frankly, I couldn't give a shit. You're not wanted here. Get on your way and don't come back."

Jacinto saw a man emerge from the hacienda behind the three guards and walk to the side of the hacienda.

"Come on, maestro, we're not going to get anywhere here."

"Are you sure I couldn't just come in and have a look? I don't mean any harm."

"Get out of here." The man made a show of releasing the safety catch on his gun. Before Jacinto could do or say anything else, Marisol had jammed her foot on the accelerator. They left in a shower of gravel, lurching round the circle and back the way they had come.

"Marisol!"

"Well, what would you have me do? That man was seriously trigger-happy. He looked like he was going to shoot us on the spot."

"Wasn't much fun, was it!"

"*Por lo contrario* — on the contrary — *eso fue una pesadilla, de los peores. ¡Qué susto, hombre!*" It was the worst kind of nightmare. What a shock. It'll take me a bit of time to get over that!" She had slowed down, and for a minute, neither of them spoke. "And you know what puzzles me?" she said.

"No." He needed to regain his composure

"Those guys were wearing the colours that Isabel Gutierrez's supporters wear."

"Yeah, well, I wouldn't imagine they would be Ocampo people!"

"It looked like they were more than just supporters, don't you think? Guards, more like, a little army. But why there," she gestured behind them, "why would there be a Gutierrez outpost in the middle of nowhere?"

"You know what?" he replied, remembering, "the police chief — I remember him from all the volcano drama — came out of the front door just before we left."

Maestro Perez," she glanced across at him, "my dear Jacinto, "she had regained her composure, "I think we should see if we can find out a bit more, what do you say?"

"You are incorrigible, Marisol."

"That's what you admired in me, you said once."

"Marisol!"

"Look, there's a turn-off here. Do you think if we go left, we can get round to the back of the property?" and before he could answer, they were heading off, bumping down a path past a row of trees which hid them from sight.

"I'm not sure I want to meet those thugs again. Do you have a plan?"

"If my guess is right, there'll be different guards round the back so they won't have seen us before. We can 'start again'. I'm sure we won't get into the place, but who knows, we might see something interesting from the outside. Sadly, I don't think you'll get what you want from this experience, but I'm curious to know more right now. Listen, after what just happened, I know it's a risk, so just say no if you don't want to. But if you're up for it?"

Jacinto didn't answer. Marisol took that as consent.

"Do you have your stick with you?"

"Yes, you saw me put it on the back seat. I always have it. My walking's nearly back to something like normal, but still."

"Well, get it," she said, and then told him the plan that was beginning to form in her mind.

Ten minutes later, they were following what seemed like a farm track. They had reached the back of the hacienda, and Maria stopped the car behind the trees as close to the building as she could.

"Sure about this?" she asked.

"Absolutely not. You're one hundred per cent crazy. But you don't look like someone who's going to be stopped."

"Okay then. Let's get out. Remember to be pathetic."

"I am pathetic. And scared."

"You are neither of those things, you lovely man. Come on."

They walked through the trees. As they agreed, he was hobbling along beside her, prodding the earth with his stick, adding years to his age and his injuries and looking older and even more decrepit than he was. She had the bag she had retrieved from the car hanging from her shoulder.

They emerged from the tree line. There was a large wooden door in the centre of the wall that surrounded the building. There were barred windows, typical for this kind of architecture, on the first floor. The sun was high in the sky. It was like a scene from a film set, and just like a movie, two men wearing the same balaclavas and colours as the guards at the front of the building came striding towards them. Marisol waved and shouted a greeting. "What a beautiful place she said, as they came up to them, "this must be the famous Vista del Volcan hacienda. I read about it in a book when I was a child, and here it is." She was laughing, little trills of delight escaping like birdcall.

"Marisol, my dear," leave these poor gentlemen alone. Good morning," he said, "how nice to see you. We're just having a wander round, though with my legs, I'm not much of a wanderer, ha ha" he coughed, "not long for me now, I suppose."

"Don't be silly, darling," Marisol laughed gaily, "you have years to go, more time for us to, you know…" and she winked grotesquely.

The guards, who, like their colleagues from the front of the building, were cradling assault rifles, were watching open-mouthed.

"I suppose you work here," Marisol asked them.

"You shouldn't be here." One of them said, trying to gain control.

"I'm so sorry," she said," we didn't mean to do anything wrong. We'll go if you want us to."

"That would be best, Señora, and soon if you don't mind."

It was at this moment that Jacinto gave out a loud groan. He coughed and then groaned again. He seemed to be about to fall. "Forgive me," he said in a rasping, weak voice," do you mind if I lean on you. I feel as if I am about to…." And without waiting for a reply, he put his hand on the shoulder of the man nearest him and seemed to half fall.

219

"This won't do," one of the guards barked.

"Oh no, please help, officer or whatever you are," Marisol squeaked.

"I'd like to just sit down," Jacinto whispered feebly, "please help me to sit down."

"Give me a hand," the guard that Jacinto was holding on to appealed to his colleagues.

"S'pose it won't hurt. He's just an old guy. We'll help him down and decide what to do."

Two of the men slowly lowered Jacinto to the ground. "Thank you so much. You men are heroes." He was breathing heavily. "Water," he gasped, raising his arm to Marisol. "Water."

"Darling, I don't have any with me," she said, clearly panicking, "I don't suppose," she said beseechingly to the men, "that one of you could bring us some water. I'm so frightened he's going to get a lot worse."

"Lady, I don't know what you think you are doing, but this isn't a hospital."

"Quiet, Taco," one of the men hissed, "we can't have this old geezer pegging out on us. Not here. Not now. Go on, go and get something for him to drink quickly, and then we can get these two out of here."

The guard headed towards the doors, and Marisol followed him. When they got there, however, he turned to her. "Stay here," he barked.

"But I thought—"

"Lady, just stay here. Wait, all right."

"All right," she said meekly. She stood there gazing up at the walls and all those windows. She thought she saw someone looking out of the one just above her on her right. A moment later, her suspicion was confirmed when a hand came through the bars and dropped something white to the ground below. Marisol glanced at the doors where the man had just disappeared. Turning, she saw the other two guards looking down at Jacinto. She just had time to reach down and pick up what the unknown hand had thrown out of the window and stuff it into her capacious bag when the doors opened again. The guard came back carrying two bottles of water.

"Thank you, oh thank you!" she trilled and got only a dull stare in return as they made their way back to Jacinto and his two companions. Glancing back, she could see no sign of life behind the first-floor windows.

Jacinto took the water and emptied one of the water bottles in quick gulping swallows. He wiped the back of his hand across his mouth. "Thank you," he croaked.

"What now?" one of the men said to his companions.

"Please, oh please," Marisol said, "could you just help me get this poor man back to the car. I will take him straight to the hospital. They know him there. They'll know what to do. I just hope it isn't too late."

The guards looked at each other uncertainly. The one who seemed to be their leader shrugged. "Come on. Let's get this over with," and they lifted Jacinto Perez to his feet and half-dragged him back through the trees, Marisol leading them with a constant stream of 'thank yous' and cries of worry until they came to the car, where they bundled the professor into the passenger seat and almost threw his walking cane at him as he sat there. Marisol got behind the wheel.

"Now, you two," growled the apparent leader of the trio, "get the hell out of here and don't come back You hear? This is not the place for you. Get him to the hospital," and, with his companions, he stood and watched as she turned the car and headed off back along the tack they had arrived by.

Back on the main road, Marisol finally let out a great wordless shout, and Jacinto started laughing. "Maestro Jacinto Perez," she said when she had calmed down," in all the years I have known you, that is without doubt the best performance of yours I have ever seen."

"Only matched by yours, my dear Marisol," he countered exultantly.

And now they were both laughing, and it seemed like they couldn't stop.

Chapter 36
Silverio

He didn't want to raise the subject with Genoveva. He wasn't sure he had the nerve. They had been lazing around, slouched on the sofa, eating popcorn and watching a particularly mindless programme which they both enjoyed. Then his phone had gone off. He groaned, got up, and left the room. *Damn, damn.* Just one day, please.

Things had become so much better since that evening in the square when he had joined her and Angelita. Not as good as they had been right at the beginning, obviously, but Genoveva's bleak despair was less frequent. It had been replaced with a kind of repressed excitement. He worried about that. He felt so bad that she was constrained from telling the friends and families of the disappeared what she knew and they suspected, but she was quite astute enough to know that she had to. So it wasn't as if he could relax. The campaign was nearly swallowing him whole, but at home, at least, the spark had been rekindled between them, and their intimacy was once again thrilling when it happened. Damn. Damn.

"If that was who I think it was and he's demanding your pres-

223

ence, I think I may have to kill you both," she said when he came back. It was only half a joke. He didn't know what to say. "Okay, go on. I don't need you. Our one day without the wretched campaign! To be expected, I suppose. I'm eager for all this to be over. Then we can see if −" she paused, as if she was changing her mind, "just go. Get out of here."

"I am upset about this, too, Genny. I really am. I want to stay here. With you. This is agony."

"Oh, poor you."

He didn't want to say this, but he felt he had no alternative. "Silvestre has heard something about, and he wants me there right now."

"About them?" They both knew who she was talking about.

"Please don't say anything. He especially asked me not to tell you."

"Great. That's all I need."

"No, because of the pressure it puts you under. No, to be able to say anything about it — whatever it is. I know how difficult that is. I really do. I mean, this is me talking."

"Some news? Silverio! News?"

"It could be. Not sure. I'll find out when I get there. I am so sorry."

"Me, too. But if it is, I don't know, just leave, and I'll have such good fun all on my own. I can't wait to be on my own all over again!"

He went, and it wasn't until he was nearly at Silverio's campaign headquarters that the shadow of Genoveva's frustration lifted from him.

When he got there, Silverio came up straight away. "Get Pablo," he said, "and come outside. I don't want anyone else to hear about this. Not yet."

The others, who were there, looked puzzled and unhappy, but they returned to their tasks as the three walked out.

Once outside, Silvestre could hardly conceal his excitement. "Listen," he said, "I have a story."

Not again, Silverio thought. The candidate became increasingly eccentric as the campaign progressed. The endless round of interviews, rallies, and TV appearances kept him permanently occupied, and he was hardly getting any sleep. His voice was going, and sometimes in his sleep-deprived state, he said things that were a bit unusual for him.

"Señor?"

"Silvestre?"

"I have a friend, maybe you both know her. Her name is Marisol Cardova. She organised that concert all those months ago." No one had to ask which concert. "I've known her for a long time. She's one of the community, and what is more, she isn't a Gutierrez supporter. She's with us if she's with anyone."

Silverio knew who he was talking about, although he had never met the woman in person. Pablo just looked blank. "Why are you telling us this, Silvestre?"

"Well, because," the candidate was enjoying himself and being deadly serious at the same time, "two days ago, maestro Perez — you know the musician who nearly died in the eruption?" They nodded. "Two days ago, Marisol Cardova agreed to take the maestro out into the country to the hacienda where that religious so-called cult hung out."

"Religious cult, señor Alcalde?"

"Ex-alcalde!" Silvestre smiled, "I mean those 'Sons of Perpetual Light' or whatever they called themselves, you remember, and their leader was killed, murdered, more like by the maestro's sons. For some bizarre reason, he wanted to go and see the place. So she drove him out into the middle of nowhere, out beyond the volcano, to see the place. Which just happened to be surrounded by armed guards wearing colours which identified them as Isabel Gutierrez's men."

225

"Why on earth would they be out there? Wherever there is?" Silverio asked, though he wondered if what he was thinking could be right.

"Well, that's just the point. From what I understand, Marisol and this musician put on quite a show. They think they managed to convince some of the 'army' there that they were just old tourists and somehow — I didn't quite understand all the details — Marisol saw someone at a window and that someone chucked something out of the window. This!" he said, pulling a white woollen balaclava from his pocket."

"We've found them," Silverio shouted, "We've found them. Come on, let's go and get them."

"Hold on. Not so fast. Not so fast."

"What?!"

"There was something else. Maestro Perez saw Rivendeira there. He's involved in all this. We already know he's involved with Gutierrez. Still, if this hacienda is where they've taken the EAS, well, he's at the very least complicit and probably more than that."

"Yes, but–"

"Listen, Silverio, you will think me heartless. But hear me out. Suppose Rivendeira is in on this, even organised it. In that case, we can't be sure we can get any police in there, at least not the state police, because they are probably compromised, and if we go charging in and they, I mean the Gutierrez faction, if somehow they manage to suggest that we had something to do with this, then we are sunk."

"But if we don't do anything and the members of the EAS — assuming it's them — are killed, then how will we feel?"

"I am sure it is them. It feels right. I can't see any other reason for what Marisol and Perez saw and found," he said, waving the white balaclava. "But I am terrified of the possibility that this might go wrong and that they will try to pin this on me or worse. Look, we have to get those people out of there, but we also have to succeed in this election. To do that, we need to gather evidence that Rivendeira and Gutierrez are controlling the hacienda, and then we'll be safe. Yes, we have two witnesses, but is that enough?

"So you're saying we should wait?"

"Yes, that's exactly what I'm saying."

"But–"

"Listen, I know that waiting is difficult, and more than that, it carries two major risks. The first is that more harm will come to these people, which is unthinkable, but the other is that they will spring their trap before we are ready. Understand me, these people have to be exposed. Look, you two, I know, believe me, I know how difficult this is; it's a hard decision. Still, it's the kind of decision I'd better get used to making if I want to be president."

Silverio didn't know how to respond. He desperately wanted the EAS people to be rescued if indeed they were there. Still, he also suspected that Silvestre was right. What a choice: do something now or do something later. What were the truly moral choices? What was the safe option? First, he assured himself that instant rescue was the only justifiable course of action, but then, almost instantly, he foresaw the real possibility of a Gutierrez presidency if it went wrong, and that made him doubt himself. Then he thought of Genoveva, and he changed his mind again.

He saw Silvestre Ocampo watching him and wondered what to do. He looked at Pablo, but his expression gave him no clue how he was reacting.

"I'm going to leave you two alone to think about all this," Ocampo said, "I've told you what I think — though I do so with a heavy heart — but now you will both have to decide what you want to do. But if you agree with me, the question then becomes how to obtain proof. Once we have that, we must work out how to rescue everyone, neutralise the woman's lies about me, and destroy her campaign. I apologise for putting you in this situation. Still, it's very, very exciting — even if it is also extremely frightening," he turned to go, "but meanwhile I have to go back and meet the woman who's going to pretend to be Isabela Gutierrez — to prepare for the TV debate - but you know that. Come along, Silverio, when you have finished here." He walked back into the building.

For a moment, neither of them said anything. Then they both tried to speak at the same time and stopped. Finally, Silverio said, "Look, whatever we decide, the big question is 'how to find out if what we think is true IS true."

"I'll get back to my cousin's lot to see what they can find out. We already have people watching Gutierrez's house in the city, but this hacienda may pose a bit more of a problem. I'll find out."

A short time later, he excused himself and headed off, who knew where, to follow up on what they had discussed. Silverio stayed at the campaign headquarters for two or three more hours until finally Silvestre let him go.

"See you here tomorrow, early," the ex-mayor said. "Our guests are arriving at half past eight in the morning, and I want you to be in those meetings. If it goes well, my administration — that is, if we win," he grinned, "will be on its way."

Back at the flat, Genoveva was on the phone. She looked up resentfully when he came in. She finished her call. "You came back," she said.

"As soon as I could," he said, "but it was well worth going."

"Yeah, yeah. The campaign. I know."

"No, Genoveva, listen. Something amazing–"

Then he stopped. He was desperate to tell her what he knew. He hated keeping things from her. *I'll tell her,* he thought, but almost instantly, he knew that he would not.

Chapter 37
Maria

It was another scorching day. The cars roared up and down the avenues. Great trucks and buses thundered along the main arteries in and out of the city.

I recall a day like this, Maria thought. It had been the day she finally walked out on Juan after one too many abuses. Today was different, though. There was a breeze, and she wasn't trapped in the fetid cell of a miserable marriage.

Entering the park, the traffic noise was muted, replaced by the happy sound of children and the laughter of lovers as they rowed around the ornamental lake. She stood and watched the scenes around her, feeling a sense of comfort and peace. She looked for something that would help her find her way to the rendezvous they had discussed.

She was a bit nervous. This was the first time she had gone out just for pleasure for as long as she could remember, and she hadn't been in this park since she and Juan had been teenage sweethearts.

People were wandering around the lake, cycling on the path, and men were selling roasted corn on the cob, chestnuts, and all manner of snacks. There were ice cream vans and stands offering chicharron, crispy fried pork belly, stands full of musical instruments, toys, and a range of trinkets.

Something was intoxicating about seeing families out for the day, enjoying themselves. At the same time, the sellers shouted for customers, and wandering bands offered to sing songs for any occasion. Amazingly, amid all the urban chaos and happy park noise around them, birdsong sounded from the trees in the occasional silences.

Maria smiled to herself. True, she did not know how things would turn out, and she still carried the weight of a complicated past hanging heavy on her shoulders. But on a day like today, for the first time in ages, she felt lighter and more alive than she usually did. She found herself humming to one of the songs a group was playing to her left. It was a song she recognised from her childhood, and it lifted her spirits even more.

She walked round the edge of the hill, which dominated this vast space. Two hundred yards ahead, she could see the house of culture, and to its left, the small amphitheatre. This is where plays were performed and groups gave evening concerts.

She headed for the bridge across the narrowest part of the lake. As she was crossing it, she saw Santiago leaning on the parapet with a man — presumably his friend Tonio — next to him. They were pointing at the boats and laughing.

She stopped. She was embarrassed and didn't know how to announce her arrival. The friend turned round and looked at her. Then, he turned back to Santiago, nudging him and saying something.

Santiago turned, and his face lit up. "Maria! Hello. So good to see you. Come and meet Tonio."

She walked over to them. They were both leaning against the stone parapet, smiling at her. "Maria, this is Tonio."

"Hello, Tonio," she said shyly.

"Come on, let's go and get a refresco or something, a snack, who knows, then we can take it into the park.

"I hope you don't mind. I've brought a few things I thought you might like. Do you want to see?"

They came over then, and she showed them the bag she was carrying. There were tortas filled with chicken, salad, chiles, and cream. There was a bowl and spoons. "Beans," she said, "like my mother used to make them. Oranges, that kind of thing."

The two men were laughing like children.

After buying some soft drinks, they found a place on the slope overlooking the lake and sat down. Families, lovers, friends, indeed a whole parade of the city's mixed population moved past them on the path. Children ran down the slope, squealing as they tried not to fall over.

She tried to think of something to say, but he didn't know where to start. There was a dynamic between the two men that she couldn't quite place, and it made her uneasy. They took some of the food that was offered. In the awkward silence that followed, no one seemed to know what to talk about, which surprised her because when she and Santiago met after class, conversation was never a problem. Now, however, if this meeting was not to be a disaster, she had to think of something. In the end, the best she could come up with was, "How is that employer of yours?" Santiago picked up the lifeline with the eagerness of a drowning man.

"You won't believe it," he said. "Something has changed. Armed guards everywhere. More and more people are coming to the house in those big cars. It's crazy."

"You've been stopped, Tonio said, laughing.

"Stopped?"

"Yeah. These armed guards, security people, or whatever, they're not the same every day. Well, to be honest, I couldn't tell. They had those things on their heads to cover their faces, so maybe they are the same. Anyway, they've stopped me and demanded to know who I am and why I am there. Imagine!"

"You were scared," Tonio said, laughing.

"No, that's an exaggeration."

"I would have been," Maria said. "Scared, I mean. But what about you? Are you going to stay there? What are you going to do?"

"I'm not sure, to be honest. Something very odd is going on there. All the people and the guards and, well, it's all a bit, I don't know." His voice trailed off.

"Señor Federico does not like your employer. He says if she becomes president, things will get worse. We will all be less free. She will make everything more unfair than it already is."

"Isn't that just the truth!" Tonio commented.

"Well, what can I do?" Santiago said, sounding defensive. "She's just the person I work for. I don't take any interest in all that stuff, just do my job."

"That's not true," Tonio said.

"Well, maybe. But anyway, if she wins, I might be working for the president. Imagine that! Perhaps I'll get a raise. I might even go and work in the presidential palace. That would be something!"

"That's all you care about, is it, how good it will be for you."

"Well, isn't that why people vote for certain candidates? They hope it will be better for them if they choose right."

"I can see right through you!" The two men exchanged glances beyond mere friendship. Watching them, Maria realised something she had known all along but hadn't wanted to acknowledge. Of course — *Madre Santo*, what a fool, what an idiot. It explained everything. She had completely misunderstood what was happening. She had even thought of romantic possibilities that were now impossible. How humiliating. She blushed, thinking about what Santiago must feel about her now — God in heaven.

"Maria?" He looked at her with that beautifully sympathetic face.

"I have to go." It was all she could think of.

"Maria, my friend. Maria?" He sounded urgent, even a bit angry.

She couldn't look at him.

"Maria, you're my friend. Does it matter to you that I am—" He left the question unfinished.

She started to cry.

He came over then and took her hands. "It's okay," he said. "We're friends," he insisted again. "Come on, let's go for a walk," and he almost dragged her to her feet while Tonio collected their things.

On the way back to Señor Federico's apartment, she had a lot to think about. She convinced herself that she was an idiot and that she had made herself look foolish. Looking back, it should have been evident that Santiago's friend Tonio was more than a friend, but it hadn't been clear to her. On the contrary, she had thought, perhaps even hoped, he might see something else in her, maybe even some kind of — I am a complete idiot, she reflected miserably as she walked.

Yet Santiago had done his best to be nice to her when he had seen her consternation. He'd tried to talk to her about their classes and to recover something of their easy banter. It had almost worked, too, but maybe he was trying too hard, or perhaps she couldn't get over her feelings of embarrassment. She left as soon as she could and saw Tonio watching her, a slight smile playing across his features. Maybe she wouldn't go back to her classes.

Unlocking the front door of the apartment, she wondered whether Federico was around, and if he was, would he be wandering around with the miserable look that had taken him over in the last few weeks? She wished he would cheer up. He was such a wonderful person to work for when he was in a good mood.

She understood him, of course, and now better than ever. She knew how close he had become to Vicky, a woman whom Maria had always had a great respect for and who had been so forcefully sympathetic and supportive when her life with Juan was ending. But now? It was difficult, sometimes, to understand why life was so confusing, and not just for her and her people but even for those who seemed to have everything.

She had not liked Alexei Kassoliniki. He had always treated her respectfully, but he was strange. He had piercing eyes and a questioning stare, which sometimes made her feel uncomfortable. But that didn't mean she wasn't shocked to hear that he had fallen off a tall building and was in mortal danger.

How would Daniel and Sarah cope? she wondered.

Señor Federico was sitting in his armchair in the sitting room. There was a bottle of beer on the table next to him, and he was smoking.

"Good evening, Señor Federico."

"Hello, Maria," he responded listlessly.

The doorbell rang. She opened the door to see Angelita standing there. She let her in.

"How is he?" she said to Maria.

"The same."

"Papa!" she called as she walked in. "How are you?" There was concern in her voice.

"Hola, mi amor."

"Smoking? Again?"

"Why not?!"

"Papa, for Heaven's sake!"

"Have you talked to Martin?"

"Of course I have." He didn't look up. "Papa, I hate seeing you like this. I wish I could help."

I should leave the room, Maria thought, but she wanted to hear how the conversation would continue.

"Look, Papi, all I know, all that Martin told me, is that they have planned a quiet funeral for Alexei and Martin will stay for that, and they are going to have a memorial or something sometime later. There are lots of people around the world who want to have something to say about Alexei."

"Yes, but…?"

"He says she is still being very silent about everything else, very - how did he put it — closed off about anything else, me, you, everything. He just hopes that when the funeral is over, things might be different."

He had died, Maria thought. The poor children. She should go to them, but she couldn't.

She wanted to ask more, but this wasn't her conversation, and, in the end, she worked here. She wasn't one of them. She shouldn't be standing there. But if Alexei had died, what would have happened? What about her and Santiago? Her head hurt.

She left the room as quietly as she could, went into the kitchen, and grabbed a glass of water.

Chapter 38
Silverio

HE FELT as nervous as if it were him who was going to be on camera, in front of the entire nation, debating with people who wanted to destroy him. He believed in Silvestre Ocampo with all his heart, though by now he was quite conscious of his various idiosyncrasies. But, he knew that the man he had been working for and with ever since the volcano eruption had brought him to the broader public's attention was a decent man. Moreover, he might have a chance to improve the country. He did not doubt that Ocampo was more suitable to lead a nation than the irredeemably awful Isabela Gutierrez, or any of the four minor candidates. They had no chance of winning, but they could affect the eventual outcome.

Nothing had come from Pablo's contacts so far. Every time he asked his colleague for news, his friend would say they're on it, and Silverio would say, "But is there any way they can be on it faster?" But it was no good. Pablo just kept putting him off and trying to calm him down.

When, to the ex-mayor, he went on again about the damage Gutierrez was doing to the campaign with her wild and completely unfounded accusations, Silvestre Ocampo would call him a 'young pessimist, glass-half-empty' kind of person.

"Listen, Silverio, we know what we know. Sooner or later, we will be able to use it, and then we'll have her. Just you wait. This is only the first debate" He wanted to believe him, but in the last few days, and ever since he had heard about the hacienda in the countryside, his confidence had evaporated. Now he feared that they would be eaten alive by the voracious sophistry of his opponent, who was strengthened by seemingly having no regard for truth or integrity.

He left Silvestre alone when they got to makeup. He was worried that he was letting his nerves show, and that was the last thing the man needed, so now he was standing in the corridor, security badge attached to his jacket, trying to get himself in the right frame of mind to be of use. He was finding it difficult. He looked at his watch. It was only fifteen minutes before the programme was due to start. His place was at Ocampo's side. I'd better get on with it, he told himself. He cleared his throat, stiffened his shoulders and made his way towards the makeup suite, but before he got there, a studio assistant came running up to him. "You are Silverio Plat, that's right, isn't it?"

"Yes, why?"

"There's someone who is insisting on seeing you. He's outside."

"Who's that?"

"One of your campaign co-workers, I believe. 'Pablo'. I didn't get his other name. He said it was urgent."

"Tell him to come here."

"No, sorry. Our instructions are clear. We can only bring in the people on the pre-notified list, like you, a candidate's assistant. All of the candidates have assistants." He knew this. He'd seen the other 'Silverios' walking around, glowering at each other.

"I'll go and see him then."

"I'm afraid you have to stay in this area until the show is over."

"Why are you telling me this if I can't do anything about it?" She didn't answer. "Look, I'm sorry to be a pain, but it's vitally important that I see him." He wasn't sure this was the case, but he knew Pablo wouldn't be trying to get to him for no reason.

"I completely understand, but rules are rules."

"Okay, okay. But could I ask you a huge favour?"

"I've already said you can't leave, and he can't come in. I'm sorry."

"Yes, I know. I'm sorry if I was a bit over-the-top, but could you possibly go — I really wouldn't ask unless it mattered — could you go and ask him what he wants?"

The woman looked about to refuse. But something about his pleading expression must have changed her mind, and she hurried off.

He made his way to the makeup suite.

"There you are, Silverio! I thought you had deserted me."

"You know I would never do that. Ready?"

"As ready as I will ever be." He got up from the makeup chair and smiled unconvincingly. "Come on, let's go and do this."

As they followed a studio manager down the corridor, the assistant came running up to him.

"Señor, your friend asked me to give you this." She handed him a bulky envelope.

"Silvestre, wait!" he stopped him. The studio manager tried to get them to move on, but Silverio summoned up all the reserves of his persuasive personality. "Wait just a few minutes. This might be something important for the debate. I promise you that we'll follow in just a minute. Just wait!"

The manager was about to protest, but Silverio was ripping open the envelope, tearing at the bulky tape that sealed it.

Silvestre was impatient and about to get angry, but the envelope split open and documents and photographs spilt onto the floor.

"Silverio, what are you doing?" Silvestre started, but he caught sight of the photograph that was at the top of the pile. *"¡Dios Mio! No puede ser!* This can't be!"

Silverio grabbed the rest of the pile and started sifting through its contents. Ocampo was gradually getting increasingly nervous, but he seemed to be looking at as many of the things Silverio was showing him as he could and listening to the torrent of whispered commentaries on what he was seeing as they were being hurried towards the studio.

"No!" he would exclaim and then "Yes!" and in this highly enervated state, he passed through the double studio doors and out towards the stage. "Here, give me those," but the studio manager, seeing this, reminded him of the arrangements the different campaigns had made: only two pages of notes were permitted.

"All right, yes, of course you are right. I apologise. Silverio, take these and give me those two."

"But they've got the points you wanted to highlight."

"They do indeed, so I am relying on you for telepathic communication if I get stuck."

Isabela Gutierrez sailed past them on her way into the studio.

"Nerves getting to you, Silvestre Ocampo? They should be. I'm going to eat you alive. But don't worry, it's all in the spirit of good fun."

She strode onto the stage, where she was shown her place. The invited audience gave her a boisterous welcome. There was loud applause and a few cheers. "This is going to be fun," Silvestre laughed nervously and followed his opponent onto the stage to the accompaniment of his own enthusiastic reception.

"Can you come this way, please?"

He followed the young woman up to the media gallery, where

campaign workers and journalists were gathering to view the proceedings. He was shown to a seat in front of a large monitor.

The candidates were arrayed in a semicircle, standing at lecterns. Silvestre was second in from the left (as he looked at them), and Gutierrez was right in the middle — a highly advantageous position — but that was the luck of a ballot they had been told.

On the monitor, Silverio could see the studio manager beginning the countdown. On the stage, the moderator shuffled her papers, the counting finished, and for the last few seconds, the studio manager's fingers took over the work until, with a flourish of music, the programme began.

Chapter 39
Genoveva

On her way home from the hospital, she could hardly contain the frustration she felt. She knew that Silverio was not telling her something — something important. She loved him, but she wasn't sure how much longer she could sustain a relationship with someone who kept secrets. These secrets were not just the typical little omissions and obfuscations that all couples live with.

He said repeatedly that it was to protect her, that even the slightest possibility of a leak would be disastrous. They had all been expressly forbidden from telling partners and families anything at all. All this secrecy, he said, was temporary, but there was a possibility that her colleagues might be found and saved. Nothing should get in the way of that.

He spoke so passionately, but all she heard was that he didn't trust her to keep a secret. She thought it so unfair, especially after how he had seen her behave when he was a member of the EAS. It was all very confusing. Her boyfriend was very loving and needed her, yet his behaviour was beginning to alarm her.

Something fundamental seemed to have changed. At the beginning, she thought they might be equals, despite her admiration for him, and despite the melting feeling he inspired in her. He understood her pain over the death of her brother, Julio. As things stood, however, it was as if he no longer felt those things.

Perhaps it was the campaign and the candidacy of Silvestre Ocampo that had caused the problems. What had started as a burst of naïve optimism had gradually morphed into a deadly serious game, a vicious contest which seemed to eat up all who were involved in it. Silverio was permanently exhausted, sometimes ratty and often absent. Worse still, from her point of view, was that her apparent importance to him was only intermittent since for large parts of the day or week or month, he probably didn't think about her at all. Then she reasoned that you could say the same thing about her. In the middle of a tense operation or a desperately serious bedside conversation with a sick patient, she didn't think about him either, except that he was always there in the background. The question that was beginning to obsess her was whether she was always present in his life like that, too.

Tomorrow she was meeting up with the families of the disappeared and, as the de facto leader of the group, she longed to know what to tell them, which, as things stood, was virtually nothing. She was sure that there would be demands from them to do something more, anything to pressure the authorities, the presidential candidates, the media, anyone who might help to redouble their efforts to get their friends and loved ones home.

She knew, of course, that the Gutierrez campaign was trying to pin the blame for what had happened — whatever that was — on Silvestre Ocampo, and listening to the powerful rhetoric from Gutierrez herself and the rest of them, she almost found herself wondering if there might be something in that. But then she thought about Silverio and Ocampo himself and knew it to be false.

But now, at last, she was hopeful. Silverio's air of suppressed excitement had got to her because she knew that this time it wasn't just the campaign itself that had fired him up. There was something else, something big, and that was good, but in her head, she was screaming, "But why won't you tell me what it is?"

She let herself into the flat. She checked the clock on the kitchen wall. There were still a few minutes to go before the live broadcast of the first presidential debate. She had time. She had a quick shower and dressed in a T-shirt and loose trousers. She made herself a sandwich, opened a beer, and sat on the couch. She reached for the remote and powered up the screen.

The debate had just begun. A woman representing an environmental party was talking about the danger of fossil fuels. She was instantly interrupted by Isabela Gutierrez.

GUTIERREZ: That's all very well, and we all want to do what's right by the natural world around us, no one more so than myself and my team, committed as we are to the environment. But what about the countless hundreds and thousands of people who depend on the oil and gas industries for their livelihood? What about all of us, all of us who rely on the fossil fuel sector to get us around, power our economy…?

MODERATOR: Señora Gutierrez, you must not interrupt. You will have your turn, I promise, but in the meantime, you must allow the previous speaker to have her say.

GUTIERREZ: Willingly, but only if she promises to stop offering us naïve rubbish and blatant untruths.

Genoveva was astonished by the combative nature of this encounter, but it was only a foretaste of what was to come. Gutierrez intervened frequently and often brushed aside the moderator's attempts to control her. Later, in answer to a question about the agriculture sector, she tried to silence Silvestre Ocampo.

> OCAMPO: And, we must ensure that our farmers are well supported whilst at the same time having a concern for the land for which they are custodians. If I am elected to serve as your president, I will do my best—

> GUTIERREZ: Do your best to emasculate this great country with regulation and restriction, more like choking the lifeblood from the industrial sector, whether manufacturing, farming, or anything else.

> [applause]

> OCAMPO: Well, isn't that just typical! Mrs Gutierrez has real trouble with the idea of debate. Her campaign relies only on interruption and bullying, as you have just witnessed. What I am offering, by contrast, and alone amongst this gathering here, is a kinder, more grown-up politics where different opinions can he heard respectfully and where consensus becomes the way to move this country forward.

> [applause]

Genoveva had expected a dry and lifeless encounter, but this was turning into anything but. Even through a television screen, the atmosphere was electric with everyone on the stage joining in as the emotional temperature and the rhetoric rose. The moderator was finding it almost impossible to control the situation. Without noticing it, Genoveva had finished her beer and ran to get another. When she returned, she didn't have time to sit down before what was happening on the screen commanded her absolute attention even more acutely than before. She stayed standing, looking down at the screen.

> GUTIERREZ: And the question we must ask about the disappearances near the town of Calixtlapan, the burning question in front of us and one that should invalidate his fitness to lead this country, is what does Silvestre Ocampo know about this? Because make no mistake, he is involved somehow. Either he orchestrated the events to protect his candidacy, or he was so weak and inefficient as the hapless mayor of San Miguel that he allowed this to happen under his watch and has no idea how to address it.

> Listen, my friends, when I am president, things like this will never happen again. We are the party of law and order, and our control over the thugs and vandals will be absolute. What do the other candidates on this stage have to offer? Nothing but weak-willed promises that absolutely nobody believes.

> [strong applause]

> MODERATOR: I will come to you next, Señor Ocampo. Do you have a response to the grave allegations that have just been made?

> [audience restlessness]

> OCAMPO: My answer is to ask my *own* question. And, my burning question is: Why is the supposedly kidnapped leader of the Ejercito de Arturo Sanchez visiting Señora

Gutierrez in her house in the city? We all thought he was a victim of an abduction or, heaven forbid, something worse.

[audience clamour]

GUTIERREZ: What a vile and monstrous accusation. Typical of someone who–

OCAMPO: I have here two photographs—

MODERATOR: This is most irregular. The rules all of you candidates agreed to—

OCAMPO: Two photographs. Señora Gutierrez, you look a bit unwell. Is anything the matter? The first of these photographs shows my opponent Isabel Gutierrez's garden here in the big city — bear with me, everyone — and in the garden, leaving by a door are two people who are visible even though it is night. One of them is the police chief of San Miguel, official Rivendeira, and the other is Guillermo Vargas, the leader of the EAS. What's going on? Why would an abducted protester and a compromised police officer be in Señora Gutierrez's garden two days ago?

[silence in the auditorium]

OCAMPO: Nothing to say now, Señora? You've been so vocal up until now, yet you appear to be struck dumb. Before you say anything, I should mention the second photo I have. It shows a hacienda near Artemio's Fire, the volcano, as everyone in our republic will know. It has a name, this place, the 'Hacienda Vista Volcan', and what this photo shows is a bunch of armed guards wearing the T-shirts that Isabela Gutierrez's supporters all wear.

There's nothing wrong with that except that they are supporting the wrong candidate, but I was just wondering what these armed men might be guarding. There couldn't be anybody held inside against their will, could there? Such as a group of protesters who vanished into thin air that the nation is desperately looking for?
You see, everyone, it is our firm belief that if you go there right now, you will find the members of the Ejercito Arturo Sanchez being held against their will. Believe me, we are going there, even as I speak. My question to you, dear Isabela, is what is going on, and what on earth are the kidnap victims doing there?

[sustained audience uproar]

MODERATOR: Ladies and gentlemen. Ladies and gentlemen, please. Señora Gutierrez, do you have anything to say about all this? I think I should give you the right to answer the charges that Señor Ocampo has levelled against you.

GUTIERREZ: Isn't this just typical of the low tricks my opponents use?! Fake photographs, wild accusations, a ridiculous farrago of falsehoods and lies.

Genoveva screamed at the screen as Gutierrez desperately tried to regain the momentum, but she never managed it before the programme finished. The other candidates were distressed that they had been sidelined in the psychodrama that had played out, unexpectedly, in front of them, but there was nothing they could do. Tomorrow's headlines were already being written.

Genoveva tried to ring Silverio. She was jumping up and down with excitement and outrage. He didn't answer. She tried twice more. Her frustration threatened to drive her completely insane, and she waited for the signal message.

"Silverio!" she screamed. "Call and tell me what the fuck's going on!"

The Song That Drives
Us On

Federico

HE HAD CONVINCED himself that learning to live with disappointment was something you had to work on. It wasn't something he hadn't faced before. Many of the cases he had been involved with had fallen far short of his ideals of justice. He no longer found it unusual. The compromises and under-the-table deals that had resolved legal battles, as well as the way that corporate greed went unpunished, should have bred in him a deep cynicism. Instead, they only reinforced a deep world-weariness and a belief that things would never work out for him. It was just the way it was.

Vicky's refusal to talk to him was just another example of life's injustices. Some people were born lucky, while others just struggled along as best as they could. With a father like his, what can he expect? He often comforted himself with this convenient excuse for his melancholy. Still, in moments of honest reflection, he berated himself for trying to excuse the flaws in his character, which were almost certainly of his making.

Had Angelita inherited a set of character traits from him? It was difficult to tell, but it didn't seem like it. After her mother had left, he had done his very best not to oppress her with his gloom. As far as he could see, he had been reasonably successful. She was, he had to admit, beautiful and, what is more, despite some of the experiences she had lived through in her short life, lucky.

She was outstanding as a violinist, and apart from that horrible experience with the professor, she was clearly in love with her art. When he watched her play, her joy as the music flowed from her was infectious, and not just to him as her loving father, it seemed, but to everyone who witnessed it. When he thought of how he had nearly lost her that day on the volcano's rim, he could hardly bear it. Even though he had lost her, in a way, to someone else, the fact that she loved Martin and he, in return, obviously worshipped the ground she walked on was a source of profound satisfaction to him.

He liked Martin a lot. He had something of the lawyer's melancholy about him, and that endeared the younger man to him, apart from their shared love for his daughter. Maybe there was something about his character, too, which he shared with his sister.

Now he was thinking of Vicky again and wallowing in his misery. Why wouldn't she speak to him? He didn't understand it. They had established such a strong connection from the moment she had appeared at the hacienda to ask for help for her confused husband. Since then, every time they had talked, the connection had become stronger and more necessary.

He had allowed himself to imagine that they would always have this connection and that his life would be complete. Then, since Alexei Kassoliniki's death, his dream had evaporated. When Martin had finally returned four weeks ago, he had been forced to find reserves of self-control that had almost physically hurt. Otherwise, he would have subjected his son-in-law to an endless cross-examination, which would not have been fair. It would have made him look as needy as he knew he was.

What he had found out, though, was that there had been a memorial gathering for the dead vulcanologist, which a couple of hundred people had attended. Most of them, Martin had said, were as weird as his brother-in-law had been. He had blushed shamefacedly at this and apologised for being disrespectful.

About Vicky, he would only say that she was beginning to remind him of the sister he had once had. This was before everything had been disrupted when she had discovered her husband in jail after that famous volcano concert. "Ever since she lost her balance and I lost my anchor," was how he put it. He was less forthcoming about her thoughts about his father-in-law. She doesn't talk about you that much, Federico. I'm sorry, but she doesn't seem so angry anymore, at least."

"That's something to be grateful for, I suppose!"

"Papa, for heaven's sake, you sound like a lovesick teenager," Angelita interrupted, "who has taken over the spirit of my father? Where has my father gone?" and he had been about to protest. Still, he saw her face, and he couldn't help laughing.

He guessed he would just have to live with it and chalk it up to yet another of life's disappointments. Right now, though, he had work to do, and he was being paid handsomely for it. He squared his shoulders and walked into the courthouse in San Miguel.

"Licenciado, good morning. It is a pleasure to see you again."

"The pleasure is all mine, Professor. How have you been?"

"Never better! Well, that's not true. I'm burnt like a prune, and I can't walk as well as I used to, and my hands are still a mess, but apart from that?" He laughed. "Come, Licenciado, we have a bit of time. Let me buy you a coffee."

They sat in a café near the courts and discussed what was about to happen. Federico warned him of the almost certainty that the judges' apparent empathy for the twins' situation might not be translated into favourable action. He warned his client that incarceration in some loathsome state penitentiary was still a possibility. It was what the prosecution had been pressing for after all. On the other hand, there was a chance that the law might be more merciful and that some other arrangement might be made. "The main thing, Maestro Perez, is that no one can say that you have not done everything you could for these boys."

"The best thing is that I persuaded you to take the case."

"Thank you, but that is not necessary. Changing the subject, what are your plans when this is all over?"

"Do you know, Licenciado, I had absolutely no idea before, but since that trip to the hacienda, everything seems to have changed."

"Yes, you've become something of a hero!"

"Of passing interest only. Everyone will get tired of the story soon, and I will be completely forgotten — and Licenciado, that is fine by me. My days of trying to be a star are long gone, I can assure you, and not just because I can't play anymore but also because I do not any more wish to be that person. Although I don't deserve it, it appears my luck has started to change. Not many people get a chance to start over, but I appear to be one of them."

It appeared that he was blushing, but it was difficult to tell under his burnt skin.

"Not many people have to nearly die and be badly injured for that either, Professor.

"Be that as it may, I have made a lot of new friends. I have been asked to be an honorary president of the Ejercito de Arturo Sanchez. They have credited us with being the agents of their rescue, Marisol Cardova and I. Do you know one of them, a rather attractive woman, who turns out to have been the one that

Marisol saw at the window that day? But really, all Marisol and I did was tell someone what she imagined she saw. I did not think much about it, really and then suddenly there it was on a presidential debate — I watched by the way — and it turns out that what Marisol and I saw, and what she told the Ocampo campaign, set things in motion. That and other things. Isn't that good?"

"What I can't understand," Federico said, "is how that awful woman Gutierrez is doing her best to wriggle out of this."

"If you lie long and loud enough, some people start to believe you - or maybe it just dulls down their critical faculties. Like piped music versus the concert platform! Do you know, a few months ago, I might have felt sympathy for her? I thought I hated those people, those protesters, when they ruined my concert and your daughter's big moment. At that moment, I would have agreed with everything Gutierrez says about them being enemies of the people. But that was then. Now I am amazed about all the stories she has been telling to make it seem that she wasn't as involved as she was — she even has the nerve to say that even if she was, it was in the service of some higher patriotism, for God's sake."

"Nothing surprises me anymore. Some people will believe anything! Look, the main thing, and it was a fantastically providential thing, is that what you and that woman saw helped to get those people out of there."

"Yes, I'm rather pleased about that! Do you know, Licenci-ado? I have decided.

"Really?" he was obliged to say.

"Yes. I'm staying here. I'm going to buy myself a place and sell up in the city, get divorced. I should have done it years ago, and given that woman whatever she wanted. When that's all done, there will still be enough for me to get a nice property in San Miguel. I like it here. My past recordings still bring in money.

I've agreed to join the staff of the local music school, and I'm starting my music programme on the radio here."

"*Profesor,* we'd better be going."

"Yes, let's go. Do you want to know something else?" he said as they strolled towards the court. "My other son has been in touch. He wants to come and see me, for 'healing' he says or whatever mumbo-jumbo his mother has planted in his ears. I've no idea how it will all turn out, but any contact is better than no contact!"

They had reached their seats. The lawyers nodded to each other politely. The twins were brought in, and they rewarded Federico and their father with a smile and a quiet 'hello'. The lawyer felt the professor beside him respond with gratitude.

Then the judges came in. They all stood. They all sat.

"Members of the court, we have come to a decision, difficult though it has been. There have been two competing claims we have had to face. On the one hand—"

He knew he should be listening intently because a future appeal — if that's what Jacinto Perez asked for — would depend on precisely what was said. But he could read it in detail later, and he was tired from his early morning flight, and he wanted to go back to wallowing in his melancholy. Chiding himself for unprofessionalism, he forced himself to pay attention.

"Would the accused please stand?" The twins were encouraged to their feet.

"There can never be a justification for taking the life of another person. The crime of murder is one of the most heinous crimes there is. For that reason, the two of you must be punished. The law allows for nothing else. However, with any crime of this kind, mitigating circumstances must be considered. At their most persuasive, they can amount to a plea of self-defence. We are not persuaded that this applies in your case. However, there is also a possible mitigation plea of extreme provocation, and thanks to the assiduous efforts of your counsel, we *are* persuaded about that. What happened to you in this cult and how your lives were impacted gives your heinous crime a context that we are unable to ignore.

This, then, is the court's sentence. You will be sent to a place of confinement for people of unsound mind for a period of five years. During that time, you will receive treatment for the damage you have suffered. If, at the end of that period, it is the considered opinion of your minders that you are sufficiently changed for the better and that you present no danger to society, you will be released into the care of a responsible guardian. You will be required to attend re-education sessions, and you will report weekly for a further two years. Only if tests judge you to be competent at the end of that time will you be released entirely. Maestro Perez?"

This surprised Federico. He had not been expecting it. "Stand up," he whispered to his companion, and the professor got to his feet.

The judges continued, "Maestro Perez, quite apart from the admiration this court feels for you, given recent events, we are obliged to ask you whether you would undertake the guardian-ship of these two young men if they are released at the end of five years."

Federico looked up. There were tears in Jacinto Perez's eyes. "Yes, I would!"

"This case is now closed."

Outside the court, the professor looked at him questioningly.

"It is about as good a result as we could have wished for. Let us hope the boys are finally fully restored."

"Thank you, Licenciado."

"I'm just doing my job. Now, if you will forgive me." He left the professor standing in the corridor and hurried away. He still had the matter of Tia Rosario to sort out.

Angelita

She said goodbye to the other three members of the quartet and climbed into the taxi to take her to the hacienda. She was feeling good about the programme they had just performed. There had been a reasonable audience, and they had done the music justice, she thought. Yes, of course, there'd been awkward moments. She hoped no one had heard the wrong notes that had got away from her and was about to berate herself for screwing up, but then she smiled. Her professor — she insisted on thinking of Maestro Perez in that and as nothing else — had told her at the very beginning of her studies that mistakes were there to be forgotten about until at least a day or two after you have made them.

"If you think about them at the moment they happen, you will make many more. If you show that you are making mistakes through facial expressions and body posture, it will detract from the audience's enjoyment. That's a pity, especially since most of them probably wouldn't have noticed them otherwise, unless they were musical experts. There aren't many of us around now, are there? The only good thing about mistakes is that after a performance we can work out why they happened so that maybe, just maybe, with practice they won't happen again."

Whatever else that man was, she thought wryly, he was undoubtedly a good teacher. Pompous and certain of himself for sure, but full of performance wisdom and musical insight, much of which she was still relying on.

It had been a surprise to see him in the audience tonight, but as strangely comforting as it was unexpected. He looked better than when he had been in the courtroom a few months ago. There was a new energy about him and something which looked a bit like kindness. Of course, she should hate him, but that hatred had been burnt away by volcanic fire and its terrible aftermath for Jacinto Perez, especially. So when he greeted her after the performance, she was almost pleased to see him, something she would have previously thought of as completely impossible.

"You are making the violin sound nice, Señora," he said. "It brought tears to my eyes."

"I should return it to you, maestro."

"What for?" he held out his damaged hands, and she was about to look for some words of appropriate sympathy, but he didn't give her the chance." I do not miss the violin. If I could still play, I would love to make music, of course, I would. It is a calling, and it will never go away. But the life I led and the things I did? I do not miss them even for one second of the day. If I did make music again, it would be in private, with friends. For now, I have a different life planned, and for the first time since I can remember, I have hope in the future, however long or short I am granted since that day on the mountain. You give me hope, too. I did not, it seems, entirely ruin your young life, and as a result, you will give enormous pleasure to the people who hear you and will, if there is any justice, live for many, many happy years. Thank you, my dear, for the music."

She had been about to reply, but he left as someone else came up to talk to her.

When she arrived at the hacienda, Tiacuri was waiting in the hall, looking worried.

"Hello Tiacuri."

"Señora Angelita. Did you have a good concert?"

"I did. One day you must come and listen."

"Oh no, Señora. I am sure it is not the right thing for people like me."

"It is exactly the right thing for people like you, Tiacuri. Next time you are coming, I won't accept any excuses!"

"Next time Señora? Will there be a next time? What is to happen, I mean, if my employer.....? And to Marcelita? Because I need to think—"

"Tiacuri, no one's moving anywhere at the moment. My father is putting plans in place so that Tia, Señora Rosario, will be well provided for - for as long as it is necessary - and as for Marcelita, she will live here with you, if you are happy to do that until we have decided what will happen. But that won't be for some time, and whatever happens, we will want your advice, and I can promise you, Tiacuri, we will do our very best for her and just as importantly, we will do our best for you."

It was clear the girl was about to thank her, but she walked away from her across the hall.

In reality, she did not know what would happen. She and Martin had talked to Federico since the lawyer's last visit a few weeks ago, when he had come for the resolution of the case about those twins. He now had the authority to look after Tia Rosario's affairs and had hired specialists to help with her care. As for his aunt, she seemed reasonably content, he told them, but he still didn't know what to do about the hacienda, let alone his niece. Whilst Tia Rosario was living there, things would go on as before. But afterwards? The hacienda would make a lot of money if they sold it, whether for the land it stood on or, who knows, converted into a hotel or some kind of centre. To be continued, Federico had said.

She got changed quickly and went down to wait for the taxi she had ordered. She had agreed to meet Genoveva after the nurse's shift before her own ten o'clock flight back to the city. They chose the same bar in the centre that they had visited the last time they had met. She arrived first and ordered a soft drink.

The first thing she noticed about her friend as she approached was that Genoveva was walking differently. There was a freshness in her step, and a smile was playing across her face. She greeted Angelita warmly, and they hugged like sisters.

"You're looking well!"

"So are you."

"Well, yes. I feel good."

Genoveva ordered a beer, but Angelita declined. "Maybe later."

"So how are you?"

"Since my friends came back, things have been so good. It's as if a great weight has been lifted from me. The campaign is nearly over, and then maybe, just maybe, Silverio will return to normal. Well, I mean, of course he won't, and when Silvestre Ocampo is president, who knows what Silverio will do, but still."

"You sound confident!"

"I am. No one can vote for that dreadful woman after what she did, can they? She can try and get out of it any way she wants, and she's been pretty good at that, I have to admit, but too many people know her for what she is. I mean, we know a lot are still going to vote for her, but…"

"How are they, your EAS friends?"

"Yeah, they're getting over it in their different ways. There's a terrible sadness over Gloria."

"The one who died?"

"Yes, she was shot in the kidnapping. They swore it was an accident, but it doesn't matter if it was or wasn't, does it? They did it, and they will pay. And as for that rat Vargas—"

"Your so-called leader?"

"Yes. Vargas has been arrested, and it serves him right. I don't fancy his chances. Angelita, so much has happened, so much is happening. I get dizzy with it all sometimes. But what about you?"

"You know what, my life's just great at the moment."

"I can see that. You look gorgeous. I'd say radiant!"

"Are you mocking me?"

"Of course not." They laughed. "But seriously, you look happy."

"I am. Martin's back, and it is good to have him there. I'm

never going to let him out of my sight again — except for when I jet round the world being a star!"

"This is so good! Come on, we have to drink to that. What do you want?"

"I'll stick to this."

"Angelita, in the time I have known you — granted, not a long time — but in all that time, I have never known you to refuse a drink. It's almost as if you–" she stopped. "Oh my God, are you...?"

"Look, Genoveva, it's early days, so please don't tell anyone. We haven't even told my father yet, so please?"

"Of course not. I am happy for you both."

"We'll see about that. I mean if everything goes okay."

"It will. I know it will."

It wasn't meant to happen. Not now, anyway, but Genoveva — no wait — there's something I want to tell you. Something I want to ask you."

"What? You've got me worried."

"Martin and I have talked. We don't know yet whether this," she pointed to her stomach, "is a boy or a girl. But whatever comes along, we want to call them Julio or maybe Julia. Your brother was my best friend. I think of that little scar above his eye, his wonderful smile, and his beautiful playing. I think about him all the time. Genoveva, will that be all right?"

For a moment, there in the centre of town, the world stood still.

Vicky

"Let me answer the door," she said, and they agreed.

It was worth it. When Maria saw who had let her in, it looked as if she was going to faint, as if she had seen a ghost. For a moment, she couldn't speak.

"Señora Vicky! Señora Vicky! In the name of all the saints, what on earth are you doing here?"

"Visiting my brother and his wife. Is that all right with you?"

"Yes. I mean no. I mean, I don't know what I mean. Señora, I am so sorry to hear about Señor Alexei. May his soul rest in peace." She was almost in tears.

"Thank you, Maria. It has not been easy."

"Oh. And the children? How are they?"

"Very excited."

"Señora?"

"Maria, you should see your face."

"My face Señora?" Maria put her hand up to check. "Is there something wrong? I—"

"Come here, Maria," and to the maid's confusion, she hugged her, "I am so sorry to be teasing you. And I am very pleased to see you again. I'm not the only one. Daniel and Sarah are very, very excited to see you again, too."

"Señora, you have no idea how much I would love to see them. I have missed them."

"I know you have."

"But what is happening? Have you come back? Are you -?"

"Maria, there'll be time for all this later. I don't know whether I am visiting or returning, coming or going. Everything completely up in the air. But for now, you will find the children in the fast-food restaurant down the street. They are with their uncle Martin. But he needs to get going — he has things to do. Martin and Angelita rang you to ask if you could look after the children for a couple of hours, in the park, in the shopping centre, or anywhere. I just need a couple of hours. Would that be all right?"

She watched Maria trying to process the surprise and shock she felt. She was hesitating. She looked nervous, completely off balance. But then she seemed to recover. Eventually, she left, confused, happy and uncertain.

When she had gone, Angelita came up to Vicky. "I'd better go now, I think."

"Angelita, I am so sorry to kick you out of your flat."

"It was our idea!"

"True. You have been so lovely to us and –"

"It's okay, Vicky. Yes, this is strange for me, obviously it is, but I love your brother, and you are my family. We are in this together, I think. I just hope things work out okay, whatever happens."

"Thank you. I think he is fortunate, my brother."

Now she was on her own, and suddenly she was starting to panic. What was she doing here? This wasn't right. She should go. She should never put everyone through this. Never do anything after a bereavement, not for a year at least, that's what they all said. So why had she dragged the children back here and imposed them and herself on the young married couple? She was pacing up and down in the small sala. What if I have made a terrible mistake?

For the thousandth time, it seemed she rehearsed the speech she was going to make. She would say, "Look, I'm sorry about everything, and I'm sorry I haven't spoken to you. I don't know why I was angry with you. You're the kindest person I have ever met. Maybe we can be friends. I haven't yet got over what happened. I may never be able to love anyone else again. If we could just talk, I know I would feel comforted. If you are not too upset with me, can we just sit down and talk?"

When he arrived and she opened the door, however, she said none of these things. They stared at each other, and she managed to say 'Federico' in a strangled voice. Then they just stood there.

A television programme

There was nothing more anyone could do. The voting was over. The exit polls, which had proved remarkably unreliable in the past, were predicting an Ocampo victory. Still, Gutierrez was not too far behind, and until things were sewn up, no one on Silvestre's team could get too excited, especially as many results would not be in for another eight or nine hours. That had not stopped the TV stations from assembling their panels of experts to discuss what they thought was going to happen. Many of the chamber of deputies, mayors and gubernatorial candidates were there to be interviewed about what they thought was going to happen and whether they had a political future. The same clips of the candidates casting their votes were played repeatedly.

In this motionless period between the campaign and the results, Channel Eight had chosen to screen its two-part examination of the events surrounding the eruption of Artemio's Fire and the deadly earthquake that had followed months earlier. For those who had been involved in the drama on the day, it was either compulsory viewing or, on the contrary, something that they could not bear to watch.

In the city, Angelita and Martin sat down in front of the TV, their nerves getting the better of them. Vicky appeared and disappeared as the programme continued. She needed to help the children sleep. In a week, they would be moving into her new house, where she hoped to start anew and possibly have a future with Federico.

Federico joined them just in time for part two.

Jacinto was nowhere near a television set, but he wouldn't have watched it even if he could. He was mostly looking forward to visiting hours at the secure hospital where his twin boys had been incarcerated.

As for Silvestre Ocampo, who might be the national president the next morning, he was floating on a fading tide of exhausting adrenaline, answering calls from well-wishers, falling asleep in his chair, and coming to guiltily when he thought of the many things he might soon be called upon to undertake and which he really should be preparing for.

Silverio got back to the flat he shared with Genoveva some-time before the exit polls were announced. She dragged her attention away from the TV, looked up, and smiled at him. He kissed her." I want a beer. Have you got one? Shall I get you one?" He went to the fridge. When he came back, he sat down next to her.

"What are you watching?"

"It's the programme about the earthquake."

"Won't it make you sad?"

"Because of Julio?"

"Yes."

"It happened, Silverio. We were there. I'm not going to forget it. Now be quiet. I want to listen."

A man who seemed vaguely familiar was being interviewed by the famous broadcaster Gaby Aguirre. The two of them were sitting in a comfortable room on a hill above the town, judging by the view through the window.

"Anselmo," Gaby Aguirre was saying, "you have told us about the night your grandmother woke you up—"

"Yes, yes, when the volcano burst through the earth on Artemio's land. You know the dogs were terrified. Blanco y Negro. They were never terrified."

"Yes, yes, I understand that, and we've had a good chance to talk about it all. You are, we know, a special witness to those events." The man on the screen smiled self-consciously. "But as one of the people who was there at the birth. I wonder if you could tell us about the day of the eruption, the day of the earth-quake, many years later. Your perspective will be unique."

Silverio looked at Genoveva beside him. She seemed very vulnerable sitting there. These last few months had taken it out of her, he thought. The strong, bubbly person he had come to know at those EAS meetings all that time ago now had worry lines creasing the centre of her forehead. She hadn't lost her effervescent charm and radiant beauty, at least not in his eyes, but something was noticeably different even if, since the EAS had been discovered and rescued, she had come back to life. But their relationship was still not entirely back to how it had once been in the heady excitement of their mutual discovery.

It hadn't been easy for him either. There was the exhaustion he and the team felt in the throes of the campaign, along with the fierce pressure they had all been under — the pressure of always being under attack from opposing forces and the need for instant rejoinders. In the light of the vicious comments that had been directed at the campaign, they had all had to find reserves of energy and resilience that he, at least, hadn't known he possessed.

It hadn't helped him, either, that the gradual awareness of what had been going on and the need to keep the details from Genoveva — or so he thought — had come close to driving a wedge between them. That was all over, of course, and Isabela Gutierrez and her clan had been exposed. Better still, the EAS members who had been kidnapped that day had been freed, though that knowledge was of course tempered with the grief over the one fatality.

The truth of what had gone on should have been enough to wipe Gutierrez's candidacy off the map. However, there was a sizeable proportion of the population who were still prepared to believe her claims that it was all a fake accusation and that, anyway, those demonstrators were enemies of the state. How on earth had it come to this, he wondered, a country divided, the truth bartered like some kind of squalid currency. He reflected that whatever the final results showed, Silvestre Ocampo — or whoever won the poll — would have a difficult time trying to knit the country back together again.

He looked at his companion on the sofa, engrossed in the programme in front of her. He loved her more strongly than ever.

He told himself he had been changed just as she had. Their experiences — the experiences of everyone around them — had eaten away at their younger selves, and maybe they were a bit wiser and sadder. Still, things have to be better, and Genoveva would again be the happy, carefree, hopeful person he first met.

Genoveva interrupted his thoughts. "That man," she said, indicating the screen, "I've seen him before. I've just remembered. When we were kids, he used to sell his toys in the square. And now I think about it, he was there at Angelita and Martin's wedding — everyone was, of course."

"Is he interesting?"

"Sort of. He's telling our story. Feels like he's us and — please don't be cross with me — I've had enough of all the arguments and the crap and your campaigns and all the disgusting, horrible wickedness for a while. Can you understand that?"

He didn't answer but instead turned his attention to the screen.

"...terrible day, a terrible day," the man Anselmo was saying.

"Could you tell us something about it? If you can bear it. Honestly, I don't want to make you upset all over again."

"No, no, it is all right." Anselmo looked at the ground and cleared his throat. "I will, I will."

"Go on," she said quietly.

He looked at her, as if making a judgement about her motives, and then, apparently satisfied, he started speaking.

"I was in the office catching up on a bit of work — though I am in the process of stopping working, you see. More time with my wife. The family. I always think…" He paused. "Yes, the office started shaking, files fell off the shelves, the ceiling fan was swaying wildly from side to side, a picture — a family picture which I always have with me to — the picture fell off its hook, and I heard the glass smash. That was it! I got out of there in a flash."

"Quick thinking."

"Not really. It wasn't my first earthquake. I remember one in Siete Vientos many years ago, and one near the capital. Anyway, I was there, you see, when the volcano arrived on Artemio's land."

"So you knew what to do."

"Yes, I suppose so."

"When you ran out of your building?"

"Awful. Awful. All that dust and concrete and people running around. Panic everywhere. You can't help that. The world turned upside down and sideways — nothing was sure anymore. The ground. It should be the one thing we can depend on. Shaking. Moving. An angry god. We are powerless. Shouts, screams." His voice was rising now. "And the bodies. I will never forget the bodies."

"No."

"And the aftershocks. That's almost worse than the real thing, you know. Very frightening." He crossed himself. "I was frightened," he admitted, shamefaced.

He stopped. He seemed lost in thought.

"Go on, Anselmo."

"The lighting gantries. You know, for the football stadium. They just came down. I wouldn't have imagined it possible. They just fell."

"And that's when you came across the young man? The one you told me about"

"Yes, that young man. Such a good-looking young man. At

least so young. His long, black hair was all covered in dust. He wore a little medal on a chain — maybe it was a St Christopher? Yes, that was it. Why would I remember this? He had a little scar above his right eyebrow on that lovely face — it was like a saint's face. I don't believe in saints. God forgive me. I think of him often. I wish I knew who he was so I could pass on his message to the person he was talking to. Was she his sister? He talked about his sister. He was desperate for her to know something before he…. He knew, he must have known."

"Go on, Anselmo. What was the message you told me about?"

"He was dying, the poor boy. I could see that, and I think he knew it too. People do, you know."

"Please don't stop now, Anselmo. I know this is hard, but you have got this far."

"Yes, I'm sorry. But this has affected me, of all things I saw that day, even after all this time."

"I can see that."

"He died. Right there." He had to stop again. He cleared his throat and pulled his palm across his forehead. Gaby Aguirre waited. Beside Silverio on the sofa, Genoveva appeared to be not breathing.

"He pleaded with me to take a message to tell someone something. He could hardly speak."

"And what was that message?"

"It was for his sister. I can't remember the exact words, but I'll never forget that moment. He wanted her to know how much he loved her. Something about nothing else mattering. Except for that. That was all. I can still hear his voice, weakening as he faded away from me. Dust. I wish I could tell her that. He wanted her to know that. His last wish. Love. That's everything, isn't it, love? Isn't that amazing?"

"Anselmo, my dear man, thank you for sharing that moment,

and to his sister, if she is watching, I just want to express my sympathy, the whole nation's sympathy for your loss".

On the sofa next to him, Genoveva started to sob quietly. He reached for her, and she burrowed her face into his chest. "Julio," she whispered, her voice catching in her throat, "Julio. Julio," and Silverio thought that beyond the triumphs they had achieved so far, beyond the injustices they were fighting against and the struggles still to come, he loved this woman with his whole heart and that would see him through, whatever happened, as long as she wanted him there.

A dinner party

"So is she still going to those classes?"

They were talking about Maria, who had moved back, with Federico's approval, to work for Vicky and help with the children.

"Yes, thanks to your father," Vicky said, looking over to Federico, who was sitting opposite her at the table.

"I thought she was talking about giving up."

"There was something, not my place to say, really, but she was uncomfortable with her friend for a bit — you know the one who worked for Isabel Gutierrez."

"I hope they lock that woman up," Federico interjected. "Poison. She just pumped poison into the system. Quite apart from what she did with your friends, Genoveva."

They were all crowded into Angelita and Martin's flat, celebrating the fact that Genoveva was in the city visiting Silverio, who should have joined them by now, but still hadn't arrived.

"But you said Maria returned to her classes."

"Yes, I'm pleased to say, and do you know she's making a lot of progress. And the children are so pleased to have them back in their lives. After everything they've been through, she's a steady point in their turbulent lives."

It didn't seem that long since Silvestre Ocampo had become the president. His victory was narrower than it should have been, in the view of everyone in the room, and the campaign's legacy was a sharply polarised population. The new president, however, had started with huge plans and a steady stream of events and policy statements, and was away on his first foreign trip. Rivendeira and Guillermo Vargas were in custody, and Isbaela Gutierrez was under house arrest to the outrage of her many fans, who believed her when she said it was unfair persecution.

"He's got a difficult time on his hands," Federico said. "I've never known it like this. The level of anger from both sides is quite unlike anything I've ever experienced. Talk about a country divided."

At that moment, someone rang the bell and Martin went to see who was at the door. It was Silverio. Hi, he said, and went straight over to Genoveva. "I'm sorry, I'm so late," he told her, and she just rolled her eyes. "No, really, Angelita, Martin. I got away as soon as I could. It's just that there's so much to do. Especially now that Silv— *El Señor Presidente* is away."

Later, as they were eating and the atmosphere grew more convivial with the beer and the whisky, Angelita turned to her friend. "So, have you made your decision?" she asked, arching her left eyebrow.

"Not really. I mean, now that Silverio is here permanently, I'm coming as much as I can, and sometimes," she looked over at Silverio meaningfully. "We get to spend time together." He heard that and started to say he was sorry, but she stopped him. "Of course, we want to be together, and his job in the president's office has to be here in the city, so obviously I should move down instead of coming at weekends or whatever. But I have a good job in San Miguel, and my parents need me, now more than ever. The amount I spend on plane tickets, though, is ridiculous. I'm earning a lot of points though."

They laughed.

"And I love my job, I do. I've always loved it. And I love San Miguel, and I know you'll think I'm being stupid." She stopped.

"Try me."

"I don't want to leave Julio behind."

At the other end of the table, Federico was talking to his son-in-law. "I'm no nearer a decision, Martin, you know that. I'd love to move up to the hacienda, but I'll never get Vicky up there," he blushed, "I mean, not that she'd come just because of me anyway, and we're not even—"

"Stop it, Federico!" She was laughing at him. "One step at a time, remember."

"Sorry."

"But you're right. I don't want to go to San Miguel. Not yet. It doesn't hold happy memories for me, sorry Federico. I know that's where I met you, and I am grateful for that, you know I am, but San Miguel, where Alexei first…" she trailed off. "Anyway, I love this city, and I always have. They want me back at the radio station, too, and the kids are getting used to seeing their friends again and gradually settling into a routine. The last thing I want to do is uproot them again."

The future.

Martin went round the table serving drinks to anyone who had run out.

"More of your juice?" he said to his wife.

"Oh God, do I have to? I know it's good for me and the baby, but can't I just have a beer?"

"You can have whatever you want, Angie," he said. Shall I get you one?"

"S'pose not," Angelita said despondently. "Give me some more of that stuff if you must."

"Any news on whether it's a boy or a girl?"

"No," Martin said firmly, "we've decided we don't want to

know. We just want to love whoever survives and give him or her the best life we possibly can."

"I'll drink to that," said Federico.

"You'll be a ridiculously sentimental grandfather, Federico," Vicky said, laughing at him.

"I am already," he admitted, with a grin." I can't wait to meet my grandchild."

"Something to look forward to", Genoveva said, "the future".

"It's the song that drives us on," Silverio said suddenly. "Hope —the future. We don't know what's waiting for us, boy or girl, progress or stagnation, conflict or peace. But I tell you what, if the president has his way, our lives will be a whole lot better than they have been, and we'll have a lot to celebrate by the time your baby, you two, grows up."

"Let's drink to that," Federico said. "To the future."

And so, they did.

Cast of Characters
(In alphabetical order)

- *Alexei Kassoniliki*, a vulcanologist, married to *Victoria*
- *Angelita Hernandez Remedios*, a music student, a daughter of *Federico*, now married to *Martin*
- *Anselmo Gonzalez de Luna*, a retired seller of toys
- *Arnulfo*, a habitué of a club in San Miguel
- *Don Estaban (deceased)*, a landowner, brother of *Tia Rosario*; the father of *Federico*
- *Don Venustiano Heredia (*deceased*)*, a landowner
- *Dr Martinez*, one-time member of the *EAS*
- *Ejercito de Arturo Sanchez (EAS)*, a left-wing protest group
- *Federico Hernandez Placencia*, lawyer, a son of *Don Estaban* (deceased); the father of *Angelita*
- *Francisco Pérez*, a student, a son of *Jacinto* and *Marisa*, younger brother of *the twins*
- *Genoveva Delgadillo Aceves*, a nurse, a sister of *Julio* (deceased)
- *Guillermo Vargas*, leader of the *EAS*
- *Isabela Gutierrez*, candidate for the presidency

- *Jacinto Pérez, a* music professor and violinist, married to *Marisa*, the father of *the twins* and *Francisco*
- *Julio Delgadillo Aceves*, a music student (deceased), a brother of *Genoveva*
- *Marcelita*, a woman with learning difficulties, a daughter of *Tia Rosario*
- *Maria Moreno Cochinaba*, a maid married to Juan (deceased); she worked for Vicky, and now works for Federico
- *Marisa Sepulveda de Pérez*, a singer, married to *Jacinto*. Mother of *the twins* and *Francisco*
- *Marisol Cardova*, a festival organiser and one-time lover of *Jacinto*
- *Martin Caldecott*, a language teacher, translator, and writer, a brother of Vicky, married to *Angelita*
- *Rivendeira*, Chief of Police in San Miguel de las Colinas
- *Silverio Plat* (no 22), one-time leader of the *EAS*
- *Silvestre Ocampo*, the *alcalde* (mayor) of San Miguel de las Colinas, now a candidate for the presidency
- *The Sons of Perpetual Light*, a quasi-religious sect led by the 'Halo'
- *The twins*, sons of *Jacinto* and *Marisa*, brothers of *Francisco*
- *Tia Rosario* (deceased), a sister of *Don Estaban*
- *Tiacuri*, a maid, works as the carer for *Marcelita*
- *Victoria Kassoniliki (Bicky)*, a radio presenter, married to *Alexei*, a sister of *Martin*

About the Series

Three volumes comprise this series:

Artemio's Fire, published in early 2023,
Old Gods, published in late 2023
Burning Questions

Available at all major online retailers in both ebook and paper formats.

* * *

The volcano called Artemio's Fire appeared outside San Miguel de las Colinas some fifty years ago, pushing its way into the life of the valley where beauty and ugliness, kindness and avarice, old beliefs and new urgencies, and repression and hope uneasily coexist. People are drawn to the town to celebrate the volcano's 50th anniversary.

The mayor is there, as is the young nurse, Genoveva, who may not be exactly as she seems. Heading towards the volcano is

Alexei, a vulcanologist, pursued by his wife, who is sure something is wrong. The beautiful young violinist Angelita heads to her grandfather's hacienda as the old man lies dying. So, too, does Jacinto, the music teacher who has taken advantage of her and is on a mission of his own. Don Esteban's sister wonders what the point of anything is.

Political rivalries simmer like the mountain's restless core. When it is all over, new challenges and injustices rear their heads, and among them, these characters have to negotiate a precarious, loving, but dangerous future.

The *Volcano at San Miguel* trilogy is a riotous, moving, sad, but eventually uplifting tale of lives weaving in and out of a unique and wonderful tapestry. As many make the journey to San Miguel, the reader is called to share their loves, triumphs, and tragedies.

www.ingramcontent.com/pod-product-compliance
Lightning Source LLC
Chambersburg PA
CBHW021003260626
47169CB00006B/1925